Madd INLET

a novel

TIM SWINK

Relax. Read. Repeat.

MADD INLET
By Tim Swink
Published by TouchPoint Press
Brookland, AR 72417
www.touchpointpress.com

Copyright © 2022 Tim Swink
All rights reserved.

Softcover ISBN: 978-1-956851-38-0

Editor: Kimberly Coghlan
Cover Design: ColbieMyles.com
Cover Image: Painting © Renee Swink

Connect with Tim Swink online: http://www.timswink.com/

First Edition

Printed in the United States of America.

For Hugh

I dedicate this book to Hugh Fordham Myrick, my dear, lifelong friend, the person who first opened my heart to Sunset Beach and Bird Island back in 1963. This is where the story is told. Where we danced on her waves . . . where we dared Madd Inlet . . . where we plied the waters and slews in the marsh . . . where we explored Bird Island . . . where we watched sunsets over Sunset with salt water heads and felt contentment. These memories, and Hugh, will always remain in my thoughts and in my heart.

Here's to you . . . my kindred spirit.

Until we meet again, where the sky meets the sea.

Bali Ha'i

(From Rogers and Hammerstein's Broadway musical "South Pacific.")

Most people live on a lonely island
Lost in the middle of a foggy sea
Most people long for another island
One where they know they would like to be.

Bali Ha'i may call you
Any night, any day,
In your heart, you'll hear it call you
Come away, come away

Bali Ha'i will whisper on the wind of the sea
If you try you will find me
Where the sky meets the sea
Here am I your special island
Come to me come to me.

Map of Sunset Beach

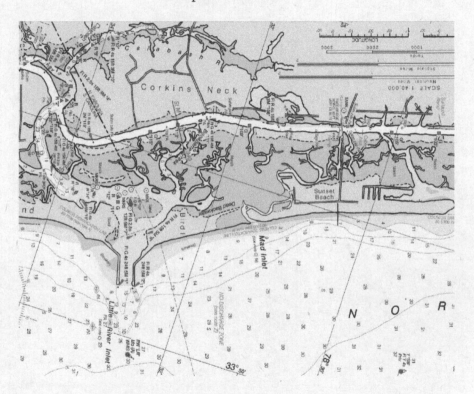

CHAPTER 1

THE FLAT BLACKTOP AHEAD SHIMMERED as the Chevy's snow tires whined along the North Carolina two-lane road on an unusually hot early spring day. They were approaching Laurinburg, which meant that the coast was about two hours away.

"You wanna beer?" Bobby Huff mumbled through lips that held the stub of an Old Gold filter cigarette. He reached into the cooler in the back seat.

"Not right now. It's a little early for me," Jack Tagger said. "Hell, let me get that, Huff! You pay attention to your driving."

Huff took the Laurinburg exit and pulled up to the state-run liquor store that sat on the outskirts of the little town. Faded posters advertising fish fries, pig pickins, and gospel sings were taped to the front windows. The events were several months past and, in some cases, several years past, but the posters were no doubt left there to block the sun as it rose up in the east, down where the Atlantic released its waves upon the white sand at Sunset Beach. The thought of the ocean stirred in Jack as it always did when he was nearing the surf after a winter spent inland, a place where he was never meant to be.

Turning toward Jack, still holding the cigarette stub in the corner of his mouth, Huff asked, "You coming in?

"Naw, I don't need anything. You buying this for Paul or yourself?"

"This is for Paul. What'd he say to get . . . a half-gallon of Ancient Age?" Huff asked.

"Yeah, I think that was it. He likes to start out hard, doesn't he?" Jack said.

"Guess it's the cancer. He lives like he ain't got much time. I reckon I would too, if it was me," Huff replied.

"You gonna meet him at the beach?" Jack asked.

"Yeah. Ocean Drive. Be back in a minute."

———•———

SOUTHEAST OF LAURINBURG, NC HIGHWAY 15/501 levels out and skirts the South Carolina border, and the landscape takes on a totally different look and feel. Absent are the rolling hills of the central Piedmont that harbor cities like Winston Salem and Greensboro. The cities become *towns* here, interspersed along the two-lane road with names such as Rowland, Fair Bluff, and Tabor City. Pastureland, cotton, and tobacco fields open up along the way, dotted here and there with dignified white painted old home-places flanked by empty unpainted wooden shacks where the families of Negro farm help once resided. The fields with tilled rows of dark, rich soil run out behind the occasional farmhouse, stretching out away from the road, some with young tobacco plants just set, others dotted with early white cotton blossoms, while others show newly sprouted stalks of corn. Iconic old tobacco barns, isolated sentinels that kept watch over the fields, occasionally revealed themselves from kudzu encasement. It can be desolate. Run out of gas in this neck of the woods, and it's a long walk. A short ways past Laurinburg, the road turns south and NC 904 eastbound eventually deposits traffic onto one of Brunswick County's beaches.

Jack, watching the rural landscape ease by, settled back in the passenger's seat and felt contentment.

———•———

THE ONCOMING WESTBOUND CAR shuddered back and forth until it decided to occupy the eastbound lane and career head-on toward their beige Chevrolet Impala.

"Holy shit! Hang on!" Huff yelled out, slamming on brakes and pulling hard right on the big steering wheel, muscling the car over onto the sandy shoulder.

"Oh, God! He's gonna hit us!" Jack cried.

The big blue Continental continued their way, barreling straight for them. The Chevrolet, forced into the ditch, bounced up on the far shoulder and continued along the embankment. As the blue car closed in on them, Jack braced for the impact and found himself focusing on the driver's face. But the image that found its way into Jack's eyes was strange and distorted. Where there should have been a face was a pulpy red blur, seen through a shattered hole in the driver's side front windshield.

The Chevrolet continued eastbound astride the embankment. Incredibly, the Lincoln nosed by the Chevy as it shot past, exploding up into the air as it crossed the ditch. The blue top of the big car was visible just seconds before it disappeared in a cloud of dust before coming to rest in an open field. Huff pulled hard to the left, and the car responded, moving off the embankment and coming to stop in the eastbound lane.

Both boys said nothing, staring straight out the front windshield until Jack asked, "Huff. Did you see that thing?"

"Hell yeah, I saw it. That fuck'n *thing* damned near killed us just now!"

"No, I mean that *thing* that was behind the steering wheel."

"That damned driver in the car back there? I hope the son of a bitch is dead. If not, he deserves to be!"

"Huff! The driver of that car didn't have a face!"

"I'm sure he doesn't, *now*."

"No! I swear to God, Huff! There was a hole in his windshield, and behind that was a red pulp where eyes, nose, and mouth should have been. I even saw the wind blowing the hair back. But it didn't have a face. He was fucked up before he ever got to us! Come on," Jack said as he opened the passenger's door and got out. "We gotta go back and check on him."

"What the hell are you talking about Jack? I'm sitting here with a cooler of beer, not to mention the beer on my breath. The last thing I want to see or talk to is a State Trooper. No way I want to get involved in this. Get back in and shut the damned door! We gotta get the hell out of here before the whole county gets here."

"Huff! I mean it. That person back there didn't have a face. And there was a hole in his windshield the size of a basketball! I swear to God! That guy was messed up before he ever parked it out there in that cotton field!"

"I'm telling you one more time, Jack! Get in and shut the fuck'n door! I ain't getting involved. I'm getting out of here. I just got my license back a month ago, and I *ain't* about to lose it again. Especially for something I didn't do or have a hand in. And you, dodging the draft. You don't need to get involved either, with Uncle Sam looking for you. But if you wanna play Boy Scout, be my guest. But I ain't staying around here any longer."

Jack looked back at the settling dust in the field. He didn't see any movement in the blue car. Thinking Huff might be right, he gently closed the door. "What if somebody saw us and got our tag thinking we caused the wreck?" Jack asked.

"Look around, dumb ass. You see anybody out in this deserted God-forsaken land? I don't, and that's the way I want to keep it," he said.

Suddenly the wreckage in the field exploded, sending a dirty orange flame upwards, backlit by a brilliant blue April sky.

"Well, I guess that settles that," Huff said, slamming his foot down on the accelerator, driving down the two-lane toward the Atlantic Ocean.

———◆———

"STOP AT THE DAYLILY FARM DOWN HERE ON THE LEFT."

"You're shitting me! Daylily farm! Why in the hell would you want to stop at a daylily farm? You turning queer on me or something?"

"My nerves are shot, and I just feel like I wanna get out and stroll through the daylilies. I've always wanted to stop there but was always in too much of a hurry to get to the beach. They say a person should stop and smell the roses every now and then. But I guess daylilies will do just fine. After what just happened, I need to get out of this car and settle down some, and a field of daylilies sounds just about right."

"How about we compromise and stop at one of the peach stands a little further down? I mean to get away from this part of the county as fast as I can. You cool with that?"

"Yeah, all right. I guess putting some distance between us and this place makes sense."

CHAPTER 2

Earlier that day

THREE YOUNG MEN ENTERED THE back of the store, letting the rusty screen door slam behind them. An older man was already there, waiting for them.

"Damn you! How many times have I told you boys about catching that screen door on your way in?" the older man said. He lit a cigarette and filled a small, slender glass with Southern Comfort. As he lifted the glass to his lips, the three younger men could not miss the slight tremor in his hand.

"What's the story? Has he left yet?" the older man asked the smallest of the three men.

"He just left, boss. He should be crossing the causeway right about now."

"Good . . . I wanna get this thing done today. My nerves can't take dragging this thing out much longer. And this liquor ain't helping 'em any. Greer and Johnson in place?"

"They left a while ago," the smaller man said.

"That's cutting it pretty close, ain't it?"

"They got it all staked out. Been up there several times and picked

7

out a place on a rise beside Highway 904 . . . only high spot out there. Nothing but dirt farmers and flat farm land for as far as you can see. They'll be able to see him coming from a half-mile away."

"What if there's traffic behind him? Can't have no witnesses," the older man said.

"That's some desolate road out there. And it's about twenty miles this side of Fair Bluff. Being that it's Tuesday and the beach season hasn't started yet and except for locals, there'll be very little traffic of any kind," the short man said. "Anyway, we've already thought of that. Greer's son is parked along 904 . . . on a side road. When he passes by, the boy's gonna pull out behind him and drive real slow so that any car coming up from behind will be held back."

The older one smiled and said, "I knew there was a reason I put you three on this little project."

━━━━●━━━━

THE RED PICKUP SPED WESTBOUND along NC Highway 904 in the afternoon heat. The early spring weather had uncharacteristically produced a scorcher. Greer glanced into the rear-view mirror. His son followed behind.

"We outta be getting close, best as I recall," Jimmy Greer said to Easley Johnson.

"Yeah, I believe you're right. The daylily farm is up here on the right, and that little bluff is about five or six miles beyond it. You ready for this?" Johnson asked.

"I reckon I am. Ain't much difference in this and some of the other things we've done. Only difference is we ain't got a white sheet over our head this time," Greer said, laughing.

"That, and this ain't no poor nigger share cropper we're dealing with this time. Being who it is would definitely put a different spin on things if we was to get caught," Johnson said.

"We ain't gonna get caught. How can we? Ain't gonna be no witnesses. Can't get convicted of something if there ain't no witnesses, now, can we?"

"Still . . . makes me a little bit nervous, seeing as who we're dealing with," Johnson said.

"You damned well better lose those nerves once you pull out that twelve-gauge of yours," Greer said.

"I said a little bit. That's all."

"Well, you can be a little bit nervous for the next five or six miles. Then there better be nothing but ice water running through your veins," Greer said.

"It will be," Johnson said, "cold as a mountain spring. When I put that wood up against my cheek and site down the barrel, I get my comfort. And then it's all business."

Greer smiled sideways out his mouth and said, "That's what I want to hear. Now *I'm* feeling the comfort." The truck traveled a couple of miles more before Greer started slowing and said to Johnson, "Stick your hand out the window and motion him to pull over up at this side road up here . . . Wiregrass Road. My boy will wait on him there."

"What the hell! We've been up here three or four times now. He knows what to do," Johnson said.

Greer gave Johnson a serious look and said, "They've all been dress rehearsals up to now. This one ain't. I'll be right back."

"All right. But hurry up. I wanna get on down the road," Johnson said.

Greer approached his son's truck and stopped at the driver's side window. He pulled his ballcap down over his eyes and looked both ways, up and down Wiregrass Road before he spoke. "You know what to do now?"

"Yeah Daddy, I do. We've been over this enough."

"Tell me again," Greer said.

"When I see the blue Continental round that curve back there, I wait for it, and soon as it passes, I pull out real slow. If a car comes up behind me and he looks like he's gonna try and pass me, I speed up to keep him behind me."

"That's right. Same as we do on Friday nights over at the dirt track," Greer said.

"I got it. Ain't no problem."

Greer looked at his son and said, "I'm depending on you. We'll all be in a world of shit if something goes wrong. You hear me son?"

"Yeah, I hear ya," his son said looking up at his daddy, shielding one eye with the flat of his hand while squinting up at this father with the other eye.

"Good," he said patting the bottom of the window opening before walking away.

———●———

RICH PIERCE TURNED UP THE volume on the radio. The song was unmistakable . . ..

"I don't wanna say goodbye for the summer,

Knowing the love that we'll miss

I'll send you all my love, every day in a letter

Sealed with a kiss."

He thought of Cassie, who was a long way away. Maybe he should have put up more of a resistance to her wanting to move back to Maine for the summer. Perhaps he should have fought a little harder. Already, he was feeling the void. But that was just like him . . . to take the path of least resistance. Even with something as important as her.

He rounded a curve and headed into a straightaway just outside Fair Bluff when he observed the shimmer of something reflecting up on a rise to his right. The reflection dissipated, and a red pickup truck appeared.

The Continental's driver had just enough time to think, *that's strange,* when a white flash exploded from the direction of the truck. The sound of exploding glass was all he heard before his world went black.

———————•———————

THE BIG BLUE CONTINENTAL VEERED over into the other lane, barely missing an oncoming beige Chevrolet.

"Son of a bitch!" Greer said. "Where'd that damn car come from?"

Johnson remained leaning over the front quarter panel of the truck with a toothpick extruding out of the side of his mouth. "I don't know but I damned near got me two birds with one stone, didn't I?" he said with a grin.

"We ain't got time for you to gloat. Grab that spent shell and get in the fuck'n truck!" Greer said, turning the key.

Johnson put his shotgun in back in the leather case, placed it in the truck bed, and walked around, looking down at the ground.

"What the hell you doin?" Greer bellowed.

"Looking for that spent shell like you said to."

"Get in the damned truck! We gotta move!"

The pickup eased down the far side of the bluff and stopped in a stand of trees beside Highway 904.

"Where the hell are they? You figure they went over to check on him?" Johnson said.

"I can't see them from here," Greer said. "Don't wanna pull the truck out any further in case they . . ."

"Oh hell yeah! There they are! They stopped their car," Johnson said.

"Oh fuck! I see 'em now," Greer said looking around Johnson.

"Back up! Back up!" Johnson yelled.

Greer shifted the gear shift into reverse, spinning tires in the sand saying, "Fuck'n long-haired hippie. Can't mind his own business! But he may damned well wish he had. I know what he looks like."

"Get down! Here they come," Johnson yelled.

Johnson, the bigger man, lay over in the seat resting his head in Greer's lap. Greer put the truck in neutral and slid his torso down so that only his ballcap peered out through the steering wheel as the Chevy approached.

"That them?" Johnson asked from below.

"Yeah, that was them."

"Did they see us?"

"I don't know. They were driving real slow. Looked like the driver was looking straight ahead down the road. But I swear, I think the other guy was looking up this way. I could see his face. But I doubt they could see us ducked down in the seat like we were." Greer said.

"You weren't, damn it. I saw you. Your head was sticking up above the dash," Johnson said.

"Bullshit," Greer said, and he eased the truck out onto 904. "I'm gonna pull on out here and cut across Wiregrass Road, just in case they decide to get nosey and come back," Greer said. "Did you pick up that spent shell?"

"Hell no. You were hurrying me so damn much I never got it. No big thing, though. It'll just look like some dove hunter's left-over shell."

———◆———

"I SAW A CAR BACK THERE. A red pickup," Jack said to Huff.

"Where?" Huff said.

"Back there . . . just a little ways up from where the car went into the field. It was parked just off the roadway up in the woods there."

"So what? All these farmers around here drive pickups. Probably out working in the field before it gets too hot," Huff said.

"It wasn't empty. I saw someone behind the steering wheel. Looked like a kid in a red ball cap. Think they might have seen something?" Jack said.

"I didn't see a pickup and really don't care, Jack. What does it matter? That driver is toast now, anyway!"

CHAPTER 3

Earlier that same morning

RICHARDSON PIERCE STEPPED OUT of his Cadillac. The brilliant sunlit sky illuminated his white hair. The two-story Polynesian-style house with its curved roof sat on the lower end of Madd Inlet and provided lodging for him and his son until the house on Bird Island was completed. When the house over on the island was finished, he would offer the Polynesian house as a guesthouse for visiting friends.

Pierce had hired a fellow named Roy James as project foreman. James and his wife lived in a little cottage that Pierce had built beside the Polynesian guesthouse. Both structures were on the mainland at the foot of the bridge that Pierce had built to carry lumber and workmen across the marsh and over Madd Inlet to Bird Island. He found James in Charleston on one of his trips to observe the early 18th-century architecture there to possibly pattern his island house after. James specialized in preserving the Charlestonian architecture on the old homes there. He liked James' craftwork and attention to detail. A tan, thin man in his late 60's, James had been considering an early retirement due to a back problem, but Pierce was able to coax him into coming to North Carolina to manage the work on his houses. The pot had been sweetened by the offer of staying on as caretaker after the island house was completed. The life of a coastal Carolina caretaker on a secluded barrier island sounded just about right for him and his wife. Pierce felt he and James matched up well.

"Morning Mr. Pierce," Roy James greeted his boss. "Didn't know you were coming down a day early."

Placing his hands on his hips, Pierce arched backward, stretching his back, and said, "I don't know, Roy. I'm finding it harder to stay inland these days. This project is near and dear to my heart. It pretty much occupies my thoughts nowadays," he said, pointing out over the inlet to bird island." Looking around as he stretched, he asked, "Any trouble from Groat?"

"Just more of the same. His men sit out there on the road watching us. They're over there now," he said, pointing over Pierce's shoulder. Pierce turned and saw a pickup truck parked a ways back from the gate at the entrance to the bridge.

"Nothing we can do about that. That's a public road. But I *am* surprised I didn't notice them when I pulled in. Was the truck there when I arrived?"

"Been there all morning. I have to believe they come over onto the island at night after we've left to check on the progress of the house. I see beer cans strewn around. They weren't there the day before when we were working, and my men don't drink on the job. I worry as we progress with the house. We may need to keep someone over there at night."

"You're probably right, Roy. He worries me too."

The Groat family were substantial land owners at Sunset Beach. The family bought up land after the devastating Hurricane Hazel at dirt cheap prices. And with that ownership came power—power that Horace Groat was not afraid to use. He had a group of followers, but most on the island were not, but those kept their mouths shut and tried to stay out of his way.

"Well, we'll just proceed, but continue to be very aware of him," Richardson said.

"I'll get out of your way now and send this crew out to the island house," James said.

"No, Roy. Let's put the finishing touches on this house so we can put everybody out there," he said, turning his gaze out over the marsh toward South Carolina. "What have we got left here?" Pierce asked, looking up at the guest house.

"Just the trim and molding," James said.

"Good. I'm ready to start the push on the island house, and so is Rich Jr."

"We've been lucky. The weather has held so far, this spring. It's early, but I hope it will carry into June. I'll get one of the guys to get your bags."

"That's all right, Roy. I have only the one. I can get it. I'm going in to change clothes. How about getting the skiff ready? I want to go over and look at the dock on the back side of the island. That's finished now, correct?"

"Will do Mr. Pierce. Yeah, the dock is finished. We can unload more supplies starting with the next boat."

"Good. Where's Rich? Has he left?" Richardson Pierce asked just as a big, somewhat beat-up late model car backed out from the car port under the Polynesian house.

Rich spotted his father and broke into a broad smile. "Hey, Dad. Glad I got to see you before I left," he said as he got out of the car and gave his dad a hug.

"Me too. Whose car is that?"

"It was Cassie's mother's car."

" I like Cassie. I look forward to getting to know her better."

"I'm afraid that's not gonna happen, Dad. At least not for the summer. "

"Why's that?"

"We had a long talk before I left Greensboro. Things were kinda coming apart for us, and we both thought the time away from each other might be good. We decided to cool it for a while and see where we're at come fall. She's taking her mother's death pretty hard, so she's going back up to Maine this summer to work on her art."

" I'm sorry to hear that. But why are you driving her mother's car?"

"Her car wasn't in any shape to drive that distance. And my Scout had more room to carry her frames and easels and stuff. I'll only be going to and from Greensboro after I get back from Greece. She needs a more dependable car more than I do, so we traded."

"Well, I hope things work out. I thought she might be the one. I'm sad to hear she's having such a hard time with her mother's death."

"Yeah, me too. Cassie has a lot on her mind right now, and that's part of the reason we're gonna take some time away from each other. She needs space to sort some things out. If there's anything serious between us, it'll still be there at the end of summer."

"I wish her well. How long do you think you'll be in Greece?"

"Not sure, at this point. Two-three weeks. A month at the most. I really don't want to go. I wanted to be here for the entire summer, with the building of the island house and all. I'm going earlier than I first thought so I can get back here sooner."

"I understand. Your mother can be quite insistent. Do whatever you need to do to keep the peace. This entire project's stuck in her craw. The whole family's, for that matter. All except you. If you weren't as involved and as enthused as I am, I don't know if I would continue this pipe dream."

"It's not a pipe dream, Dad. It's your dream. And oh . . . the plans for the upper floor are back. They're in the house on the living room table. I really like what you did with the widow's watch. Sealing the west end off with that partition is a great idea. It'll block out the light pollution from Ocean Drive and Myrtle Beach."

"As best as it can. We'll still have some light in the night sky, but it won't be directly in our eyes," Pierce said.

"Yeah, probably. But still . . . great idea. I really like the change. But I best be going. Get this trip over with as soon as possible so I can get back here. Love ya, Dad, I'll miss you. Leave some work for me," Rich said as both men hugged their farewells.

"I'm sure there'll be plenty to do. Have a safe trip, Rich."

"I will, Dad. You stay safe, as well. But I need to tell ya. I had a run-in with Groat night before last."

"How so?" Pierce asked.

"I was in Milligan's store and ran into him there. He mumbled something as I walked by him, and I asked if he was talking to me. He said he was and then reiterated so I could understand him. He insisted that we're not gonna build the house out there. He said again that he doesn't like our bridge going across public fishing grounds. And then he made a threat."

"Made a threat? How's that?" Pierce asked.

"He said your money may have sway with the state, seeing that you cowed them into letting you build your bridge over Sunset Beach waters but that your money doesn't have any sway with him. He said you don't intimidate him. Then he said your bridge could end up into the water just as easily as any other bridge could."

"I've told him the marsh does *not* belong to Sunset Beach or any landowner. It belongs to the *state*, and I have a lifetime right-of-way *over* it. Not *on* it. He knows that. I don't want you dealing with that man, Rich. In the future, just walk away when he or his men tries to engage you."

"He's not gonna push us around, Dad. If he thinks he can, it's gonna be a long, hot summer. But all right. If it will put you at rest."

"It will put me at rest. Love you, Son. I'll see you when you get back."

"Love you too, Dad. Can't wait to get back and roll up my sleeves. Remember, save some work for me."

Rich eased the car through the gate and headed for Greensboro. He didn't notice the pickup was gone.

CHAPTER 4

THE BREEZE PUSHED BACK AT RICHARDSON PIERCE'S FACE. Sitting in the front of the skiff, he surveyed the sound side of his island. Scrub Pines sloped down to near the edge before giving space to a white, sandy beach, lapped upon by clear sound water. The treated hardwood of the landing dock glowed golden in the late afternoon sun. Three-fourths of the island lay in North Carolina, with the western tip in South Carolina. Sunset Beach and Bird Island faced south, not east like most of the beaches on the Atlantic seaboard. Thus, the positioning of the barrier island set up sunsets toward the Western end of the beach, making for stunning color arrangements as the sun dips below the horizon. Thus, the name Sunset Beach.

Roy James cut the skiff's engine, and the boat glided to the nearest piling. Arms extended, Pierce rose from his seat and met the piling with his hands. James steadied the skiff as Pierce ascended the wooden ladder and tied the boat off on a cleat.

A sandy road led from the landing, winding through a mix of pine and yaupon trees before opening at the foundation of the house. Some of the workers were now erecting scaffolding, preparing to go up with the structure. Looking over the work, Pierce commented to James, "This looks nice Roy. I really like how you matched up the brick. Nice. Very nice."

"Thank you, Mr. Pierce. As I said, the weather *has* cooperated."

They remained, discussing various aspects of the coming construction before Pierce took leave for his customary walk out to the beach.

Cresting the tall sand dunes that fronted the island and provided protection from storms, Pierce paused and surveyed the vista. To his left ran Madd Inlet, and beyond lay Sunset Beach. The two rows of cottages began some distance past the inlet and ran down the beach, eastward. Beyond, the Vesta fishing pier extended out from the beach. The pier was named for the Southern Civil War blockade runner, The Vesta, which was laden with needed supplies for the Southern Army, including a new uniform for General Robert E. Lee. A Federal squadron had been set up outside Fort Fisher near Wilmington to intercept steamers attempting to enter the Cape Fear River. The Vesta was spotted by the Federal fleet and was pursued by eleven Yankee cruisers. Soon, the Vesta was completely surrounded. She turned and ran the Federal gauntlet and headed for a sandbar where she ran aground in ten feet of water at Sunset Beach.

Bruce Kinnard was the original owner of the pier, and in deference to the South and the Confederate steamer, he had the pier built over the grounded vessel. The only part of the ship that was now visible was the top of the smokestack, which stuck about four feet out of the sand.

Beyond the pier and across Tubbs Inlet, at the other end of Sunset, lay Ocean Isle Beach. To his right was Little River Inlet, a slice of water that separated the South Carolina beaches of Cherry Grove and Ocean Drive from Bird Island. The western end of the island ended with a rock jetty that the Army Corps of Engineers had built in the late fifties as a result of the eye of hurricane Hazel coming ashore, its eye riding the inlet inland where it deposited its legendary rage, destroying property from Long Beach, North Carolina to Myrtle Beach. He remained in awe of the ocean's potential fury, especially on calm, beautiful days like today.

The soft, afternoon on-shore breeze momentarily soothed his worry as it always did when he stood atop his sand dunes and viewed the panorama. His social and financial status in the world did not come without a sense of privilege. The family had made its fortune in the banking business, founding one of the first banks in North Carolina. But he had a sensitivity that the rest of the family did not. He saw a bigger picture and was interested in things outside the financial world. That sense of character was a double-edged sword, though. His nature allowed him to appreciate the gentler side of life but did not lend itself to the aggressive world of free enterprise and commerce. So much so, his family and the bank's board had initiated his early removal from his turn as the family CEO of the bank. He was just not cut out for the rough and tumble world of banking. So, he took his millions, went into early retirement, and quietly headed in other directions, searching his own peace. And that peace included Bird Island.

Pierce had just turned his back to the ocean again to observe the progress of his house from the higher perspective of the sand dune when a deep rumble vibrated in his chest. He put his hand to his heart and paused, waiting for what might follow. Seconds passed . . . eventless. Relieved, he turned to the ocean, scanned the horizon, and thought *damned sonic booms!* Beachgoers and locals had long been hearing the deep unexplained sounds from out in the ocean for some years now, but nobody really knew what they were or what caused them. It was thought jets from the Marine base in Sunny Point, practicing maneuvers for coming sorties in Vietnam, were the cause of the "sonic" booms. But that was well disputed by the authorities that had conducted tests in the area. More times than not, when the boom was heard, it had been established that there were no jets in the immediate area. Over the years, folks lost interest in its cause. Many of the locals laughed it off as Davy Jones looking for his locker. But on this day, it bothered Richardson Pierce, considerably. He had heard the rumble many times, like all the other locals. But something about this one stayed with him. This one was more of a *feeling* than a *sound*. The *feeling* rumbled deep in his chest. It was a feeling he had never really experienced before.

CHAPTER 5

THE FAIR BLUFF VOLUNTEER FIRE DEPARTMENT responded with two tankers. The first to arrive got stuck in the loamy soil while crossing the field. Its two rear tires had to be dug out by hand and shovel. By the time it arrived at the burning car, there was nothing left but a frame.

The fire captain approached Highway Patrol Lieutenant Paul Berger. "You make anything off the license plate? I can't. Burned so damned hot it melted it."

"Naw, I'm afraid that ain't gonna do us much good. One of my men was able to make out the first six digits of the vehicle identification number in the left corner of the dashboard. We'll have to run it through Raleigh to see if we can match up the numbers. That's gonna take some time, though. They'll have to run it through Central Data in Dallas. As far as that poor creature sit'n there in the car . . . what's left of it . . . ain't enough to tell squat. We're just gonna have to work with what we have and try and ID the car through the partial VIN. Maybe this person will turn up missing, and the family will contact us in a few days. That would save us some considerable leg work," Lieutenant Berger said.

"Think it could be ID'd through dental records?" the Captain asked.

"Paramedics already checked on that. From the looks of it, the person in there doesn't have any teeth left. Looks like the face was all but destroyed in the impact," the Lieutenant said.

The two men stood silently for a moment before the fire captain asked, "You got any idea what may have caused this?"

"Probably some tourist coming back from the beach fell asleep. Car veered off, jumped that ditch, and ended up in this field. You have any thoughts as to what might have caused such an intense fire?" the Lieutenant asked.

"This *was* one hot fire. Probably ruptured the gas tank when it crossed that ditch."

"I don't know, Captain. I gotta gut feeling about this one. I'm gonna impound the entire car, not just the dashboard. I'll radio Lee's Towing to come tow this thing out of the field. He can keep it safe in his lot until we can get something back from Raleigh and Central Data."

CHAPTER 6

THE BLUE LIGHT IN THE REAR-VIEW MIRROR caused Huff to skip several breaths. At the same moment, Jack blurted, "Oh shit Huff! How fast are you going?"

Huff looked down at his speedometer and responded, "fifty-five, damn it! What the hell is this trooper's problem? Give me some gum. It's in the glove compartment."

"Here," Jack said, after taking the wrapper off the stick of gum. "Pull the hell over."

"I will soon as I can get to a place where I *can*."

The trooper popped his siren once, and Huff responded by immediately pulling his car over into the tall grass that lined the road. Rolling his window down, he looked up into a pair of sunglasses with shiny reflective lenses.

"Yes sir, Officer," he said through a stick of Juicy Fruit, "Is there a problem?"

"There could have been. You rolled through that stop sign back there. That's a bad curve back up the roadway on 904. That stop sign was put there for a reason. Been a lot of wrecks there, caused by what you just done. What you got in that cooler back there?"

"Just some beer cooling down for the beach, Officer."

"You mind if I have a look?"

"No sir. Go right ahead."

The trooper opened the back door and opened the lid of the cooler. Satisfied, he joked, "I just wanted to make sure you weren't transporting moonshine. Then, I *would* have had to put you under arrest. But I'm gonna let you go with a warning about the stop sign thing. But remember, a stop sign means just that. Stop all four wheels. Be careful and enjoy your trip down at the coast."

"We will, Officer. And thank you very much," Huff said with much relief and gratitude.

"Oh my God," Jack said through an expulsion of air. "That was too close! Whenever 'the man' shows up nowadays, I bout mess my pants!"

"No shit, buddy-boy! State Troopers aren't normally that nice. We've gotta get down there and get this trip behind us."

———————•———————

THE ONE-LANE PONTOON BRIDGE was closed when they arrived at the backside of Sunset Beach. Once an hour, the wooden barrier arm would come down and stop traffic traveling on and off the island, and the barge-type bridge would swing out allowing boat traffic to move up and down the Intracoastal Waterway. Spring boat traffic consisted mainly of northbound yachts making their way back north after wintering in Florida.

Jack lit a cigarette, tied his hair back in a ponytail, and settled back in the passenger seat. The sky over the causeway was a brilliant blue with white puffy clouds out over the ocean. The boats that had been waiting for the bridge to open started passing through the narrow opening. A yacht with a tanned woman on the bow passed through.

"You see her?" Huff asked.

"Yeah. All tall and skinny," Jack replied.

"Did you see her smile and wave at me? I guess this is where you and I part old friend," Huff said opening the driver's side door.

"She was waving at the guy in the Corvette behind us! Shut the door, dumb ass. The bridge is starting to open," Jack said.

They crossed the one-lane bridge as the traffic on the other side waited their turn. Jack and Huff couldn't help but notice the white puffy clouds becoming an ominous black.

They continued across the causeway and came to the end of the road where Beach Road intersected. Bruce Kinnard's Vesta pier sat directly in front, extending its wooden appendage out into the Atlantic Ocean. The Impala turned right onto Beach Road, and then right again, a few yards down, into the Sunset Beach Motel parking lot.

"I'll come in with you. I need to stretch my legs," Huff said.

"This shouldn't take long. I've already reserved the room."

Jack and Huff entered the slip of a lobby and smelled fried bologna wafting down a hallway that appeared to lead to the living quarters in the back. Two plastic chairs sat across from the counter against the far wall of the lobby. Huff took a seat.

"Hello," Jack said into the hallway. "Anybody here?"

"Yeah, hold on, Hon," came the reply from the darkened hallway. "I'll be right there. Let me turn off this bologna affore it burns." The sound of bare feet making their way up the linoleum hallway preceded the appearance of a large woman wiping her face with a dishtowel.

Laying the towel on the counter after one last swipe of her mouth, she took a deep breath and said, "What can I do for ya?"

"Yes ma'am. I'm Jack Thompson from Charlotte. I spoke to you on the phone a while back and made reservations for April."

The sound Huff made behind him was indiscernible between a laugh and a cough.

"Let's see here," the woman said, her meaty hand thumbing through the Rolodex. "I remember that one 'cause we don't get many requests for a month. Oh here it is . . . yeah, Jack Thompson," she said looking up at Jack. "I believe I've seen you before. You've stayed here before, haven't you?"

"Yes ma'am. I've come down and stayed with you on weekend surfing trips," Jack replied.

"Well, you're paying up for a month. Can I see your credit card so I can imprint it on my machine?"

"Uhh . . . Ahh . . . I'm gonna pay cash," Jack said reaching into his back pocket for his wallet.

"That'll work. Room 23 on the second level to the right of the stairs," she said.

"Thank you, ma'am," Jack said, taking the key.

"No loud music or parties is all I ask. You can have all the women you want, but one at a time," she said with a smile. Then she added under her breath, "And I'm sure that's a problem for a young buck look'n like you do."

"Jack Thompson from Charlotte?" Huff said as he and Jack climbed the stairs. "What tha hell . . . ?"

"You gotta remember. I'm on the run now, Huff. Gotta lay low. Selective Service would just love to know that Jack Tagger just checked into the Sunset Beach Motel, as indicated by his use of his credit card. For any business that may give me away, I'm Jack Thompson from Charlotte, and I pay cash."

Arriving at room 23 as indicated by rusted metal numbers on the door, Jack inserted the key attached to a green plastic tongue. The stuffiness from the winter permeated the one-bedroom kitchenette.

"Pretty damned nasty smell," Huff said walking over to the window air conditioning unit, turning the knob to the high setting. "How bout you unpack right quick, and then let's step across the street and check out the surf. If it's any good, we'll have us a session before I head down to O.D."

"That sounds about perfect. Best idea you've had all day, Huff."

———•———

THE OCEAN SETTLED AND ROLLED GENTLY beneath them as they straddled their boards. The dark, purplish clouds had receded and were now a backdrop out at sea.

"How long you gonna give it to get a job down here?" Huff asked, turning his gaze out onto the horizon for any swell that may be rising out in the ocean.

"As long as it takes. Since I'm getting a jump on the season, maybe I can land something soon. I've got the room for a month. After that, my money starts to get pretty thin."

"Sure you don't wanna try it farther south? Maybe Ocean Drive or Myrtle Beach? Or even Charleston. At least Charleston don't close down at the end of August. *And,* more people. Makes it harder for the draft board to find you, I would think."

"I don't need the crowds right now. Sunset's home."

"You ain't *beginning* to get over her, are you?"

"It's not that. I just need to get away, and there's no other place I'd rather be right now."

"You know Sunset ain't always gonna be just a two-row beach cottage beach, don't you? Old man Groat's gonna see to that. I hear Bruce Kinnard's been approached by him several times about selling the pier. Wants to extend it out further so's the end ain't sticking just twenty feet out in the ocean at low tide. He wants to put an amusement park on one side of the parking lot and charge people to park on the other side," Huff said.

"He's not gonna do that. Not with the Vesta parked directly under the pier. That's history. It's a Civil War relic," Jack said.

"I doubt he gives a damned about the Civil War. Don't no Southern relic mean anything to a man like him if he can't make money on it," Huff said.

"It's people like him . . . greedy bastards. Before it's all done, Myrtle Beach is gonna cross the state line and run all the way to Ocean Isle Beach. Won't be nothing but cars and lights up and down this part of the coast," Jack said.

"Exactly what I'm talking about, Jack!"

"Well, hopefully it won't be in my lifetime."

"Hopefully you'll meet some young thing, and you can quit thinking about her. But then, you've still got the draft and the war to think about. And I hear those drill sergeants love nothing better than to get their hands on a long hair," Huff said smiling.

"If they find me down here, I'll head for Canada. I'm not gonna fight in this damn war! It's an unjust war that drafts mostly poor black and white boys as fodder to go fight and die for them. To hell with that," Jack said. Changing the subject, Jack asked, "You hear what Richardson Pierce is planning to do with Bird Island?"

"Who's that?"

"That guy from Greensboro. He owns the island across Madd Inlet from Sunset. Bird Island," Jack said.

"Oh yeah. I've heard of him. Rich guy, right?"

"Yeah. He's gonna build his dream home over there. He's building a bridge and road across the marsh and inlet connecting to the island. Already started on it, I hear. It'd be nice to get on with one of his crews, but I may be too late. More than likely he's got all his crew lined up."

"I don't see how it can be any more of a dream home than that mansion he lives in Greensboro. I've seen it," Huff said.

"They say it's a pipe dream; he's going soft in the head and is embarrassing the family. That's what my busy body aunt says, anyway," Jack said.

"I didn't know about all that. I guess then it'll be off-limits and no more surfing that nice right break down by the rock jetty."

"Maybe so. Word is though, that he's a cool guy, even though him coming from that well-to-do family and all. They're all big-time socialites, but I hear he's different from the rest of them. He's involved with that group called Create Global Peace. He's got their decal on the back bumper of his Cadillac. I've seen it. It's just a decal of the whole Earth. Lord knows, with what's happening in Nam we could use some help from the bourgeoisie," Jack said.

"DuPont Chemical is making too much money on that war! And

the DuPont family has way too much money and power. Much more than the Pierce's, I'm sure," Huff said.

The surf built again, and the two surfers rode into the ending of the day. The sun was starting to set when they left the water. Jack and Huff stopped and turned.

"Geez, what a hell of a good end to this day," Jack said as the last golden rays of the day danced across the tops of the waves. "I hope this is a sign of things to come this summer. I could use a good omen."

"It's gonna happen. Give it some time. You're gonna find her again. It's just not gonna be Kathleen," Huff said.

"I know," Jack replied. "But man, it sure is good to be here and away from Greensboro," Jack said sniffling back the salt water in his nostrils.

"This place is you, my man! This is where you need to be," Huff said slapping him on the back. "Come on. I need to hit the road. Paul's gonna be getting shitty about not having his bourbon."

As the two turned to walk back across the beach and over the sand dunes to the hotel, they observed a man walking towards them from the direction of Bird Island.

"How ya doing?" Huff said to the man as he passed. "Nice evening, huh?"

The man turned his head in their direction but made no response.

"I said, nice evening, ain't it?" Huff reiterated.

Again he said nothing but appeared to look directly at Jack.

The man passed on by them. When he was about ten yards beyond, he stopped and turned around. Jack turned at the same time and saw him standing there looking back at them for few seconds before the man turned and continued on down the beach.

"Holy shit! Did you see that, Jack? That man didn't have a face! Huff said.

"That *face*," Jack said, as if to himself.

"No shit! Poor guy. Probably a Vietnam vet . . . Napalm," Huff said.

"That *face* . . . that face looked like the face I saw driving that car!" Jack said.

"What are you talking about Jack? You saw that car blow up. That guy's dead-er'n hell right about now," Huff said.

"You didn't see the driver, Huff. I did! That face looked like the face I saw through the windshield," Jack said.

"*That* face looked like a product of Napalm bombs. We drop it on the Viet Cong in Nam to crisp their ass. Nasty stuff. It's like jelly, and when it gets on you, it burns through you, and you can't get it off. I've heard about some of our guys coming back . . . guys who were in the wrong place at the wrong time . . . those who survived it . . . with their hands, arms, legs . . . in that guy's case . . . faces melted off. A result of Uncle Sam's friendly fire!" Huff said.

"Yeah, I've heard about that stuff. But you didn't see the face in that car. I *did*. That face! I've seen that face before," Jack said, still looking down the beach at the departing figure.

"Don't you think you're overdoing it, Jack? Let's get the hell outta here," he said grabbing and turning his friend by the arm. "I gotta get down to Ocean Drive!"

CHAPTER 7

HUFF SHOWERED FIRST, AND THE TWO said their temporary goodbyes.

"See you on your way back home?" Jack asked.

"Yeah, Man, if I can. I'll try to stop back by on Sunday on my way back from Ocean Drive. But it depends on what time I get away from there."

"Good," Jack said. "If so, maybe we can catch another session on your way home."

"Will do it. If not Sunday, I'll be back down in a few weeks," Huff said and the two slapped hands on it.

Jack went up to his room, showered, put on fresh but worn jeans and a white embroidered Mexican peasant shirt, and stepped into flip-flops and out onto the porch with a Budweiser in hand. Dusk was fast setting in as he leaned over the railing and looked out into the pier lights that were just coming on, illuminating the white, cresting tops of the waves.

The waves were still pumping. He decided to take a stroll out on the pier.

He drained the last of his Budweiser and lit a cigarette. Crossing the street, he came to the steps that led up into the bait shop at the front of the pier. Sitting on the steps were two fellows in denim overalls, each nursing a tall Pabst Blue Ribbon. One, a big, rotund man, the other short and skinny, but with sinewy tanned biceps and forearms. Jack noticed the carpenter belts on the steps.

"Nice evening," Jack said as he reached the first step.

"Ain't it though?" the big one said.

Jack paused, took the last drag off his cigarette, and thumped the butt out into the sand beside the steps. "You two carpenters?" Jack asked.

"How'd you guess," the big one said looking down at the belts beside them.

"I've been known to strap one of those on myself," Jack said, nodding over at the leather belts. "Started out as a laborer on a crew building houses back in Greensboro. Worked my way up to carpenter. I'm Jack Tagger," he said extending his right arm.

"I'm Big Tom," the larger one said holding out a rough, beefy hand to meet Jack's. "This 'un here's Little Tom," he said cocking his head to his side.

Jack responded with a smile.

"Our mommas gave us our first names, but the Big and Little part is our own artistic effort. Pretty creative, huh?" Big Tom said.

Little Tom held out his hand and met Jack's hand with a firm handshake. "Tom Gregory. Nice to meet you, Jack."

"Same here, Little . . . Tom."

"You'll get used to it after a while," Big Tom said. "It'll start rolling off your tongue smooth as butter and sweet as honey. Least it does with the women."

Little Tom chuckled.

"You guys work on the island?" Jack asked. "I'm looking for work."

"Yeah, we work on the island," Little Tom answered. "We came down here last year . . . last winter to be exact and were lucky enough to get hooked up with Horace Groat to do all the repairs on the cottages he owns and rents out through his realty company. He'd just fired his other crew right before we got here. Guess you could say we were in the right place at the right time."

"You just work in the off-season then?"

"Naw," Big Tom inserted. "We work all through the season. This salt air does a number on these cottages. Something to do all the time. We're trying to finish up with everything we've had to do over the winter in time for the start of the summer season. We're behind, though. Come to think of it LT, we could use another swinging hammer. Think old man Groat would see fit to dig into those deep pockets and spring for another hand to help us finish up?"

"I don't know," Little Tom said. "Wouldn't hurt to try, though." He looked at Jack and said, "You understand it would be temporary, though. Might be two-three weeks of work, and then you'll have to find something on your own."

"Fine with me. That's two or three weeks of work I don't have right now. It'll keep me from tapping into what money I brought with me."

"You staying over there?" Little Tom asked, nodding his head across the street to the Sunset Motel.

"I am," Jack said.

"We'll talk to Groat tomorrow. If he's willing to put you on, he'll probably want to meet and grill you first. He's a strange, old codger who's suspicious of everyone. Don't trust anyone when it comes to money. Meet us here tomorrow evening."

"I appreciate it, fellas. I really do," Jack said as he walked up the steps to check the surf on out at the end of the pier.

———•———

THE FOLLOWING EVENING, Jack approached the steps of the pier where the two Toms sat nursing their beers. The heat of the day had broken. A breeze blew in off the ocean.

"Y'all have a chance to talk to Mr. Groat?" Jack asked.

"There he sits, right there," Big Tom answered pointing behind Jack to a silver Cadillac parked in the pier's parking lot.

Jack followed Big Tom's finger back over his shoulder and observed a man wearing aviator sunglasses, sitting with all the car windows down, staring at the three of them.

"We put in a good word for you, hippie. Now don't fuck it up. Agree with everything he says and don't go rippling the waters. That there's a man that don't like no stone unturned. He don't want no consternation in his world."

"Consternation? Where'd you learn such a big word," Little Tom asked, poking his friend's oversized belly.

"You forget my momma taught at Tabor City Elementary. I come from a highly educated, distinguished family."

"Educated, maybe. Distinguished? I doubt it," Little Tom replied.

"What'd he say when you asked him if he needed another worker?" Jack asked.

"He asked about you. Where you was from. How much experience you had. If we thought you could be trusted."

"Trusted? How come he asked . . ."

"You better go on over and talk to the man, Jack. You don't keep men like Horace Groat waiting," Big Tom said.

"Yeah, okay. Thanks again, you guys," Jack said.

"Think nothing of it. We can use the help getting done before the season starts," Little Tom said as Jack started toward the Cadillac.

"Mr. Groat? I'm Jack Tagger. Nice to meet you," he said extending his arm through the window.

The gesture was not returned. "Get in," Groat said. Jack crossed the front of the car and got in the passenger's side. Looking straight ahead, Groat said," I hear you're from Greensboro."

"Yes sir."

"Ever hear of a fellow up there named Pierce? Richardson Pierce," Horace Groat asked, now turning his head toward Jack, aviator sunglasses tipped down on his nose exposing a set of steely eyes that studied Jack intensely.

Jack thought of Big Tom's warning.

Jack paused before answering, "Seems like that name rings a bell. Can't say as I've ever met the man, though. Just a name to me."

"He's a big shot up there. His family's high-society folks that come from old money."

"Like I say, seems like I've heard of him, but never met him."

"I'd a thought you'd been right familiar with that name, coming from Greensboro and all. You seem to be an intelligent boy . . . city boy . . . someone with some education behind him. Am I correct in my assumption?"

"Two years junior college."

Groat peered ever so more intently at Jack over his sunglasses, "Thought so. Don't ever doubt my assumptions, Boy. I can see through people and get to the heart of matters. You in college now?"

"No sir."

"How come your ass ain't in Vietnam then? You got some kind of physical deferment?"

"Just layin' low trying to avoid that scene right now," Jack said.

Quiet settled in the car. Jack looked out the front window. Groat held his stare for a few seconds before he broke the silence.

"Draft dodger, huh? Well, you just keep your political opinions to yourself. I don't wanna hear 'em." Changing the subject, Groat said, "I got big plans for this place. Them two there," he said looking at the two Toms. "They're good boys. Work hard, but ain't got the brain between the two of 'em for what I'm looking for. I'm gonna need someone in the future. A foreman. A right-hand man that I can trust completely."

"Big Tom said the job was for a few weeks . . . three at the most," Jack said.

"As it stands right now, that *is* correct," Groat said.

"Well, I don't want to take anybody's job away, if that's what I am getting here," Jack said.

Groat frowned, took a deep breath, and then exhaled it while looking out the front windshield. "You ain't taking nobody's job. For now, you got the job as a laborer, starting at minimum wage. You do and fetch whatever they ask you. Just don't forget, I'll be around."

"I won't. And thank you, Mr. Groat. I'll do you a good job," Jack said, extending his arm out to Groat. Groat ignored his hand.

"You start tomorrow, seven AM. Meet them here on the steps. They'll already have the work schedule for the day."

"Will do," Jack said swinging his legs out the passenger side door. He closed the door just before Groat sped off, leaving sandy dust in the air.

"Well, what'd he say, Jack?" Big Tom asked, the steps to the pier shaking a bit as he descended towards Jack with a fresh Pabst in his hand. Little Tom followed.

"Surly fellow, isn't he? But . . . he said I have the job," Jack said grinning up at the two. "I'm your laborer. I'm to fetch whatever y'all ask me to fetch. I reckon I'm your Stepin Fetchit."

"My what?" Little Tom asked.

"You know, Stepin Fetchit . . . that black actor from back in the thirties. 'Yowsa boss, I'll fetch it for ya.' Kinda like . . . you know . . . during the Amos and Andy era."

Big Tom laughed and slapped Jack on the shoulder. Turning to Little Tom he said, "I told you I liked him from the beginning . . . I believe we can work with this boy."

"I don't believe I'd go calling him *boy*," Little Tom said.

"I'm not worried about that," Jack said.

"We'll be here around seven in the morning," Little Tom said. "Don't be late."

"I'll be here," Jack said.

———◆———

HORACE GROAT WATCHED FROM a distance as Jack and both Toms

left in little Tom's pickup truck headed down to the east end of the beach to tear out some rotten siding on one of the front row cottages. Jack had arrived at the pier first. It didn't go unnoticed by Groat.

CHAPTER 8

ROY JAMES LOOKED LEFT AND RIGHT AS he walked across the bridge. He did not take the threat made by Groat lightly.

The bridge left Sunset Beach about three-fourths of the way back on the sound side and ran from the bulkhead across the marsh, interspersed with open water, finally crossing Madd Inlet, and ending at Bird Island. It was a magnificent structure, with several open passageways underneath for low-profile boats to pass under to allow fishermen and crabbers access to the sound beyond. It was close to being finished. Some planking and railing were all that was needed before trucks and supplies could access it and cut construction time considerably. The boats that brought lumber from Wilmington would not be needed as much.

"Hugh, you and Lucky keep your eyes open for anything suspicious around the pilings and underneath the bridge," Roy James shouted over the side to Hugh Wyrick and Lucky Whitley, two of his laborers who were poling a shallow draft boat underneath the bridge. "I'm not so concerned about nuts and bolts being loosened, but it don't hurt to double-check. My feeling is that if that son of bitch is gonna do anything to this bridge, I see him dynamiting or setting fire to a section at an opportune time."

"Nothing unusual so far, boss," Lucky answered. "But we ain't gonna be able to pole clear across today on account the tide will be going out directly."

"I know. But let's make it as far as we can; then we'll tie up and come back tomorrow and the next day til we've covered the entire bridge. I'm thinking about putting a crew on it, nightly. I just don't trust that fella."

"Might not be a bad idea," Hugh said. "Leastways til this thing simmers down some."

"I hope it will, and soon. I don't cotton to having to look over my shoulder when I'm working," James said. He looked back over the bridge's span and spotted the silver Cadillac sitting at the gate at the entrance to the bridge. "There he is again," James said.

"Who?" Hugh asked looking up at him.

"Groat."

"You want me and Lucky to go and run his ass off?"

"Lucky, you stay here. Keep poling and checking the underneath. Hugh, you come up, and let's you and me walk back there and find out what Mr. Groat is looking for."

Hugh stood up in the boat and raised his hand. James grabbed him by the wrist and pulled him up onto the bridge. He brushed off his jeans, and the two men walked down to the silver Cadillac.

They approached with James in front. He lifted his arm as he walked, pointed at the Cadillac, and shouted, "You got some business with us, Groat?"

"Well now that all depends on who *us* is," Groat answered.

"I'm Roy James, foreman on this project."

"Just fucking with you, James. I know who you are. My sources have already provided me that bit of information. In answer to your question, I'm just here observing the goin's on here on my beach. Now I got a question for *you*."

"And what might that question be?" James said.

"I'm just curious as to what might make a man wanna leave a nice place like Charleston and come up here and get involved in something that he has no business getting involved in?"

"I'm afraid I don't quite understand your question, Groat."

"What part don't you understand?"

"The last part. The part about me getting involved in something I don't have any business getting involved in."

Horace Groat slid his Aviators down on his nose and eyeballed Roy James and said, "I don't know if you know this or not, but this is *my* land, Mr. James. My family once owned this entire island. And more on the mainland. We owned it all at one time, until my daddy decided to sell off lots. I disagreed with him about that, but I was just a young man then. We still own most all of the land you see around here. But the thing is, I own *all* the oceanfront on the western end of this island. From the end of Sunset Beach all the way to Madd Inlet. There's a lot of empty beachfront out there. Sixty-five acres in all. I could fill in the backside of the beach and extend this island all the way to the inlet and put in more lots on the ocean side. You have any idea how much money that potentially represents? Serious money.

"Only thing that stands in my way is Richardson Pierce and this damned wooden contraption he's built across the marsh there. I need to do some dredging to fill in on the backside so I can develop those lots on the beachfront. I told Pierce he needed to take down that section of the bridge that crosses over the inlet so I could bring a dredge in up through the inlet from the ocean side. I said I'd replace it just as I found it. He refused. Said he needed that bridge to connect to the island so he could bring in supplies and start developing the island. Well, one word led to another, and then he proceeded to be a smart-ass and told me not to put a foot on his bridge or his island. What sticks in my craw more'n his meaningless threat is that he proceeded across this marsh and never spoke to me about it. He had the gall to come across here and never mentioned a thing to me.

"This ain't no small thing, James. And when it comes to money, there ain't no playing involved. I've had an architect look at the possibilities, and his survey says at least twenty-one more cottages could be built on the oceanfront, all the way to Madd Inlet. Like I said, that's a lot of money. It's a serious matter. Very serious."

"I've heard about the Groat family and all the land you own. But the thing is, there's limits, Groat. And from what I hear, limits is one thing you don't seem to understand. This marsh is state-owned. You don't own it. Richardson Pierce negotiated with the state to lease the right-of-way over the marsh and build his bridge over to the island. Sounds like a matter between the state and Mr. Pierce, and it really doesn't concern you. And by the way, he has no plans to *develop* Bird Island. He's building a house over there for his family's private use. He's planning on moving down here full-time once the house is completed. It's been a dream of his for some time and ain't nothing you can do to put an end to his dream," James said.

"Let me just say that anything that concerns this island concerns me,

46

and that includes the marshland that backs up to my beach. Don't say I haven't warned you, James. The project you're working on just ain't gonna happen. You're on the losing side . . . working for the wrong man. I've got plans for Sunset Beach. Big plans. This ain't gonna remain the sleepy little beach it is now. Soon as this bridge and his high-minded plans end up in the water, I'm gonna be needing a foreman to run *my* projects. You may wanna think about that, Mr. James. But you don't have a lot of time to consider it. Time's running out, and once the hourglass is empty, there ain't no turning it back over."

"Consider it considered, Groat, and I'm not interested," James replied.

"Very well. You've made your bed, and now you're gonna have to lie in it. I suppose up where Pierce comes from, they have to play by the rules when making their money," Groat said, sliding his sunglasses back onto his face. "Down here, we play by different rules. The rules are made by a few. The rest follow. And if they don't, things can get rough."

"You 'bout finished with your threats, Groat?"

"You can take them as threats. But most people down here take what I say as un-written law."

"Good day, Mr. Groat. I'm certain this won't be the last meeting between us."

Groat stopped halfway into his car, looked back over his shoulder at Roy James, and said, "You can count on that."

———•———

"JACK, GO ON UP ABOUT TWO more rungs. There's a piece of siding up there that's worked its way out," Little Tom called up to Jack.

Jack wiped the sweat out of his eyes and dried the palms of his hand before moving up the ladder. The morning sun was starting to bear down.

"Hot as hell for April, isn't it," Jack said, balancing himself on the ladder while he re-tied his ponytail.

"Can't never tell," Big Tom said. "Some years, spring can break the first days of March and summer's here by early May. Other times the weather can last and it be a chilly and rainy June. Just can't never tell. But the sooner it breaks nice, sure enough, the vacationers will start coming down, if just for long weekends. And it looks as if that may be the case this year. If so, we got a lotta work to do before they start coming. Groat can get right ill if he thinks we're lagging."

At that, Horace Groat's Cadillac pulled into the driveway of the cottage they were working on. Groat stepped out of his car and said, "Boys you're gonna have to step it up if we're gonna have these cottages in shape by the time the season starts. By the looks of things, that might be sooner than later."

Big Tom wiped the sweat from his brow with the bandanna he kept in the back pocket of his bib-overalls and winked up at Jack.

"Jack, come down off that ladder and talk to me," Groat said.

"All right," Jack said.

Jack met Groat at his car door.

"Let's walk," Groat said.

"Something wrong?" Jack asked.

"Not yet. And I wanna keep it that way," he answered.

The two men walked a ways on Main Street before Groat said, "Jack, you know the other day when I asked you if knew Richardson Pierce?"

"Yes sir."

"You said you didn't know him. That you'd only heard of him."

"Right," Jack said.

Groat stopped and turned to confront Jack. "You sure about that? You sure you've only heard of him?"

"Like I told you, seems like I know the name."

"If you know the name, then you've got to have more information than you've given up," Groat said. "You being a city boy from Greensboro, and all."

"I'm not sure what you're getting at," Jack replied.

"What I'm getting at is this. I find it somewhat coincidental you showing up here from Greensboro just about the time Richardson Pierce is about to finish construction on his bridge across property he don't own and is about to go full swing on that development he is building out there on Bird Island. I won't stand for a plant in my business."

"Sir?"

"Someone Pierce planted here to keep an eye on me and my business plans," Groat said as he lowered his sunglasses and looked Jack in the eye. "Believe me, boy. You don't want to go against someone like me in that capacity. Back in the days, you know what was done to a spy when he was found out?"

Jack looked back at Groat and swallowed but did not respond.

"In the olden times, the penalty for spying or treason was death. In such a case, I'm inclined to still abide by the old way. You know what I'm saying here, Jack?"

"No, I really don't, Mr. Groat. But I have to say I don't appreciate the tone of what you're saying."

Horace Groat stood silent, intensely observing Jack for several seconds before he broke into a snide smile and he said, "Naw, Jack, that'd be awfully harsh retribution, wouldn't it? I wouldn't do that. We don't live in the olden days, and I do believe death for betrayal would be against the law in this day and age. I was just trying to get a rise out of you. I tell you what I'm gonna do. I'm gonna believe you, Jack. And by believing you, I'm gonna put a lot of trust in you. So much so, I got a special job for you. And if you're successful in what I'm about to ask you to do, it could possibly lead to bigger and better things. I'm looking for a right-hand man. Someone I can trust and who'll do what I say, when I say, and will complete the job I give him. I'll ask a lot. But I can assure you the reward will be well worth it. Now, I ask you, Jack. Do you think you could be that man?"

Jack's life lately had been like chasing after its tail. Since his breakup with Kathleen Green, he'd dropped out of college and gone from menial job to menial job, just getting by. It was once thought by his friends that by now he would have had the world by the tail. That the world was his to shape. Or so it was thought. Before Kathleen left and Vietnam arrived on the horizon.

"Do you, Jack?"

Groat's voice brought Jack back to the present.

"Well, Mr. Groat. My daddy always told me never to agree to anything until you know all the ins and outs. I'd like to find out more about what you're proposing. Could we talk more about it?"

Groat stared at Jack for a few seconds before he answered, "Them two you work with . . . the big un and the little un . . . they'd jump and ask questions later at what I just put out to you. But I guess that's why I'm talking to you about this. You're smarter'n them. Meet me tonight at my office. You know where that is?"

"No, I'm afraid I don't."

"Behind Milligan's store. It's on the main road going out just after you cross the bridge, on the left. I own that building too."

"What time?"

"Let's make it seven."

"I'll be there."

"WHAT DID HE WANT?" Little Tom asked when Jack arrived back at the site.

"A bit cantankerous isn't he," Jack said

"Why? What'd he say?" Big Tom asked.

"He asked me again if I knew Richardson Pierce. He seems to think I have some connection with him."

"Don't let that bother you, Jack. He's got it in for Pierce. Don't like him or what he's doing over on the Bird. And since you and Richardson Pierce are from Greensboro, he's gonna think you have some connection with him until you prove to him you ain't," Little Tom said.

Jack thought about that last sentence. Why was Groat suspicious just because he and Pierce happen to be from the same town? It really didn't make sense. He hadn't been on the job for a full week and already Groat's talking about taking him into his inner circle. Jack was curious to find out what the "special job "was that Groat has in mind.

CHAPTER 9

JACK ENTERED MILLIGAN'S STORE THROUGH the front door, causing the bell to jingle above the doorjamb.

"We're closed," came a terse female voice came from within the depths of the store.

"Ma'am?" Jack looked up and responded.

"I said we are closed. I just haven't had a chance to lock the front door. Read the sign on the door. We close at seven o'clock. Open tomorrow morning at nine. We aren't into summer hours yet. Won't be till the first of June."

A smallish woman wearing glasses too big for her face, looking somewhat akin to a mouse, stepped from behind the counter. Hands on hips, she stared at Jack and waited for him to leave.

"Ma'am, my name is Jack Tagger, and I have a meeting with Horace Groat at seven."

"Well I'm Alice Millikan, and me and my husband own this store. You need to go around back. His office is back there," she said pointing at the back wall.

"Out the front door and around back?" Jack asked.

"Once you get around back, you'll see a door in the back of this building. He's in there."

52

"Thank you, Ma'am."

Jack walked out the door and turned right and found himself facing a rusting aluminum screen door. He knocked twice before he heard, "Who is it?"

"Jack. Jack Tagger."

A few seconds elapsed before the wooden door behind the screen door opened and Horace Groat appeared. "Thought it'd be you. But a man in my position can't be too careful. Have a seat." Groat motioned to four chairs positioned around an oval Formica table in the center of the cinder block room. A lone light bulb hung from the ceiling over the table.

Horace Groat continued, "There's *some* folks 'round here that'd like to take a poke at me. I think the word is jealous. They've always been some folks who don't like the fact that we Groats have held, and still hold, so much real estate around here. And with that holding comes power. But I know who they are. That's what tips the scales. Knowing your enemy. As long as I know who they are and what they're up to, I can control the situation. Understand what I'm saying here, Jack?"

"I don't know about that . . . ah . . . I really don't want to get into that kind of thing. I'm new around here and I . . ."

"That's right, Jack, and that can be to your advantage. And maybe mine too, if you decide to work with me."

"But I'm already working for you."

"Note the word I used. Not *for* me. I said, 'If you work *with* me.' There's a difference."

"I'm not following you," Jack said.

"Jack, the job you have now ends in a few weeks. As soon as all the repairs on the cottages are finished. After that, Big Tom and Little Tom will do just fine. I'll have odd jobs to keep them busy all summer. But I'm afraid there won't be no place for you. Least not on their crew."

"I know that, Mr. Groat. And I'll look for more work when we get to that point."

"Doesn't have to be that way, Jack, if you don't want it to be."

"I'm listening."

"Jack, I already told you there's folks here that don't like me. But I know who they are and what they're up to, so I can keep them under control. But there's one person that I can't get under my thumb. Know who that might be, Jack?"

"From what you've said and the questions you've asked, in the past, I have an idea."

"And just who might that be, Jack?"

"If I had to bet, I'd bet you're talking about Richardson Pierce."

"What made you think it was him?" Groat asked, an arched eyebrow aimed at Jack."

"Well, he seems to be a point of contention for you."

"How's that?" Groat asked, his eye still peeled on Jack.

"You've asked me several times if I knew him, us both being from Greensboro, and all. I gather he must be a pebble in your shoe."

"That's why I've had my eye on you, Jack. You're smart and pick up on things pretty quickly."

Groat smiled and pushed back from the table, his stare softening.

"I got a proposition for you, Jack—one that can mean more money in your hip pocket. If this thing I got in mind works out, it would mean you getting paid double, while working just one job. You interested in hearing more?"

"Getting paid double for the same job? Like I said, I'm listening," Jack said.

"I don't like Richardson Pierce or his type. Not one bit. Big city man from big money coming down here, buying his own private little island. See, Jack, I don't really know what he's doing out there. What his true plans are. A man can't tell me that he's planning on building just one home on that island. That don't make sense when he can develop that entire island and create his very own resort. *Bird Island Resort*, next to Sunset Beach. And he's doing this just when I'm trying to bring this beach into the modern-day by gearing up to expand Sunset and put up more of my own cottages. But I can't build on my oceanfront property out there because the state has refused to let me buy up that marsh on the backside and fill it in for development.

"They say doing that would disturb the sea turtle's natural habitat as a breeding ground. Since when did a damned Loggerhead Turtle's rights become more important than a man's right to prosper? I need the rights to the backside of my beachfront property so I can extend Main Street down the beach. If I don't have that roadway, I can't develop the lots and build the cottages I intend on building. The state sure stepped aside when they let him buy a lifetime right-of-way out on the marsh. And that's very damn curious to me. So that right there gives you two reasons I am suspicious of him. *And* the state. Plus the fact I just don't like him."

"What does all this have to do with me?" Jack said.

"I need someone on the inside of his operation. To get to know him. What he likes, dislikes, what turns him on, what don't turn him on. But most of all, what his *real* plan is for Bird Island. And then find his weak spot so I can destroy him and his plan. But most of all, I want to know if he starts moving more land over there. Land other than that parcel where he's building his house right now. If he starts disturbing more land, that would tell me he has more plans in mind. And if so, I'd wanna know about it sooner than later."

"I don't know. I don't have any argument with Mr. Pierce. Don't even know him. And I'm inclined to let people live as they please, as long as it doesn't infringe on me or my rights."

Horace Groat stared at Jack for a few long seconds and then said, "That's just it, Jack. Richardson Pierce *is* infringing on me and my rights. My rights as a long-time landowner and resident of Sunset Beach to make a living and expand my land holdings. You know, they ain't making any more land down here. He comes down here, owning his own island, and thinks just 'cause he's from a wealthy family and can get in bed with the state, he's gonna hide behind them to shut me down? Ain't gonna happen, Jack. Now, you with me or against me in this? I ain't asking you to pull a trigger or anything like that. Just get in with his crew, keep your ears open, and get paid twice for doing one job. I'll match whatever he pays and kick in an extra ten dollars a month more'n what he pays you. It'll be under the table . . . tax-free. That's a good offer, Jack. I think you're too bright a boy to turn an offer like that down."

Jack sat, fiddling with a rubber band that had been lying on the table, and said, "I can't afford to break the law right now. And as long as I don't have to, I'll consider your offer."

Groat grinned at Jack and then said, "I knew I had you pegged right when I figured you were a smart boy. Good! Now, I think you need to start trying to get onto his crew. Don't want them spotting you working with Big Tom or Little Tom. They'd know you was working for me, and that would throw a monkey wrench into things."

"One question, Mr. Groat. What if his crew is full and there's no place for me? What then?"

Groat looked at Jack through steely eyes and said, "Laborers come and go. That's why I keep Big Tom and Little Tom around. Neither one of them loaded with the smarts, but they're steady as a mule and work in the ruts without complaining. Here every day, work hard, and happy just to end the day sitting on the steps of the Vesta Pier with a tall Blue Ribbon in their hands. I can depend on 'em. They ain't no drifters. Laborers come and go. Here today . . . *gone tomorrow.* Ya just never know when a spot's gonna open up in this business," Groat said, gazing up at the single light bulb hanging over the table.

Jack studied Groat. He didn't like the idea of being a snitch, but the pay was too good to pass up. Especially right now.

"I need to know, Jack. Tonight. I'm wanting to get on with this before that bridge gets completed. Once that happens, it puts a whole different slant on things."

Jack continued in thought. *Money's good . . . very good. He isn't asking me to harm anyone or anything. Just information, that's all. Could be a good thing. Work my way up in Groat's organization and find myself a future here.*

Groat held out his hand waiting for Jack's answer. "We got a deal here or not, Jack?"

Jack slid his hand across the table and met Groat's hand. "We got a deal. I'll go see his foreman first thing Monday morning. I don't guess they work on the weekend. But if there's no opening, I still got my job here with Big Tom and Little Tom?"

Groat's eyes glazed as he gazed upwards, as if in thought, and said, "I got plans for you. Big plans."

As soon as the screen door slammed shut at Jack's departure, a door opened in the back of the room, and Jimmy Greer entered. "What'd he say? I couldn't hear all of it, but sounds like you and him got a deal," Greer said.

"Yeah, we do. For the time being anyway,"

CHAPTER 10

MONDAY MORNING DAWNED BRIGHT WITH a cloudless spring sky. Jack woke early and remained in bed, his arms bent under his head, thinking about the day and what it could mean. An excitement stirred in him, accompanied by a tinge of trepidation. He didn't know where this was going. But the unknown had always been a draw for him. This could lead to a future here at Sunset Beach. He loved Sunset just as it was . . . its quiet beauty that few people had yet to discover. But he knew it was bound to grow, and there was nothing he could do about that. As much as he hated to see it happen, Sunset would someday be an extension of the South Carolina beaches, separated by Little River Inlet. Maybe the inlet would be enough of a barrier to hold back some of the commercialization. But progress was coming, and he was thinking he was getting tired of being on the outside . . . of running on empty.

Perhaps he and his generation were destined to lose. Hell, the war ground on in Vietnam, regardless of their protests. He had felt the beginning of the caving-in sometime before. His generation wasn't gonna change the world. Greed sat at the top of the food chain. Change was simply an idea that temporarily stood in front of a machine that was too big and powerful to stop as it clawed its way forward, devouring whatever was in front of it, spitting out the remains, and continuing down the road without looking back. He was tired of being on the losing end. The machine was taking him in. He felt himself slipping towards its ugly, advancing teeth. But so be it. He'd tried it his way.

Kathleen had left him to pursue the life that was afforded proper people. She'd played the game for a while, until the machine started creeping up on her, as well. He'd been so angry at her. How could she give up the fight that both he and she had so believed in? Now, he thought he was beginning to feel the pull she must have felt. Only, once again, she was smarter than him. She saw the impossibility of fruition and gave in and went on with her life. Again, he was left behind, only to finally realize the silliness of that dream they shared.

Today was a new day for him. He would rise from his bed and begin this new journey in a different direction. It was about *him* now. What a fool he'd been.

———•———

"EXCUSE ME. CAN YOU TELL ME where I can find the foreman?" Jack asked the carpenter up on the second floor of the guest house who was putting the finishing touches on the railing above.

"He's over on the island. Should be coming back across in about a half-hour. Comes back to the mainland to check . . ."

Just then a motor was heard, propelling a boat crossing the open water between the island and the mainland. At the wheel of the boat stood a tall man with gray hair, thinning on top but thick on the sides. His arms and face burnished brown and leathery from days spent under the Southern sun.

"Well, you're in luck. Here he comes now," the carpenter said, pointing out in the direction of Bird Island. "He's coming in a little early."

"What's his name?" Jack asked.

"Roy James. Hang on, and I'll come down and walk down to the dock with you."

Roy James cut the skiff's motor on approach and let the boat glide to the wooden dock.

"Mr. James. This man here . . . what was your name?"

"Jack Tagger."

"Jack Tagger here would like to speak with you," the carpenter said as he jumped down onto the dock to meet the front end of the boat's glide into the dock.

Roy James looked up at Jack, squinting into the sun that backlit Jack as a silhouette standing on the dock. "I'll be right up, soon as I tie up here," James said.

He threw a line up to the waiting laborer, who then attached the line with a figure eight around a cleat that was nailed to the dock. James then climbed the wooden ladder to the dock.

"Roy James," he said extending an arm that was met by Jack's. "What can I do for you?"

"I'm from Greensboro but aim to settle here. I'm a licensed carpenter and looking for work and was wondering if you have any openings?" he said.

Roy James bent slightly, brushed off his pant legs, and said, "Now that's a coincidence, isn't it," he said looking at Jack.

"How's that," Jack replied.

James straightened and looked Jack directly in the face for a moment before saying, "I just lost one of my laborers. Lucky Whitley. A good man. Lucky was on look-out walking the bridge Saturday night, and about mid-way across, it looks like some planking gave way, and he fell through. We'd already laid those planks and secured them with bolts. We're still not certain how it happened."

Jack's mouth went dry as he recalled Horace Groat's words. *Laborers come and go. Here today . . . and gone tomorrow.*

"You okay, son?" Roy James asked. "You look a little peaked."

"Yeah, I'm all right. Been having a touch of something. Must be something going around. I'm sorry to hear that. Maybe this isn't a good time . . ." Jack said, turning to leave.

"Well now, hold on a minute. Much as I hate it, I'm gonna be needing to fill Lucky's spot. Say you're from Greensboro? Ever heard of a fellow named Richardson Pierce in Greensboro?"

Jack lied. "Can't say as I ever have."

"I'm surprised. His family is prominent up there."

"Actually, I grew up in the county, just outside of Greensboro," Jack said.

"Well, he's the one who owns all this. He's building a house over on Bird Island. We've just started going up with the foundation. There'll be work here for a good while. Gotta finish this bridge and then the house. Say you're a licensed carpenter?"

"Yes sir," Jack said.

"I don't need a carpenter right now. But I can start you out as a carpenter's helper. Pay you at a helper's rate, least til I see how you swing a hammer. We pay twice a month. Cash. You interested?"

Jack's mind raced. Could Groat have had a hand in this? Jack tried to focus, but his head was spinning.

"I ahh . . . yeah. I guess so," Jack said.

"Well now don't go and be doing me no favors. I'll have plenty of applicants for the job once it gets out that we're hiring," James said.

"No . . . ahh . . . I mean, thank you. I'll take the job! And paying in cash works better for me anyway! I guess it's that touch of something that's made me a bit woozy. Sorry. When can I start?"

"Well you don't need to be working up on that bridge today, you being dizzy and all. Think you'll be ready by tomorrow morning?"

"I'll be here. Thank you, Mr. James."

CHAPTER 11

"YOU SEEN GROAT?" JACK HOLLERED UP to Big Tom who was straddled on a ladder hammering extruding nails back into the vinyl siding on a cottage.

"Naw. Not since earlier this morning."

"Okay, thanks."

"He might be back at his office. Try him there."

"Mind if I borrow your truck for a half hour or so? It's a long walk back over the causeway, and I really don't look forward to that long a stroll in this heat."

"Naw, I don't mind. I'll be here working for the rest of the day anyway and won't need it til quitting time."

"Thanks, Big Tom. Appreciate it. I'll be back shortly."

"Just make sure you're back by Blue Ribbon time."

Jack smiled. "I'll make sure of that, BT."

———◆———

HORACE GROAT OPENED THE rusting metal screen door after the second knock. "I was figuring how long it would take you to be at my back door," Groat said, smiling at Jack, chewing on a toothpick perched in the side of his mouth."

"Why's that?"

"Cause I heard what happened to one of Pierce's workers over the weekend. Word travels fast on this island. It was a shame the man fell through the planking and broke his neck. Did you go see their foreman this morning?"

"I did," Jack said.

"Well? Did you get on?"

"Start tomorrow morning."

"Good. Good," Groat said, still smiling.

"Mr. Groat. I need to ask you something."

"Ask away, Jack."

"You know anything about that?"

"About what?"

"About what happened to that laborer?"

"Now Jack, I just told you how word travels fast on this . . ."

"I mean . . . did you or any of your people have anything to do with that plank giving way?"

"I don't believe I like what you're insinuating here," Groat said.

"You mentioned at our meeting last Friday, that laborers come and go. And then this happens."

"Purely coincidental, Jack. That little bit of information would never hold up in any court of law. Our system abides by more than a reasonable doubt for a criminal conviction. There would be more than a reasonable doubt in this situation."

Jack looked deep into the man's face for assurance.

Groat responded, "I'm sorry the man met this fate. I'm sorry for his family. Maybe he was drunk and he fell in. It *was* a Saturday night. But no, I'm a businessman, Jack. Not a killer."

Jack held the stare a moment longer, and then his shoulders relaxed, and he said, "I guess it *was* just a coincidence."

Groat smiled a thin smile and said, "Don't ever *doubt* me like that again. I'll let this one slide, but no more. We clear on that?"

"I guess," Jack said.

———•———

THE OFF-SHORE WIND WAS PRODUCING swells of perfect waves. None of the normal late-afternoon chop made so by on-shore winds. This was pure glass with diamonds reflecting on the surface of each wave. They were coming in sets of five to seven with the middle waves being the biggest. Jack sat straddling his board in the lull between sets, trying not to think of his meeting with Horace Groat earlier that day. Groat's answer to his question about the laborer's death being purely coincidental sat well enough with Jack, but somewhere within him, the words had not reached. He was bothered. He tried to let the sun-rays rest on his shoulders. He breathed deep and tried to relax. But it wasn't working. He was still bothered.

A set started to build farther out from where Jack sat on his board. He waited, watching the rise of blue-green water until it built itself into a wall. Being the first wave of the set, he rose on his board as the wave passed underneath. Same with the second and third. On the crest of the fourth wave, he saw a big thick one rising from the ocean's surface, building as it came towards him. He turned his board and stroked hard toward shore.

After several powerful strokes, he looked back over his shoulder at the cresting top of the wave that was closing on him fast. Jack paddled harder to keep the wave from closing out on top of him and felt his board rise up onto the wave. He stood up in one fluid movement and flowed down the face. At the trough, he cranked his board left and looked up into a barrel that was forming directly above him. Jack's surfer heart soared as he moved his board back up the face and positioned himself for the barrel to encompass him in the green room, a place where surfers say that time and thought felt as if suspended.

The world around him turned green as he worked himself back deep into the barrel so that the only light, outside the watery world, was in the opening directly in front of him. That light started to close, becoming narrower and narrower until it became a small circular view of whitewater cascading down from the top of the breaking wave just above, and out in front of him. And then the opening closed completely, and the light went out.

Jack's body tumbled over and over in the darkness. He knew not to fight . . . just relax and let the turbulence pass. He was down deep in this one. He waited, but the washing machine tumbled on, turning him over and over. The air in his lungs started to become thin, and his body started an instinctive fight against the dark that held him. He opened his eyes in search of light in the darkness—a light that would indicate the direction of the surface. But the only thing becoming light was his body. His struggle became less and less. A peacefulness came over him.

So, *this* was the way it would end. He relaxed and waited for the visitation from loved ones that had passed, as he had heard would happen from other surfers that had come close to drowning. A human-like figure appeared in the darkness and moved toward him. *This must be them,* he thought. *Here they come. The end must be near.*

But the depth suddenly released its hold, and Jack found himself bobbing, spitting saltwater from his lungs. The darkness had disappeared as quickly as it had enveloped him, and he was back on the surface . . . in the light. The figure he saw now stood in that light . . . *on the shore!* The ocean current inched Jack's body closer to the beach . . . and recognition. But it was not family. Strangely, the figure on the shore emerged as the faceless man that he and Huff had seen on the beach the day of their arrival.

The man stood at the edge of the surf, looking seaward, its featureless face . . . seeming to emit a certain sadness. And then he disappeared.

Jack struggled toward the beach just as a large set came in behind him and lifted him, moving him towards the beach. The wave crested, and he put his head down, stretched his arms out in front of him, and body surfed in the foam to the shore. Seconds later, he felt the sand under his palms and beneath his toes. He crawled up onto the beach. Exhausted, he remained on his belly and coughed up the last of the saltwater from his lungs and rubbed it out of his eyes. He turned his head to the side and tried to focus on a figure walking down the beach away from him. Just as his vision cleared, he observed the figure stop and turn around, slowly, back in Jack's direction. The figure came into focus, and once again, he saw that it was him. The faceless man had re-appeared. He looked back at Jack briefly and then turned and walked away. Jack, still prone on the beach, lifted himself up on his elbows and followed the man's retreat. *Who the hell is that guy?* he thought to himself.

CHAPTER 12

THE CREW WAS GATHERING AROUND the dock early Tuesday morning, awaiting Roy James' instructions for the day before heading over to the island to begin work. Jack approached the small knot of men and introduced himself.

One of the men standing in the group replied "I'm Bill Greeson. Carpenter. We heard yesterday that they'd hired a replacement for Lucky," he said. He didn't offer out his hand to Jack and continued, "He was a good man, a damned good worker. We're gonna miss him."

"I'm sorry for what happened to him. I'll do my best to give as good as he did," Jack said.

"That'll take some doing. Like I said, he was a good man," Greeson said.

Two men approached, descending the slight rise from the guest house to the dock. Jack recognized Roy James. The distinguished white-haired man who accompanied him must be Pierce. The men arrived at where the group had settled. The dignified-looking man took the lead, extending his arm to Jack and introduced himself. "I'm Richardson Pierce. You must be Jack Tagger. Welcome aboard."

"Thank you. Like I was telling the guys here, I'm sorry to be here under these circumstances . . . Lucky's death and all . . . ."

"That's no fault of yours, Jack. No need to be sorry. Just give a full as day as Lucky did, and you will honor him in that way."

"I'll do my best, Mr. Pierce."

"Roy says you are from Greensboro?"

"I am. Actually, from Brown Summit."

"I know the area well. Owned a farm on Reedy Fork Creek, at one time."

"The cattle farm?"

"That's the one," Pierce said.

"Don't the Hallsons own that?"

"They do. I sold it to the Hallsons about ten years ago. I didn't have any business in the cattle business. I didn't know a thing about cattle farming."

"That's beautiful land out there," Jack said.

"It certainly is. That was more the reason I bought it, I think.'

Jack was aware he was making some points here, and it couldn't help but make up for some equity with Lucky's co-workers. Still, Jack knew the reason he was there. He would give Richardson Pierce an honest day's work. The information he would supply Groat could be a mere conversation . . . . information that was obtained through simple discussion.

"Hugh, you take Jack and see how much of the bridge y'all can get done today. There should be enough lumber still out there to keep you busy til' lunch or maybe this afternoon. Let me know when you need to re-supply, and I'll get some more lumber out there for you. Still some boxes of nails out there?" Roy James asked.

"There were two boxes as of quitting time yesterday."

"I'll send a couple more boxes out with the lumber," James said

"Okay. Let's go, Jack," Hugh said.

The two men walked side by side, saying little until they reached the section of the bridge yet to be finished. Jack looked across the span of open water to the other side where the bridge had been completed, the section they were to eventually tie into. The pilings had already been set and the outer frames put down. Jack and Hugh were to cut the planks, which would become the decking, and then fit and secure them to the outer railing.

"Grab the end of that railroad tie. Gonna be nailing down the side runners anyway, so might as well go ahead and take this with us," Hugh said. "Don't want nobody running their vehicle off the side of this bridge, now do we? Already been one person to go in and not come back out alive. And he weren't in no vehicle."

Both men bent and lifted the heavy creosote tie off a pile that was stacked on the bridge. Beads of perspiration broke from their exertion as they dropped the tie at the appropriate place.

The sun rippled the top of the water as it made its way back to the sea, snaking between Sunset Beach and Bird Island. Jack bent and looked down into the water, his hands braced on the bridge's railing, waiting to start the day.

"Why do they call it Madd Inlet, Hugh? Look at it. Just meandering along . . . doesn't look mad to me," Jack asked Hugh Wyrick.

"What you see on top ain't necessarily what runs below. That's a damned bad inlet, Jack. It just don't let on, at times. Like now, at high tide, it looks nice and wide on top, running out real smooth. *Meandering*, like you say. But underneath, what you can't see is another story. The sides channel straight down in a V shape all the way to the bottom. People have lost their lives trying to cross this inlet at the wrong time. Low-tide, it runs sweet and shallow. A person can cross in water up to their knees. Kids play in it. But come mid to high tide, it's a different story. Step off the bank, and you'll slide right down the side into water that's rushing faster under the surface than on top. A person steps off the bank at high tide gets sucked down under and ends up a half-mile out there," Hugh said pointing out the mouth of the inlet to the ocean. "That's why they call it Madd Inlet."

Horace Groat's name came to Jack's mind as he surveyed the inlet, his hands still resting on the railing. "I guess it isn't what it seems, is it?" Jack said under his breath.

"Say what?" Hugh asked.

"They got it all wrong. The spelling, I mean. They misspelled it, didn't they?"

"Misspelled what?" Hugh asked.

"Mad. They misspelled it. Mad only has one D in it," Jack said.

"Hell, I don't know! Maybe whoever named it wanted to make an impression. To get a point across. Like this is a really Ma-*d-d* inlet."

"Maybe that's it," Jack said grinning, pushing himself off the railing. "Trying to get a point across. Either that, or just a bad speller."

"Come on. Let's get this bridge finished," Hugh said, laughing.

Both men turned and walked across the bridge to where workers had finished up the day before, their carpenter's belts jangling in the morning sunlight.

"Where was Lucky working when he fell? This side or the other side," Jack asked.

"He was on the other side. We weren't so concerned with this side because we knew we would be working over here and would see or pick up on anything that looked suspicious. He wasn't working. He was over there just keeping an eye on things since it was the weekend. Groat had made some threats about the bridge. So Roy had him over there at night because he felt that if anyone was going to do anything or booby-trap the bridge, it would be at night," Hugh said.

"You think that's what happened? Somebody booby-trapped it?"

"Well, the police chief don't think that was the case . . . just a loose plank that fell through when he stepped on it. Me, I don't buy it. Groat has made threats before. Me and Roy heard him make one, just recently. But Horace Groat has the police chief in his back pocket. His family's been down here since the beginning of time. They've owned land here ever since before the Civil War. Roy James knows the story better'n me, but he told me that after the war, the carpetbaggers came down here, and the Groats lost almost all of what they owned.

"Eventually, they were able to get a foothold again when they were able to buy a small parcel of land over here on the beach. Roy said they kept at it, cobbling land once it became available until once again, they owned damned near the whole island. Only exception was Pierce and Bird Island. The first owner of the island was a guy named Samuel Frank. He bought it in the early eighteen hundred's for something like ten dollars. His family held on to the island through the years until Richardson bought it in early nineteen-fifty. Roy said Richardson paid sixty thousand dollars for it. He said the Groats had tried to buy it for years, but I guess the Franks and Groats didn't get along. Roy says that's the real, underlying reason for Groat's hatred for Mr. Pierce and his son,

Rich. The feud started the day he bought the island . . . something the Groats always wanted. And it continues to this day, I guess."

"I heard that Groat's problem with Pierce is that he thinks he is planning on developing the island after he builds his house. That he will have his own resort sitting right between Sunset and Myrtle beach. Doesn't mean anything to me one way or another. But that's what I heard," Jack said.

"If he has plans to develop that island over there, it's beyond me. I ain't heard nothing like that," Hugh said. "My understanding, and I get it from Roy James, is that he and his son are the only ones in his family that are interested in his idea of a family compound. Roy says he's building it for him and his son as a retreat. A place to get away. Gonna keep the Polynesian guest house for any guests that might want to come down. Anything else, I don't know about," Hugh said. "But this ain't getting this bridge built. Let's get to work."

CHAPTER 13

FOUR O'CLOCK ROLLED AROUND WITH Jack's skin a shade or two darker than when he started to work that morning. He and Hugh had added length to the bridge. More than had been added in any previous days.

"You put in a good day's work today," Hugh said to Jack as they walked back towards the mainland end of the bridge, their carpentry belts slung over their shoulders. "You give it that much every day and I'll put in a good word to Roy," he said.

"I appreciate it," Jack said.

"Naw, I'm the one that appreciates it, Jack. The finishing of this bridge has sorta been put on me. You swing a hammer every bit as good as Lucky, if not better . . . God rest his soul. I'm anxious to get over on the island and start to work on the house. More days like this one, and you'll be coming with me," Hugh said.

"Hope so. I need the work," Jack said.

"How you getting around? I ain't seen you drive up in a car, yet. You ain't hoofing it are you?"

"I'm afraid so. Room and board takes 'bout all I have saved up, right now."

"I got a buddy who's selling his Jeep. It's an old Willys Jeep, and he ain't had too many takers. It's kinda rough on the outside, but it runs good. He might be willing to let you take up payments on it. I'll vouch for you and tell him you've got a good job here with steady work, if you're interested, that is," Hugh said.

"A Willys Jeep? My father used to have a Willys Jeep. A green one. They used to make a Jeep station wagon. He was a country mail carrier and he used it to carry the mail. He swore by Willys," Jack said.

"This Willys ain't a station wagon, but it's green. You want to go look at it?"

"Yeah, I do. You really think he would let me buy it on time?"

"It's possible. He needs the money, and he ain't seen no takers yet. Where you staying?"

"At the Sunset Beach Motel," Jack said.

"Next thing we gotta do after getting you some transportation is get you out of that old fleabag and into a decent place to live. Tell you what. I'll drop you off; go home and get cleaned up, and I'll pick you up, say around six?"

"I'll be ready. I appreciate it."

"You got it," Hugh said.

CHAPTER 14

"WHERE'D YOU GET THIS OLD bucket of bolts?" Huff asked.

"I'm buying it from a friend of one of the guys I work with. Pretty cool, isn't it," Jack said.

"Yeah, I guess so. They still making Willys parts?"

"The guy I am buying it from gave me the name of a company that specializes in Willys Jeep parts. He said they're becoming collector items."

"Yeah, collectors of used parts," Huff replied.

"How bout staying down another night? I haven't made it down to Myrtle since I've been here. We can take Nellybelle and you can head back home tomorrow," Jack said.

"Nelly who?"

"Nellybelle! Remember Pat Brady from the old *Roy Rogers Show*. He had a nineteen forty-six Willys that he called Nellybelle. Always caused him trouble and had a mind of its own. Just like a woman," Jack replied.

"Oh, hell yeah! Nellybelle and Pat Brady. I'd all but forgotten 'bout *The Roy Rogers Show,*" Huff replied.

"I loved that show. Watched it every Saturday morning, as a kid. Nellybelle was so damned ornery, he had to tie it to a hitching post whenever he parked her for fear she'd roll away," Jack said.

"I don't know if I'd call her Nellybelle, Jack. But anyway, Myrtle Beach sounds like a good idea. We'll go down, have us a few, and I'll head back tomorrow," Huff said.

CHAPTER 15

900 NORTH OCEAN BOULEVARD WAS PACKED, unusually so for a night before the season began. Peaches Corner, an open-air bar on the corner of Ocean Boulevard, across from the pavilion in Myrtle Beach had been a landmark on the strand since 1937. Its foot-long hotdog and corndogs were prominently displayed on the lighted marquee that hung above the open sliding glass doors that allowed patrons to survey the parade of people on the sidewalk in front of the bar while quaffing a frosty mug of draft beer. The ceiling fans over the bar whirred, and an occasional breeze blew in off the ocean, providing slight respite to the humid-low country night air.

"You think this job's gonna hold out for the summer?" Huff asked Jack.

"Sounds like it might," Jack said looking down into his mug of beer.

"You sure fell into that, didn't you?"

"I guess I did," Jack said, still pondering the bottom of his mug of beer.

"What's the matter, Jack? You ain't looked up from that mug since they poured it. What's bothering you?"

Jack sat silently for a few seconds before answering. "I don't know Huff. I'm afraid I've got myself in a situation that I'm really not sure how to handle."

"What's up?"

"Not only do I have *a* job; now I've got *two* jobs."

"How's that?"

"Well, you know the man I told you about. The one that owns a lot of property down here?"

"Yeah. You told me about him, and I know about *that* job. What *else* have you gotten yourself into?"

"Well, *that* man . . . Horace Groat . . . he's got a strong dislike for Richardson Pierce . . . the guy who's building over on Bird Island."

"Yeah, I know about him too."

"Well, there's bad blood there, but it's mostly Groat's. Pierce owns something Groat and his family have always wanted," Jack said.

"What's that?" Huff said.

"Bird Island."

"So, what's all that got to do with you having two jobs?"

"Groat came to me. Said in time, he was gonna need a supervisor for his business, and that time didn't look to be too far off. He insinuated that could be me. But he threw in a hitch. He said the man he chose had to be totally dedicated to him. A man he can trust. Then he said he wanted to have someone on the inside of Pierce's operation . . . to keep an eye on him to keep Groat informed of what was going on over on the island and what Pierce's plans were and how things were progressing. He thinks Pierce is gonna develop the entire Island. Then he made me the Godfather offer."

"The Godfather offer? What the hell is that?" Huff asked.

"The book . . . *The Godfather*. He made me an offer I couldn't refuse."

"And that was . . ."

"He said if I could get on their crew as a carpenter or carpenter's helper or whatever, he would double whatever Pierce paid plus an extra ten dollars a month," Jack said.

"Whoa now! Getting paid twice for the same job? And ten dollars beer money a month to boot! Where's the problem, Jack? He ain't asking you to off anybody, is he? Just be his eyes and ears. I don't see any problem with that. You're just mowing both sides of the fence," Huff said.

"I know it. And that's one of the main reasons I agreed. But there's something I hadn't thought of."

"What's that?"

"It's just . . . it's that these seem to be good folks . . . the guys I work with, Roy James and Richardson Pierce. They seem to be decent people. I like 'em. And so far, I can't see where Pierce has done anything wrong. He leased the land over the marsh and the inlet from the state. And from what I'm hearing, he *is* building a family compound, and I don't think he has any plans to change that. At least I haven't heard of any, as of now. I guess that could change, but if it does, I don't see how that has any business with me. And Groat worries me. I get a bad feeling about how far he's willing to go to get what he wants," Jack said.

Huff said, "I see where you're coming from, Jack. But it's just a job. He ain't asked you to break the law," Huff said.

"Not yet, anyway," Jack said.

"Well, until he does, why don't you ride it out and see where it takes you? In the meantime, pocket some money and enjoy life. Think about what we're talking about right now, compared to what we were talking about when we came down here. It was *if* you get a job, *if* you can make it here. Buddy, I don't see any *if*s in your life right now. And from what you're going through, with Kathleen and the draft, that's good."

"I guess I need to look at it that way," Jack said

"You know it," Huff said. "Jack, I want to tell you something. You worry too much. Always have. You worry about right and wrong, this and that. Don't get me wrong, now. That's a good quality to have. But it gets away with you sometimes and clouds your thinking. It ain't always things are either right or they're wrong. There's gray in the world, Jack. And gray is okay."

Jack took a sip of his beer, smiled, and looked over at his friend. "When did you a become a philosopher, Huff? That's good shit. Thanks."

"Contrary to what most people think, my momma didn't raise no fool, Jack."

The two men turned on the barstools and looked out into the night and the folks walking down the sidewalk. Neither said a word until Jack said, "I saw him again."

"Who?

"The faceless man."

"Where?"

"Out on the beach. I was surfing and ate it on a big one. I swear, Huff. It was one of those washing machine moments that wouldn't let go. It wouldn't end. I thought I'd bought it. I was going round and round. Then it suddenly released, and I came to the surface and made my way in, barely. I was spitting up saltwater and could hardly breathe.

I opened my eyes and saw a guy standing on the shore. I tried to yell to him for help, but I just choked on saltwater again. Another set came in, and I caught a ride, and it washed me in. I crawled up on the beach and just laid there. And I saw him. His face was a blur, but I knew it was him. It's creepy. I feel like, for some reason, I'm supposed to know him."

"Now you're giving *me* the creeps, Jack. Like I said, he's probably just a poor son of a gun who had the misfortune of going to Vietnam and having his country burn his face off. What's there for you to get to know?"

"I don't know, Huff. But one way or the other, I gotta find out," Jack said.

———•———

"YOU TAKE IT EASY GOING BACK, my friend. Especially along that stretch of 904," Jack said to Huff.

"I'll do it. You don't think you'll be coming back home anytime soon?" Huff asked

"I don't think so. Too many unpleasant memories there for me right now," Jack said.

"I understand. I hope you'll find a pretty young thing down here," Huff said.

"I doubt it. Not at Sunset Beach, anyway. Single girls haven't found this place yet."

"Yeah, but there's Myrtle Beach just down the road. Come June, they're swarming down there like honey bees," Huff said.

"We'll see. I just don't think I'm ready for another relationship right now. But thanks anyway."

"You're welcome, my man," Huff said as he entered his car. "Keep some spare parts around for that bucket of bolts, ya hear? Peace!" he said with a smile and peeled off, leaving Jack in a sandy cloud.

Jack watched his friend drive off down the main drag. At the intersection, Huff slowed, put on his left turn signal, and disappeared across the causeway. Seeing his friend's brake lights disappear around the curve hit Jack with an unexpected wave of loneliness. He thought of home, which seemed like a long way and a long time, ago. The last conversation with Kathleen came to him . . . .

"Jack, I want my freedom. I don't want to end it with you, but if there was someone I would like to go out with, I want to be able to do that," Kathleen said.

"I knew this would be coming," Jack said.

"Why do you say that?"

"I just knew it. When you transferred to St. Mary's, I knew you'd change."

"I resent that! At least I'm being honest about it. I don't want to go behind your back and do it," Kathleen said.

"I kinda wish there wasn't a need, Kathleen."

"A need for what, Jack?"

"To be honest, I guess I wish there wasn't a need for your honesty," Jack said.

Kathleen reached out and ran her hands through his long black hair, pushing it back from his forehead. Then, she moved both her hands down to his cheeks. She held him there, looking into his eyes, and said, "It's time. We've been together eight years, and you still don't know where you're going. You have no plans. I do. Don't hold that against me, Jack," she said, softening.

Looking through her framed hands, Jack said, "I guess you're right. I don't. And don't you hold that against me."

"I don't. In some ways, I respect that in you."

"What do you mean by that?"

"I mean you're different, Jack. You walk to the beat of your own drummer, and you don't let society dictate to you or put you in a box. Like I said, I respect that in you. I wish I didn't. But I do. I admire that. But that's you, Jack. Not me."

"I'm sure your momma and daddy will be happy to hear this. You go on, Kathleen. But just know this. You walk out, and I won't be there chasing you. You go, I'm done."

Kathleen stared at Jack for a long second through a sad smile, and then she turned and walked away.

CHAPTER 16

THE CALL CAME INTO THE SAMPSON COUNTY North Carolina Highway Patrol Division when Lieutenant Berger was on vacation. The dispatcher in Raleigh left a message that was received by the division secretary who wrote the message. Lt. Berger had been back three days before he worked his way through the stack of pink notepads and came to the one from Raleigh.

WHILE YOU WERE OUT

IMPORTANT: Lt. Berger. The information you requested on said Lincoln Continental has been processed. Please contact Bob Freeman in the Records Department at the Raleigh State HP office asap.

He flipped the paper over and looked at the date the note was posted. "Damn," he said aloud. "Almost three weeks since this came in!" He grabbed the note and walked out to the secretary's desk and demanded, "Mrs. White, did you not note on this slip of paper that it said 'Important' at the top?'" He dropped the pink note on her desk and asked, "Is this not your handwriting?"

"Well, yes sir, it is. I remember taking that message from Raleigh, but you were on . . ."

"Then why didn't you bring it to my attention Monday when I came back on duty?"

"I'm sorry, Lieutenant. I should have. I know . . ."

The Lieutenant dismissed her with a wave and turned and walked back into his office, looking down at the note in his hands.

"I don't really know what I'm gonna find out anyway. I'm probably putting too much into this," he said to himself as he dialed the Raleigh number.

"North Carolina State Highway Patrol Headquarters," came the voice at the other end.

"This is Lieutenant Stan Berger in Sampson County. Put me through to Bob Freeman in Records."

"Will do, Lieutenant. Hold, please."

Seconds passed before Lt. Berger heard, "Bob Freeman."

"Yeah, Freeman, this is Lieutenant Berger down in Sampson County. I believe you have something on that Lincoln Continental that wrecked and caught fire down here last month?"

"Yeah. Geez, that was several weeks ago . . . let me see where I put that. Hang on a second."

After a few seconds of paper shuffling, Bob Freeman came back on the line.

"Okay, I have it right here, Lieutenant. Sorry it took so long. Anytime we have to run a VIN through Central Data, it takes longer . . ."

"I understand. Did they have any luck?"

"Looks like they did. Your Lincoln is registered to a Sarah M.

Prebscott in Caribu, Maine. Says here that's in the county of Arr . . . Arroo . . . I can't pronounce the name so I'll spell it. It's A R O O S T O C K. How'd you pronounce that?"

"Well, I guess just the way it's spelled. Aroostook," Lt. Berger said. "You got an address for her?"

"Just getting to that. It's 23 Garden Circle."

"Okay now, that's Sarah M. Prebscott, 23 Garden Circle, Caribu, Maine?"

"You got it, Lieutenant. Anything else I can help you with?"

"I believe that'll do it. Thank you, sir."

"Anytime, Lieutenant."

Lt. Berger hung up and dialed directory assistance for Caribu, Maine.

"What city?" the operator asked.

"Caribu Maine," Berger said.

"What listing?"

"Last name Prebscott, Sarah M."

"Hold please." Seconds passed and then, "I'm sorry, that number has been disconnected," the operator said.

"Disconnected? Do you have any other listings for a Prebscott in Caribu?" Berger asked.

"Not in my listing. I'm sorry. Is there another number I can help you with?"

"Well then, how about the telephone number for the US Post Office in Caribu?"

"Hold for the number," the operator said.

Berger dialed the post office's telephone number in Caribu. A man's voice answered the call. "Station 4, Pederson. Can I help you?"

"Yes, Mr. Pederson. This is Lieutenant Berger, North Carolina Highway Patrol."

"Yes sir, Lieutenant. What can I do for you?"

"I'm trying to locate a resident of Caribu. Her name is Sarah M. Prebscott, and she lives at 23 Garden Circle. The phone number has been disconnected, but I wanted to see if that is still a good address for Ms. Prebscott."

"Hold a second and let me run that address." The postal clerk came back on the line and said, "That address is vacant, and there was no forwarding address left."

"Disconnected phone number and the residence is vacant. Where does that leave me?" Berger mulled aloud.

"Hold on, trooper. I believe the carrier just got back off his route. Let me see if he remembers who lived there."

"I'd appreciate that."

Moments passed before a different voice filled the earpiece. "This is Calvin Jones. Is this the North Carolina State Trooper?"

"It is. Lieutenant Berger."

"Oh. Well, Lieutenant. I'm sorry to say that Ms. Prebscott passed away a while back. A fine lady. I hated to see her go. When I'd get to her house, she would invite me up for a cup of tea in the summer, or hot chocolate in the winter. I'd take her up on it sometimes if I was running ahead of schedule."

"Is there anyone living there now?"

"Nope. House is locked up tighter than a tick. I don't know what the family is going to do with it. A real fine house. Three stories. They say it's been in the Prebscott family since it was built around the turn of the century. It's sat empty for about a year now. I don't know if there's any more family around or not."

"You say your name is Jones? Calvin Jones?"

"Yes sir."

"Well Calvin, keep my name. I'll give you my number. If, by a long shot, anything should turn up in the future, would you mind giving me a call?"

"No sir. I'd be glad to."

"Thank you, Calvin. You got a pen to write my number down?"

CHAPTER 17

CASSIE CAVANAUGH OPENED THE SCREEN door and held it open with her shoulder. She shifted the pile of art books to her right arm while fishing for the keys in her purse with her left.

"Damn! Why didn't I get my keys out before I got here? I always do this, and I usually have a load of something in my arms when I do," Cassie said to herself.

Unable to put her hands on them, she set the books down on the porch railing and scrounged around in her purse for the keys until she found them.

"Thank God! I was thinking I might have left them back in North Carolina. I never checked to make sure I had them before I left," she mumbled to herself.

Cassie inserted the brass key into the lock and finagled it several times before it turned the deadbolt. The door inched inwards then stopped, making a creaking sound as it did. Cassie took the round, brass door handle and pushed gently; the door continued to creak as she inched it forward. Just inside the door, standing in the darkened room, she stopped, and a sob that sounded something like a staccato laugh emerged from within her.

"Oh, Mother!" she wept, as she knelt onto the antique Persian rug in the living room of her mother's house. The scent of Tea Rose, her mother's scent, hung ever so lightly in the room. She remained kneeling and looked into the darkened living room. Her mother's rocking chair remained, unmoved, by the fireplace. The couch sat to her left under the front picture window, her mother's old throw casually draped over the back, waiting to warm the next person to be seated. The quiet in the room seemed to be waiting for her mothers' return.

———•———

THE RECEPTIONIST PICKED UP the phone call on the second ring.

"Lieutenant, there is a mailman named Jones on the phone for you. He says he's from up in Maine," she said.

Lieutenant Berger grabbed the phone from its cradle and said, "This is Berger."

"Yeah, Lieutenant. This is Calvin Jones in Caribou Maine."

"Yes, Mr. Jones. You got anything for me?"

"Well, yes and no, Lieutenant. Someone has moved into that residence you were inquiring about, 23 Garden Circle, but I don't know if she bought the house or what. I haven't actually met her yet. She hasn't been home when I get to her on the route. I've rang the doorbell several times, but . . ."

"Mr. Jones, is this my person of interest or not?" Berger asked.

"Well, that's just it Lieutenant. I'm afraid not. You were looking for a Prebscott, but this woman is named Cavanaugh, Cassie Cavanaugh."

"Just one person? Is there anyone else who's getting mail there at 23 Garden Circle?" the Lieutenant asked impatiently.

"No, no one else that I've delivered to."

"Could this person be a relative of Ms. Prebscott?"

"I really don't think so. I don't think she had any relatives. I never knew of a husband. Least she never spoke to me about them."

"What about a vehicle? Is there a vehicle in the driveway?"

"Come to think of it, there *was* a vehicle parked there. I think it was one of those four-wheel wagons. An International Scout was sitting in the drive, if I'm not mistaken."

"Did you get a tag number off the plate?"

"No. I'm afraid I didn't think to do that," Jones said.

"Well, all right . . . but keep my number, and if you can remember, next time you see the Scout, get the tag number and call me back. And if anything else comes up that you think I should know. But I think that'll probably do it for now. I appreciate your help."

"Yes sir, Lieutenant. Got your number written down right here on my letter case."

The Lieutenant set the phone back in the cradle. "Well damn! I guess my hunch that I was making too much of this was right."

CHAPTER 18

THE LIGHT BULB BURNED DIM OVER THE TABLE, casting shadows into the corners of the room. Horace Groat bent a match out of the matchbook and raked the phosphorous head across the sandpaper at the bottom of the book. The match burst brightly in his face as he lit the end of his cigarette. He blew out the match, inhaled, then blew out the smoke, which settled whitish-gray around the overhead bulb. Groat leaned back in his chair and studied Jack from across the table for a moment, and then asked, "You got anything for me, Jack?"

Jack was not ready for the question. Not this soon. He hadn't been on the job that long. He paused for a moment and tried to think of something . . . anything that would satisfy Groat's impatience.

"Well . . . how 'bout it Jack? What do ya know?"

Jack was uncomfortable with such directness. He had nothing that would be of any consequence or value.

"Well, Mr. Groat, Pierce, and the crew are just going along day to day, working on the house. I haven't seen any sign or indication of him doing further development on the island. And I hear his wife and the rest of the family back in Greensboro don't really support him in this endeavor."

Groat leaned forward, his stale cigarette breath hitting Jack

94

squarely in the face. "That's old news, Jack. I don't pay for old news. Now what else ya got? Give me something I don't already know."

Jack thought to himself, *Well if you're so damned good at getting information, why the hell do you need me?* But the money he was going to make came back into play. He gathered himself and said, "Mr. Groat, I've only been on the job a week, now and I . . ."

"I'd think a week would have given you some inclination as to what's going on over there. Or of what's *going* to go on over there."

"I'm not gonna blow my cover, Mr. Groat. I don't want them to think I'm a newspaper reporter or some nosey snoop. So far, they don't suspect a thing. And that's the way I wanna keep it. I'm building a relationship . . . establishing trust with them, and if I'm gonna get any information, that's gonna be the way I'll get it," Jack said.

"Maybe I forgot to tell you, Jack. I lean towards being an impatient man. When I want something or want something done, I want it sooner than later. Did I forget to tell you that? If I did, well then I'm telling you now."

"I'm not a pushy person, Mr. Groat," Jack said.

"Well, maybe I misfigured you, Jack. Maybe you're not the man I need to do this," Groat said.

Jack thought again of the money that was going to be coming in. He was tired of living on the losing end as everybody else pulled up stakes, forsaking their principles to get ahead. He thought of sticking a fist full of green in Kathleen's face and saying, "What do you think of this, Ms. Saint Mary's girl? Does this make me worthy in your eyes now?" Well then by God, if information is what Groat wants, and he wants it 'sooner than later,' hell, he could provide him that. If he *demanded* information, well then, he could sure as hell *supply* that information. Even if it meant him having to make up shit and sell it to him as a pack of lies, he would do that. He'd sell it to him tied with a bow. But it would be on *his* time. Not Groat's.

"You didn't misfigure, Mr. Groat. I'm your man. I just need some time. I can't just go busting in there asking a bunch of questions. I've gotta ease my way in there. They gotta trust me. And trust takes a little time to establish," Jack said.

Groat took another drag of his cigarette, studied Jack, and then said, "Okay, Jack. I'll give you some time. But I want some information to start percolating in here, and the sooner the better. I ain't used to waiting. And I don't wanna drag this damned thing on all summer, either. Now get to work and make me happy. I like to be happy, Jack."

Jack stood and put both his hands in his pockets and said, "That's what I aim to do, Mr. Groat. Just as soon as that information starts to . . . as you say . . . *percolate*."

Jack let the screen door slam behind him.

Damn, he thought. *What was that tight-ass' plans? Did he expect me to get him his information within two weeks and then shut the job down, along with the pay? 'Don't want this thing to drag out all summer.' Well, Mr. tight-ass, that's about exactly how long I plan to take. You brought me into this, but it ain't gonna be a two- or three-week job. I figure it to be a summer job . . . . at least.*

CHAPTER 19

THE SUN BURNED BRILLIANT OVER THE blue Aegean Sea. The plaster houses glowed white along the cliffs. Sunglasses were a must.

The white-haired woman sat on the couch thumbing the current copy of *Grecian Architecture* magazine while cradling the receiver under her chin. The long-distance operator said in broken English, "I'm sorry madam. There is no answer. Would you try your call at a later time?"

"Oh, all right! I suppose so," came the slightly bothered, aristocratic reply. "But I have tried numerous times, but no one answers. Couldn't you try the number periodically and call me when you connect? I will be here the rest of the afternoon . . . until my dinner engagement this evening . . . around seven or so. If you could just call me here at this number before seven when you get him on the line . . ."

"I am sorry madam. That will not be possible. You are not the only person attempting to connect with the States today."

"Well! I understand . . . but you don't have to be so terse . . ."

"A pleasant day to you madam," the operator said just before disconnect.

"No wonder they're all fishermen here. That's all they can do. They're a very lazy culture. It's no wonder they can't do better," Martha Richardson said to her traveling companion, Lotta Murray.

"I know exactly what you mean," Lotta said.

Looking at her watch, Martha said, "I would think Rich Junior should have been here by now."

"You know how young people are these days, Martha. The hippy culture seems to have permeated even our children . . . our culture. We certainly didn't raise them that way. Even your Rich. Four years at Woodberry Forest prep seems to have lost some of its polish on these kids. Their time frame is . . . *whenever*. I guess prep school isn't what it was back in our day."

"I know, Lotta. But my Rich is different. He's always been so punctual. And he is such a considerate child. Always has been. Even through our divorce. He never wanted to take either side. Didn't want to hurt our feelings, I suppose," she said, putting the magazine down on the couch beside her.

"Martha, you put that boy on a pedestal. You always have."

"He *did* have a touch of waywardness in him when he was young. Danced to a different tune, you might say. Still does, I guess. Like his father! Oh, God! Did I say that out loud? Please no! Not like his father!"

"Is Richardson still building his pipe dream out on the coast?"

"You know he is. There is nothing that is gonna dissuade him from trying to prove us all wrong about that damned castle he's building."

"Another hurricane Hazel comes through, and that place will be nothing but a memory," Lotta said. "Is he really building it on the ocean front?"

"That's what Rich says. He did say it is behind the front row of dunes. But a lot of protection they will be if that island takes a direct hit, or even a glancing blow. But listen to me. What do I care whether or not a hurricane washes his place out to sea?"

"My thoughts exactly, Martha. Can I fix you a drink?" Lotta asked, crossing the living room floor. "A vodka, perhaps?"

"Not just yet. Oh, what the hell. Yes. Yes. I'll have a Stoli. Neat."

Lotta filled the bottom third of a leaded crystal tumbler and handed it to Martha Pierce.

"Thank you, dear. This is really a little too early for me, but . . . I don't know, Lotta. I'm a bit worried about Rich. Nothing stands out. Just a mother's intuition, I suppose. But he should have been here by now . . . or at *least* called."

"Why don't you call Richardson? Then you'll find that he's still at Sunset playing with his father's toy house, and you'll relax. Remember what I said about the classlessness permeating *our* society. Their hippy time is pervasive. But that's right, your Rich isn't affected by that culture."

"Oh Lotta, stop it. I don't want to call Richardson and give him the satisfaction of thinking I've lost my influence with Rich or that I'm worried in the least about him."

"Well, it might help put you at ease. Now, let me refill that glass for you?"

"Sure," Martha said as she stared out the window. "I'll try Rich again tomorrow," she said, sipping her drink.

CHAPTER 20

THE TELEPHONE RANG TOO MANY times for Trooper Berger. "Ms. White! Can you get . . . Oh hell!" he said grabbing the receiver off its cradle. "Highway Patrol," he answered into the mouthpiece.

"Lieutenant Berger?" came the voice from the other end of the receiver.

"This is Berger."

"I thought that was you by your southern accent."

"What can I do for you? Who is this?" he said.

"Oh, sorry! This is Calvin Jones with the US Postal Service up in Caribu Main. Remember me? "

"Yes, Mr. Jones. I do remember you. Got something more for me?"

"Well, I don't know if this's gonna help you or not . . ."

"Go ahead and tell me. What did you find out?"

"You're in North Carolina? Right?" Jones asked.

"That's correct."

"Well, I remember your last question for me was about the vehicle. So I paid special attention when I was by there today and it was . . . ah . . . *is* a Harvester International Scout. Green in color."

"You didn't happen to get the tag number and state, did you?" Berger asked.

"I did! And it's a North Carolina tag."

"A North Carolina tag! Damn! How bout that! Did you get the number?"

"I did sir. You got a pen and paper?" Jones asked.

"I do. Go ahead."

"Its tag number is TJS 2323."

"TJS 2323?" Berger repeated.

"That's correct."

"And you're certain it's a North Carolina tag?"

"Dead certain," Jones said. "Green letters and numbers on a white background."

"That's it," Berger said. "Damned fine job, Jones."

"Well, I hope this helps you, Officer."

"It does; it does. Thank you, sir. Oh, by the way, Jones. Have you seen or met the person living there?"

"I've seen her from a distance. A nice-looking lady. I'd say in her early twenties, maybe."

"Well, do me one more favor if you will, Mr. Jones. If you have the occasion to meet her or talk to her, don't tell her about my inquiry. I'm not sure what we're dealing with here, and until I find out, I don't want her to know she is of interest to us."

"I got you, Officer Berger. Me working for the federal government and all, we're restricted in what we do and say as well. I'll not mention our conversations."

"Thank you, Jones. You've done a good service, and I thank you. Good day, Mr. Jones," Trooper Berger said.

"You betcha! Anytime. You have a good day down there in North Carolina."

"You do the same," Berger said.

Lieutenant Berger hung up the receiver and looked at his watch.

Four o'clock, Friday afternoon . . . *I doubt I can get anything back today. Hell, I know I won't. I'll go ahead and call in the tag number to Raleigh, and maybe I'll get something back by Monday afternoon. Tuesday at the latest.*

The phone rang in Raleigh's Highway Patrol Headquarters.

"NCHP Raleigh."

"Yeah, this is Lieutenant Berger in Sampson County. I've got a tag number that I need you to run."

The voice at the other end said, "You know this is late Friday afternoon. We were in the process of shutting down for the weekend. Give me that number, and I'll enter it before I leave. Should be Monday or Tuesday before I can get back to you."

"That's fine," Berger said. "I'm surprised I got anyone on the phone this late in the afternoon. Just get back to me when you get something on it."

"Will do. You have a good weekend, Lieutenant."

"You do the same," Berger said.

CHAPTER 21

JACK PARKED THE JEEP IN THE SHADE under one of the Yaupon trees. He grabbed a fresh pack of cigarettes off the passenger's seat and slid out from under the steering wheel. He thumped the unopened pack against the top of his left hand and surveyed the landing. Some of the guys had arrived before him and were standing on the dock talking, waiting for the foreman to crank the skiff to take the first load of workers over to the island. He didn't see Roy James. He knew he was never late. Punctuality was big on his list.

Jack walked down the slope to the dock and joined the other workers. "Where's Roy? He decide to sleep in this morning?" Jack asked.

"He's still up at the guest house. Said to tell you he wants to talk with you as soon as you arrive," Hugh said, his back to Jack. "He said first thing."

Jack's throat went dry. He looked up at the house. "Everything okay, Hugh? I didn't fuck up on the bridge, did I?"

Hugh's back remained turned to Jack, and he said, "Don't know Jack. Ain't sure why he wants to see you. But you better get your ass on up there so's we can get on to work."

Jack continued looking up to the guest house and said, "All right. I'm going."

Arriving at the house, he walked up the steps, crossed the deck, and knocked on the glass door. A moment later, Roy James opened the door and stood before Jack.

"Come in, Jack," he said. "And close the door behind you. These mosquitos are brutal. Open the door, and they follow you in. Have a seat."

Jack sat in one of the wooden chairs at the dining room table. "Hugh said you wanted to see me right away," Jack said. "Everything all right?"

"Jack, I've been hearing some things about you . . ."

Jack's throat knotted. "Sir?" was the best he could come out with.

"Been hearing things," James continued.

"What kind of things?"

Perspiration dotted Jack's forehead. He felt dizzy. Did his relationship with Groat somehow get out? Who leaked it? Groat? Because he was unhappy with Jack's progress?

"Hugh tells me . . ."

Hugh? How . . . but why?

". . . that you swing a good hammer. Work your ass off, too. I know this comes in short order, but you've impressed me, Jack. I think you should be made a full carpenter instead of a carpenter's helper. That'd be all right with you?"

"Ahh . . . well . . . I thought . . . hell yeah!" Jack blurted.

Roy smiled and said, "Because of payroll, we'll start you out on Monday. It'd be less complicated that way. Standard carpenter pay to start out with. But I've got my eye out. Gonna need a foreman when we get going with that house. Will have to hire some more helpers, and

I anticipate needing someone in a supervisory position when that happens," Roy said, with a gleam in his eyes.

Jack got the intended message.

"Yes sir! Thank you . . . and I won't let you down."

"I know you won't, Jack. Now get down to the dock. I'm taking you and Hugh off the bridge and putting y'all on the house. Tell the men I'll be there shortly."

Jack turned and walked back down the slope towards the dock.

Hugh was laughing when Jack came back down to the dock. "Scared you, didn't I? Come on and admit it."

Jack was still in thought about what had just transpired. "Say what?" Jack asked. "Oh yeah . . . hell yeah," he said.

"I figured from the look on your face. What'd he say?"

"He made me a full carpenter. I guess I got *you* to thank for that."

"Naw, you made carpenter all by yourself. It was bad timing, with Lucky's death and all. But you proved yourself in a short time, Jack."

"Still . . . thanks. *And*, he's taking you and me off the bridge and putting us out on the house!"

"Hot damn! Bout time," Hugh said. "Let's go to work!"

The boat sat low in the water with a full crew on board as it pushed water out and away from the bow. Roy cut the engine as they neared the back side of the island. The skiff glided into clear, shallow water. Hugh jumped out into waist-deep water and eased the boat up onto the beach. The workers followed. Roy sent the crew to various parts of the house. The foundation had been laid, and the framing had just begun. Hugh and Jack were to work on the front of the house.

"Grab those two-by-fours, Jack. They've already been cut and measured. We'll start with the left side and go up from there." Hugh caught himself. "Oh, that's right. You're a full-fledged carpenter. I can't be telling you what to do, now."

"That doesn't start til Monday. As of right now, I'm still your laborer," Jack said.

"In name only," Hugh replied. "You know as much as I do about hammering and cutting lumber."

Jack brought the treated lumber over, and the two men pulled out levels and hammers. They inserted ten penny nails between their lips and broke the morning quiet. The two worked silently, except for an occasional grunt. Their backs glistened in the heat. Jack was bent over, extracting a misplaced nail when he felt it. He'd had this feeling before over on the beach.

"Whoa," Jack said. "Did you feel that? What do you figure the temperature is . . . gotta be in the '90s?" Jack asked.

"I'd say that's 'bout right. Why? And whoa, what?"

"That breeze that just came through. It was almost cold. I got a chill," Jack said.

"Got a chill? You must be getting sick. Ain't no cool breeze come through here so far this morning," Hugh said.

The coolness passed, but the presence remained, and he sensed it coming from above him. Hesitantly, Jack slowly turned his head and looked up into a voided face on top of the dune.

Jack silently stared at the figure, unable to speak, before blurting out, "Hugh! Who is that?"

"Who?" Hugh replied.

"The man up there on the dune. Do you know who he is? Have

you ever seen him before?" Jack asked, desperately jabbing the air, pointing up to where the figure stood.

Hugh looked at Jack, and the two locked eyes. Hugh sensed the urgency in Jack and turned his head and followed in the direction of his arm. Jack's gaze remained on Hugh.

"What man? Ain't nobody up on that dune," Hugh replied.

Jack looked back up, and the place where the man stood seconds ago was now back-dropped by white, puffy clouds.

"Boy, you must be getting a heat stroke. I hear that's what happens. A person turns cold as ice in the middle of one. Maybe you need to go lie down under them Yaupons over there."

"I swear, Hugh. I saw this guy walking on the beach when I first got here. He has no face. Only two eyes peering out from pulp . . . where a face should've been. We thought maybe he was a Vietnam vet . . . had his face melted by napalm. Then I saw him on the beach again when I was surfing. Now, this is the third time I've seen him. I know this sounds really weird, but I think I've seen a ghost . . . and he's trying to tell me something."

"Like what? Hugh said. "That maybe you ought to do what I told you and cool off under that Yaupon tree?"

"I think I will," Jack said walking into the tree shade. Turning, he said, "And you're sure you've never known anyone like that? As long as you've been living here, you've never seen him?"

"Nope. Can't say as I have. And from what you've described, I don't think I'd have forgotten him if I *had* seen him. But then again, I don't get over to the beach much . . . maybe on the weekends me and my wife will go over and do some pier fishing."

"No, you wouldn't," Jack said.

"Wouldn't what?" Hugh asked.

"Forget him. You wouldn't forget him if you ever saw him. I wish I could," Jack said.

CHAPTER 22

JACK LIVED FOR SATURDAY MORNINGS. Two days off and a wide-open ocean in his front yard to play in. However, on this Saturday in late May, he decided to take his board and drive the fifteen minutes down Highway 904 over to neighboring Ocean Isle Beach. Although more surfers, the surf was as usually as good there as at Sunset. More surfers meant more aggression out in the water. He didn't like fighting for waves. But on this day, for some reason, he felt ready to branch out to meet some people. To hell with the aggression. He'd just hang outside the sets til he found a wave for himself.

He pulled into the pier parking lot and slid his surfboard out of the open rear-end of the Jeep. He crested the dune beside the pier and walked out onto the beach, flushing a cake of wax from the back pocket of his beach trunks that he'd owned for years. Numerous bars of surf wax had worn a hole in the back pocket.

Jack put his board on the sand and started waxing it up while scanning the ocean for waves and for surfers, but he spotted only one. *That's rare, for this beach*, he thought. He waded into the whitewater, pushed off, and laid on his board in one motion. Duck-diving under the first wave, he came out the other side, paddling and shaking the water off his face. He paddled up behind the lone surfer whose hair was pulled back in a pony tail that flowed down the center of his broad shoulders and back. Jack pulled up beside him.

"What's happening man," he said while looking out to sea for waves.

"*Man*? You leave your *glasses* or your *brain* on the beach?"

Jack turned his head and observed a female sitting astride her board looking out at sea as well.

She looked over at him and said, "I'm not *man*, dude! So don't call me that!"

Jack back-peddled as best he could. " Oh . . . shit . . . I wasn't expecting . . . I mean . . . shoot! I'm sorry. It's just that from behind . . ."

She broke into a smile and said, "Settle down. It's okay. It's not the first time I've been mistaken for a dude. It's the broad shoulders . . . from surfing, you know."

"Well . . . it's not that broad shoulders aren't attractive . . . I mean they are, really . . ."

"You're digging yourself deeper. Let it go. I know what you mean," she said.

"Okay. I'll stop there. I'm Jack. Jack Tagger," he said, reaching across and offering his hand.

"Katherine Williams," she said reaching across to meet his hand. "Friends call me Cricket. Nice to meet you, Jack Tagger."

"Cricket. Cool name. I like that. But why?"

Cricket looked down at her torso and said, "Well, I ain't the biggest thing . . ."

"Oh . . . sorry again. I didn't notice, with you sitting on your board. Only half of you is exposed . . . ."

"Shall I expose more," she smiled and said in a sultry voice.

"Geez. You're right. I keep digging myself deeper," Jack said.

Both remained quiet looking out at sea before Cricket glanced over as if checking out Jack. "I've not seen you in these waters before, pilgrim," she said in her best John Wayne voice. "Down for a visit?"

"No, not this year. I'm permanent, as of right now. I work in construction at Sunset. You?"

"My family has a house on West 3rd Street on Jink's Creek. I live there."

"Not sure where Jink's Creek is," Jack said.

"It's to the right of the pier. Come across the causeway and take a right. Jink's Creek is actually the sound," Cricket explained. "We're on the second row."

"Oh, Okay. So where are all the surfers? This beach is usually crowded with guys . . . uh . . . ahh . . . *people* out in the water."

"What time is it? What time did you get here?"

"Bout nine, I think."

"It's Saturday. Too early for most of the lame dicks around here. They're sleeping it off," she said.

Jack's face flushed.

"Oh hell, I'm sorry. I know I need to clean up my mouth," she said.

"No. Really. I just wasn't ready for that. But I like it," he said.

"Like what? A trash-talking surf chick turns you on?"

"No, but it says . . . to *me* . . .you're a free spirit. I like that."

Cricket sat up straight on her board and gave Jack a smile.

"Surf chick? Okay then," Jack said.

"Okay," Cricket said, smiling as she turning her board. "I'd better be getting in to get dressed for my lunch shift."

"Where's that?

"The Pelican's Perch on 2nd Street. It's a restaurant and bar. I work the lunch shift and the bar on various nights. You ought to come by one evening. You may get lucky."

Jack shot her an embarrassed, questioning look.

"Lucky . . . meaning a free beer or two, dumbass!"

"Oh! Gotcha! Free beer ain't as good as free ass, but it'll do," Jack said.

"Funny! I'll talk to you later. Oh, by the way. Where are you staying at Sunset?"

"A co-worker helped me out. I was staying at the Sunset Beach Hotel, but the roaches started winning. He got me a bottom-floor, guest quarters apartment at a cottage. It's on 40th Street. You know where that is?

"40th Street. Isn't that at the very end of the beach? Has great views of the sunsets over Bird Island?"

"That's it. First cottage on the left as you turn in. Come see me some time. We'll go out for a session," Jack said.

Cricket swung the front of her board around and started to paddle to catch an on-coming wave. "I may just do that, Jack Tagger. Peace!"

"Back at 'cha," Jack said, watching her carve the front side of the wave as she headed in. "And I just may catch lunch at the Pelican," he yelled.

He wasn't sure she would hear him over the roar of the wave, but when she flashed the peace sign over her shoulder, he knew she had.

THE MUSIC WAS GOOD. The Beach Boys' *Don't Worry Baby* was playing as Jack took a seat at a corner table in the Pelican Perch that overlooked the back-patio seating and the outside Tiki bar. He fired up a cigarette and pulled the menu from between the napkin holder and a bottle of ketchup. He glanced over the menu and felt a presence standing over his left shoulder.

"What'll you have, pilgrim?"

Jack looked up into a lovely, brown-skinned face smiling down at him. Her brown hair, mixed with strands of dirty-blond streaks cascaded down around her shoulders, framing her tanned face. He lost his breath for a second and then stuttered. "How's the fried Grouper sandwich?"

"My favorite. Well, a close second to the oyster Po-Boy."

"Oh hell yeah!" he said. "But I don't see that on the menu."

"We don't put those on the menu. But we still have a batch of fresh oysters in the back. The months for oysters all have an "R" in them . . . like, October through April. But we still have some of April's batch in the back. This time of year we save 'em for the locals. But Sunset Beach will do. Want one?"

"I would love one."

"Anything else?" she asked.

Jack scanned the menu, uncertain. Cricket turned the menu in his hand and pointed to the side offerings.

"The onion rings are killer. They do the trick," she said writing the order down on her pad. She stepped back and looked under the table. He was still in his wet trunks. "You stay out the whole morning?" she asked.

"Yeah, the surf didn't wanna stop pumping. It started getting crowded, and that's when I got out."

"Okay, Jack. I'll put in your order. What to drink?"

He looked at the back of the menu again and ordered a Michelob.

"Got it. I'll bring the beer right out."

He'd smoked his cigarette to the end by the time the beer arrived in a frosted mug.

"Your sandwich and onion rings should be right out," Cricket said.

"Take your time. I'm gonna drink this beer and . . . probably . . . yeah. Go ahead and bring me another one. I'll probably be ready for it by then."

"Another frosted mug?" she asked.

"Why not?" he said.

He always enjoyed a cigarette with his beer, so he lit another. He took a swig of his beer, then a drag off the cigarette. He exhaled, sat back in his chair, and relaxed. He felt content.

Cricket soon brought out his Po Boy, onion rings, beer, and mug and sat them on the table. Four surfers came through the door and called out to her.

"You missed it, Cricket. Pure glass and nothing but sets," a dark-haired boy with shoulder-length hair called out to her across the room.

"Oh, I was out there, before you lamers rolled out of bed! But some of us have to work for a living," she said.

"Oh yeah! Sure, Cricket. *You* have to work. We all know that, you poor thing," a second surfer said.

She patted Jack on the head and said, "The lunch crowd is coming in. It's gonna get crowded, and I'm gonna get busy. You gonna stay down all day? If you do, maybe I could snag us a six-pack of cold ones, and we could go out on the beach and chat later this evening."

"I'm gonna go back out and see what's going on out there after lunch. If it's not good, I may go back, shower, and take care of some things back at Sunset. But that would be nice. What time?"

"How bout meeting me on the right side of the pier around seven. Would that work?"

"Sure, that'll work. It's only a fifteen-minute drive down here. That is if the bridge doesn't catch me. But they open every hour on the hour for the boats, so yeah, I can beat it and be here around seven."

"Great! I'll see you then," Cricket said.

CHAPTER 23

JACK SHOWERED AND CHANGED INTO his best faded bell-bottoms and a white cotton Mexican peasant shirt. It stayed wrinkled due to the absence of an iron and the knowledge of how to use one. He didn't care. It was his favorite dress-up shirt. He slid his flip-flops on and headed for Ocean Isle. The scent of Patchouli followed him.

As he approached the one-lane pontoon bridge in the distance, he observed the boats floating in wait on both sides of the bridge. He checked his watch.

Six forty-five. Good. No need to kick it. I'll make it in plenty of time. Jack rolled down the window and let the breeze whip his hair. He would put it back into a ponytail when he got there.

He turned the radio on to WAVE 104. *Jumpin' Jack Flash* by The Rolling Stones was on. Jack smiled and turned it up, and his thoughts went to Cricket and the care he took in getting himself ready. He felt a tinge of embarrassment.

Settle down, he told himself. *You are not ready for a relationship . . . by your own admission. You just met a chick today, and you're getting all wobbly like a high schooler. And by her looks and coolness, she's probably got a pack of dudes following her. Just settle and make it what it probably will be. Just friends.*

He crossed the bridge, continued to NC 904 towards Ocean Isle Beach, and settled back in his seat. At that moment, *You've lost that Loving Feeling* by the Righteous Brothers came on the radio. Jack thought of Kathleen. Then his thoughts moved on.

He arrived at Ocean Isle, turned right onto the causeway, and crossed over the big bridge. From the top, he could clearly see Sunset Beach to the right. The view from here, left and right up and down the Intracoastal Waterway, the islands and the ocean in front were breathtaking, especially at this time of day. The pier was straight ahead. Butterflies rose in his belly.

Go away! I'm cool with this. Just a friend, he said to himself.

He hadn't been with a woman since Kathleen. Hell, he'd hardly talked to one since her. This was new to him. He gave himself permission to be a little nervous.

Jack parked his Jeep, pulled off his flip-flops, and put them in his back pocket. He pulled his hair back in a ponytail and headed around the right side of the pier where the ocean breeze met him. He crested a small sand dune and looked for the brown-skinned girl, but she saw him first, waving with one hand, holding up a bottle of beer with the other, a big smile on her face. Jack waved back and stumbled into the breeze and across the loose sand.

"What's up Surfer Chick," Jack said.

"Nothing but the blue sky," Cricket said. "Have a seat."

Jack crossed both legs and dropped to his hind side.

"How about a cold one," she said after he'd snuggled his ass into the soft sand. The day's warmth was retained in the sand.

"Sure," he said, "Ahh . . . this sand feels good. Still warm."

"Yeah, I think this is my favorite time of the day. Twilight. The colors are so soft and muted. You can actually feel the moment," she said.

"You sound like a poet or a writer," he said.

"Well, maybe that's because I am one," she replied. "Or attempt to be one."

"Oh yeah?" Jack said, now looking at her sideways. "I don't mean to be rude, but what are you doing down here working in a bar and grill if you are so talented? And I would think you are!"

"You're not being rude. I sometimes wonder that myself. A lot, actually. And the answer is I really don't know. I'm trying to figure that out, I guess. How bout you?"

"Me? What?"

"How bout you? Why are *you* down here and not in some preppy college getting a business degree or something like that?"

"Well, that last part of your question is easy," Jack said, laughing. "Do I *look* like someone who would pursue a business degree or '*something like that*?' The first part is a little harder."

Jack remained silent for a few seconds.

"And . . . ?" Cricket asked.

"And . . . well I guess you and I have a little something in common. I really don't know why I'm down here . . . except . . ."

"Except what?" Cricket asked.

"Except I'm just not meant to be in college. I'm not good at it right now. And . . ."

"And what?"

"I'm resisting."

"Really? You draft dodger!"

"I don't know if I'd put it that way . . ."

"You are! You aren't willing to pick up a gun for our Uncle Sam and defend us defenseless citizens against those invading red tyrants? Next thing you know, they'll be knocking on our doors here in the US of A, spreading communism . . . trying to take over the world," she said.

Jack looked at her, unsure, before she let out a deep-chested laugh.

"I'm just fucking with you, Jack. Right on! That war is so wrong. Good for you! I'm for ya! Sunset seems like a good place to hide out. Not much traffic or people. Is that why you chose it?"

"Partly. The other reason is I love that beach. Been going there since I was a kid. A buddy of mine's family has a cottage on the waterway, just down from the bridge. We used to take his boat and explore all over the place. The marsh and slews, Goat Island, Bird Island, Tubbs Inlct, Madd inlet. The whole area. I'm just out of a relationship, and the place just soothes me. I guess I just need to be here right now."

"Oh wow!" Cricket said.

"Oh wow, what?"

"Me too."

"You too what?"

"I'm just out of a relationship, too. I came down here to surf, write and get away," Cricket said.

"I'll be damned," Jack said. "Two peas in a pod, kinda."

"I guess so! So, no pressure though, right? I don't think I'm ready to get back into a relationship just yet."

"Me either. We'll be buds. And that's just what I need about now. A bud," Jack said.

"Speaking of buds, you wanna toke one?" she asked, pulling a joint out of her top pocket.

"From one bud to another . . . *and* to another. Don't mind if I do," he said.

CHAPTER 24

THREE BEERS AND HALF A JOINT MADE him a bit woozy. He turned the radio up loud and lost himself in thoughts and music. At a stop sign in the middle of nowhere, he realized, *Damn! I missed the turn for Highway 904.*

He turned left onto Old Georgetown Road and drove towards Calabash. Fifteen minutes later, he arrived at the intersection of Old Georgetown Road and Beach Drive. He turned left onto Beach Drive, and feeling much better about things, he shifted the old Jeep into fourth gear and let her run. The warm night air felt good, and his evening with Cricket went well. He was content. Again! How long had it been since he felt this good!

His thoughts carried him away . . . so much he didn't slow for the approaching turn-off Beach Drive. Here, a left turn onto Shoreline Drive would have taken him back to the beach. But instead, he passed it and stayed straight, skidding, just barely coming to a stop on the dead-end road at a place the locals called Bonaparte's Landing. A few feet more, and he would have ended up in the Intracoastal Waterway. He shifted the Jeep into neutral, pulled up on the emergency brake, fired up a cigarette, and sat, thinking about the evening he'd spent with Cricket.

"Just buds, like she said. Surf pals. Neither of us are ready for another relationship," he said out loud.

His headlights illuminated the dark, fast-moving water out in the waterway in front of him.

His mind wandered. *Bonaparte's Landing. What and how was this dead-end road and this spit of land named that?* It had always been called that. But he never knew why.

He looked to his right and saw an old fishing hut that emerged from under the cover of kudzu. As many times as he had been this way, he had never noticed it before. A sandy lane or road ran between the water's edge and the abandoned building. The place always had a spooky feel to it.

The marijuana buzz was still with him when he became aware that a fog had settled in front of his headlamps coming in from the body of water that lay before him. On the other side of the Intracoastal was a marsh, and beyond that, the back side of Bird Island. The big inlet called Little River was at the west end of the island, entering from the Atlantic Ocean.

A chill enveloped him inside the Jeep, and he attempted to zip up the plastic window beside him. The zipper hung. He finagled with it, but to no avail. Paranoia accompanied the chill coming through the open window.

"Oh hell, it's just the grass, settle down," he said. He sat for a moment and pulled on what remained of his cigarette, looking out the front window trying to gather himself. "I gotta get out of here," he said tossing his cigarette out the partially opened window.

He tried to put the gearshift into reverse, but the gears ground and jammed . . . he couldn't find reverse. He continued pumping the clutch and ramming the stick shift over and back, feeling for the open slot where reverse should be. A rumble of thunder sounded off in the distance, sounding almost like a cannon shot, adding to Jack's confusion. The sky above the fog was filled with stars.

No sign of rain up there, he thought. The buzz from the grass was intensifying the situation. He knew that . . . but still. He looked over his left shoulder back toward Shoreline Drive, and the thought of running became real as he reached for the door handle.

Run back up Shoreline Drive . . . at least to civilization and get the fuck out of this desolate place, he had just thought when he first became aware of the movement. He froze and looked down, not wanting to turn his head in the direction it came from . . . to his right . . . down the sandy lane that ran in front of the old fish hut and between the water's edge. It was from that direction he had noticed . . . no *felt*. . . the movement in the fog.

Jack turned his head to the right and saw that the fog had thickened and was roiling in the center of the path. It swirled faster, mixing directions until the form of a human-like figure seemed to emerge. It began to move . . . coming towards him. The apparition that emerged from the vapor was complete and was that of a man, but Jack couldn't make out a head.

The apparition approached, then left the sandy path, and stepped onto a grassy plot of land momentarily before seeming to walk out into the waterway, directly into the path of the Jeep's headlights, and then it dissolved into the watery night.

Jack sat motionless, breathing deeply for a moment or two, before trying reverse again. This time the stick shift slid quietly into the gear. He depressed the clutch and backed the Jeep back the short distance to Shoreline Drive. He stopped the Jeep and followed the beam of the headlight back out into the dark water.

"What the hell just happened? Either I'm going crazy, or this beach is inhabited . . . by what, I don't know. The man with no face keeps searching me out. And now this headless apparition. I gotta get back to the beach."

He turned left and hauled down shoreline drive to Sunset Beach. The pontoon bridge was open.

"Thank God," he said as he pulled up and eased out onto the one-lane bridge. About mid-ways out, he had the inclination to look to his right, down the Intracoastal towards Bonaparte's Landing, but fear locked his head. It was just too dark. And he was afraid of what might be out there.

CHAPTER 25

JACK ARRIVED AT THE DOCK FIRST THING on Monday morning. He had a new job promotion, new pay, and a new friend. Life was getting good. But the memory of Saturday night's dream or encounter . . . or whatever it was and the faceless man out on the beach was still with him.

Hugh Wyrick arrived shortly after Jack. "Hey Jack," Hugh said through a smile, a cigarette sticking out the corner of his mouth. "You have any more run-ins this weekend with that faceless man you saw up on the dune Friday?"

"Naw," Jack lied.

Jack rubbed both hands back through his hair and looked over his shoulder, back over the marsh and slews in the direction of Bonaparte's Landing on the waterway.

"Hugh. You know anything about Bonaparte's Landing over there?" he said motioning with his head. "How and why it's named that?"

"Afraid I don't. It's been called that ever since I've been here. And that's all my life."

"You know any Bonapartes down here . . . any families by that name?" Jack asked.

"I don't. I *do* know that a family once owned all that land back there. But I can't remember their name. Why?"

125

"Just a strange name to a strange place," Jack said. "I had a kinda weird experience down there Saturday night. I missed the turn to Shoreline Drive and almost went into the waterway."

"I think a lot of people probably do that . . . mostly tourists, though . . . folks who don't know the place. They miss the turn and 'bout end up in the drink. Speaking of . . .you have a few in ya, did you?" Hugh said smiling.

"Yeah, but that's not it, Hugh. It was something more than a little buzz. Something strange happened to me over there, but I'm just not sure what or how to explain it."

"I know what you mean. I have to say I *do* get a creepy feeling when I'm over there. An uneasy feeling, I guess you'd call it," Hugh said. "But if you're really interested in the history of that place, you ought to talk to Bruce Kinnard, the guy who owns the pier."

"Yeah . . . I know who Kinnard is," Jack said.

"He's been down here bout as long as most anyone. There's some other old-timers around, but he's probably the one most likely to talk to you about the history down here," Hugh said.

Continuing his gaze over the waterway to Bonaparte's Landing, Jack said, "Thanks. I just may do that."

———◆———

AT THE END OF THE WORKDAY, Jack pulled into the Vista Pier's parking lot and walked the short distance to the pier's steps where Big Tom and Little Tom sat nursing two tall PBR's.

"Well, lookie who's here," Big Tom said. "The mystery boy hisself! How you doing Jack?"

"Hey B.T, L.T. Doing okay. You guys?"

"Can't complain," L.T. said.

"How's it going, working for Pierce and all?" L.T. asked.

"Good. Good," Jack said.

"I know I'm not supposed to say this, leastwise to where Groat might hear it, but I hear he's a pretty good man," B.T. said.

"He *is,*" Jack said, moving up the steps. "You guys seen Kinnard?"

"He's up there," B.T., said motioning over his left shoulder. "In the grill. Least that's where he was when I got this beer."

"Okay, thanks. I need to talk to him. See you guys later," Jack said.

"Okay," B.T. said. "I'll let you buy me one later for that bit of information."

"Will do," Jack said moving alongside the men as he made his way up the steps.

Mrs. Kinnard was behind the bar in the bait shop when Jack passed through the little alcove that separated the bait shop and the grill.

"Mr. Kinnard here?" Jack asked.

"He's out on the pier," she said.

Jack looked through the door out to the pier and saw the tall man with white shoulder-length hair and matching white beard walking towards him. A tan, somewhat handsome face shone through the flowing mane. A storm was developing out at sea. Dark, purplish clouds framed him.

"Mr. Kinnard," Jack said.

"That's me," Kinnard answered.

"Looking pretty nasty out there, isn't it," Jack said, looking back over Kinnard's shoulder.

The salty dog turned and looked out to sea, then back at Jack. "You worried about a little blow, are you?" he said, looking down at Jack with a knowing smile . . . as if he could see through him.

"Well, no. I mean, not really," Jack said. "I'm Jack Tagger. Can I speak with you for a moment? I was referred to you by a co-worker of mine. He said you have been here about as long as anyone and you may be able to help me."

"Well, I guess I *have* been here a while. What can I help you with, Jack?" he said.

"Well, I was wondering if you knew anything about Bonaparte's Landing. I mean . . . why is it named that? It's such an unusual name and all. I was wondering about its history . . ."

The knowing smile again appeared on his face. "Why do you ask, Jack?"

"No big deal. I was just wondering if . . ."

"You had an experience over there . . . one that you don't understand?"

"Well . . . ahh . . . Saturday night I was . . ."

"I'm assuming that's a yes. No need to tell me what happened, Jack. But I *will* tell you that some people have had some . . . I'll just say strange experiences over there at Bonaparte's Landing. What I know . . . or have been told, I'll tell you. The legend or story behind Bonaparte's Landing relates back to Napoleon Bonaparte and his field marshal Michel Ney. At the end of the Napoleonic Wars, Napoleon was defeated and exiled. Ney was arrested and was convicted of treason because he was an ally of Bonaparte's. He was sentenced to death before a firing squad, but the firing squad consisted mainly of the Rosicrucian Freemason brothers, as was Ney. Thus, before he could be executed, the brothers spirited Ney out of the country aboard a sloop called the Langolier, which ended up at the mouth of Little River at the western end of Bird Island.

"The Langolier's draft was too big and was unable to enter the river, so they put Ney aboard a dingy, and he rode up a slew, behind Bird Island to what we now call Bonaparte's Creek. He eventually ended up across the waterway, at what is now called Bonaparte's landing. The story goes that Ney was confused and delirious when he landed there, and when the local oystermen found him, they asked who he was and he replied, 'Je suis Bonapartist . . . Je suis Bonapartist,' which meant something along the lines that he was devoted to Bonaparte. Well, they thought he was saying he was Jesus Bonaparte, and to a religious southerner back in those days, calling oneself Jesus was blasphemous. It was such an odd occurrence, and the locals started calling the place Bonaparte's Landing . . . where the strange man came ashore.

"No one knows exactly what happened to Ney. Some stories are that he ended up in Georgetown and later was spotted in Charleston. Others say that he died in the back waters of Sunset Beach, confused and uncertain of where he was but that his spirit remains . . . wandering about . . . looking for his devoted General Bonaparte. That spit of land is said to be a strange place with an energy that still attracts other spirits."

Jack's face paled.

"That help shed any light of the Landing and what you may have experienced, Jack?"

"I reckon so," Jack said more to himself as he walked away.

CHAPTER 26

THE PHONE RANG IN THE OUTER OFFICE late on Monday afternoon. The secretary answered the call. Seconds later, she buzzed the Lieutenant.

"Raleigh is on the phone for you Lt. Berger. Do you wanna take it, or are you getting ready to leave?"

"Raleigh? No, I'll take it. I've been waiting for this call since Friday. Didn't think they'd get back to me this soon," he said. He picked up the receiver. "Lt. Berger here."

"Lieutenant, this is Weaver, DMV. You called with a tag on Friday?"

"I did, but I thought it'd be tomorrow at least before you got back to me. That was fast," Berger said.

"Well, we serve to please our own," Weaver said.

"I appreciate it. So you got something back on that North Carolina tag up in Maine? TJS 2323, I think it was."

"That's it, Lieutenant. It comes back to a Richardson Pierce, Jr. on an International Harvester Scout. The tag was issued in Shallotte, North Carolina. But the address is listed as 1420 40th Street, Sunset Beach, North Carolina."

"Sunset Beach?"

"Anything wrong Lieutenant?"

"No . . . well, I'm not exactly sure," Berger said

"That not your car?"

"Well, yeah. But we had a car . . . a Lincoln Continental go up in flames down here . . . on a rural highway that runs to and from Sunset Beach. Turns out, *that* car was registered to a person up in Caribou, Maine. Now, I have *this* International Scout up in Caribou, Maine, but registered to a person down at Sunset Beach. The house up in Maine has been vacant for some time, but now a female, driving this vehicle from Sunset Beach, recently moves in. And her last name isn't the same last name as the owner of the woman who lived there or the owner of the Continental . . ."

"I'm sorry, Lieutenant. I'm afraid I'm not following you."

"What? Oh . . . just thinking out loud. I'm sorry. But thank you. You've been a big help," Berger said.

"I hope so. But from the sounds of it, I'm not sure . . ."

Lieutenant Berger slowly put the phone back in the cradle and thought, *I've got two cars and an unidentified woman, and all three have the house in Maine in common. WITH a connection to Sunset Beach thrown in.*

He leaned back in his chair with his hands clasped behind his neck, his feet up on his desk.

Now, what's the common thread here? I've got a Lincoln Continental that is involved in a fatal accident in my county. The car was headed north on NC 904. The car was registered to a Sarah Prescott in Caribou, Maine. But Prescott passed away, and that residence is vacant. Then, a vehicle shows up at that same residence . . . an International Harvester Scout with North Carolina tags belonging to a Richardson Pierce, Jr., and some young lady is driving it and has taken up residence in the house. But her last name is not Prescott. It's Cavanaugh.

"Interesting," he said to himself.

CHAPTER 27

RICHARDSON PIERCE STOOD ON THE DECK at the guest house, leaning on the railing and overlooking the marsh and water below. When the phone rang inside, he had just shifted his gaze to the very top of one of the walls of his house, now just barely rising atop the Yaupon and Pine trees over on the island. Pierce went in, picked up the receiver, and heard a dreaded voice. The connection crackled, but he knew instantly who was on the other end. The overdone southern accent was not lost on him.

"Reeeyuch. This is Maatha."

"I know it's you, Martha. Your accent precedes you."

"You're so clever, Reeeyuch. Always were."

"What do you want, Martha?"

"Is *my* son still there with you?"

"No Martha. I would have thought he'd be there with you, by now."

"Well, no, he isn't. How long ago . . . when did he leave?"

"Well . . . it's been . . ."

Pierce's mind went blank. Rich Junior had had plenty of time to get to Greece. He knew from past dealings with his ex-wife to limit the information he gave her. She'd invariably turn it around and use it as a weapon.

"He left here with intentions of coming over there and spending some time with you and then coming back here for the rest of the summer to work on the house. So, you're saying he's not there?"

"That's exactly what I'm saying. Did you not get his flight itinerary before he left?"

"No, I did not. He was coming to see *you*. Did *you* get it?"

"We'll no, I did not. I would have thought you'd have . . ."

"Martha! No! I did not!"

"Well, maybe he and Cassie are together . . ."

"He and Cassie have been split up for a while. He said they needed a little breathing room. She went back up north for the summer."

"Well, what's her number? I need to call her and find out . . ."

"I don't have her number. I don't even know where she's living. Somewhere in Maine, but that's all I know."

"Well, once again, it looks as if you can't be counted on. You let him leave without getting *any* information!"

"Let me see what I can do from here, Martha. What airline was he flying?"

"I don't really know. Either Piedmont or Eastern."

"Well, I'll start from here. I may have to go to Greensboro. In the meantime, why don't you check with the airlines? What number can you be reached at there?"

"You'll have to go through the operator. Oh . . . let's see. There is a number on the front of the phone. It's . . . 001 30 21 621 1139. I don't know what all that means. I suppose it may be the number here."

You don't even know the phone number where you are! And I'm the one that can't be counted on?

133

"I'll write that down. Maybe the operator will know what to do with it. Let me go, and I'll see what I can find out."

"Well, there's nothing I can do here. Get back to me as soon as you know something."

"I will. Goodbye," Rich said and added under his breath, "You can fix yourself another damn cocktail, is what you can do!"

"What was that Reeych?"

"Nothing. I need to get off so I can start trying to get some answers."

"I'll be waiting to hear back from you."

Pierce placed the phone back on the receiver and walked back out onto the deck. The ocean was unusually blue. A breeze blew in off it. It was a stiff one . . . uncomfortable in an unexplained way; it almost had a chill to it. He wrapped his arms around his body and embraced a slight shiver. Another supposed sonic boom reverberated from out over the ocean. An uneasy feeling settled in him, and he turned, opened the glass doors, and went back inside. Then, he stopped, turned back, and looked out over the ocean.

EARLY THURSDAY MORNING, Richardson Pierce was waiting on the dock when Roy James arrived.

"Morning Mr. Pierce. You're up and about early this morning," Roy James said.

"Couldn't sleep last night. Roy, did Rich happen to leave any information with you about his travel plans?" Pierce asked.

"No Mr. Pierce. He didn't."

"No chance you'd have Cassie's phone number or where she was going?"

"No, sorry. What's up?"

"I spoke with his mother last evening. She says he hasn't shown up. He's three weeks late."

"Maybe he's still in Greensboro. Did you try calling him there?"

"I did. Got his ansaphone. If he's there, he isn't responding to his messages."

"Well, I wouldn't worry. Rich is a good boy with a good head on his shoulders. I'm sure there's a reasonable explanation," Roy said.

"I don't know, Roy. I have a feeling, and it isn't a good one. Three weeks . . . that's a considerable amount of time for him to be missing, if he *is* missing. I don't know. His mother is waiting for information on him, and I don't know where to begin . . . where to search. I'm gonna do some paperwork this morning and then head back to Greensboro this afternoon. I need to finish up some business there anyway," Pierce said.

"Might be a good idea . . . a start anyway. Put your mind at ease when you find he's still there and hasn't left yet," Roy said. "We'll take care of things here so you can take care of things there."

"Thanks, Roy. I'll call you when I get there and let you know when to expect me back."

CHAPTER 28

THE RUSTED SCREEN DOOR WAS SHUT, but the lightbulb was lit. Jimmy Greer answered the knock. "What do you want?" he said.

"I need to see Mr. Groat," Jack said.

"What about?" Greer asked.

"Let 'em in, Jimmy," came a familiar voice back in the room.

Jimmy Greer turned, walked away from the door, and took a seat at the table facing Jack. The glow from the overhead bulb illuminated onto the top of Greer's ballcap. The lower half of his face was cast in an eerie shadow. Except for the glare in Greer's eyes, the shaded face reminded Jack, strangely, of that of a child's.

Groat was sitting at the head of the Formica table with a small glass of brown liquid. A bottle of Southern Comfort sat on the table beside it.

"This here's Jimmy Greer. I don't believe you've met him yet. He works for me too. Now, what is it, Jack? You got something for me?" Groat said.

"I do have a little information for you," Jack said approaching the table. He started to pull out a chair, but Groat said, "No need. You ain't gonna be here that long. Just tell me what you got. I'd say it's about time you got something on Pierce."

"It's not much, I'm afraid. And I don't know how you're going to use it to your benefit. Pierce's son was to go to Greece to see his mother, but he's not shown up. He's missing, I hear."

Groat cut an eye toward Greer. Jack thought he saw the slightest of smiles.

"And . . . because he is missing, Pierce is going back to Greensboro this weekend to try and find out something."

Groat cut another glance at Greer, and this time Jack was certain he saw a smile.

"How long's he been missing?"

"About a month, or less," Jack said.

"That might be something of value," Groat said. "Stay on it. Let me know what more you hear. And, I'm interested in any signs of him expanding and developing any other parts of that island. *Very* interested. You need to step it up, Jack. Feed me. I need more."

Jack's mind raced for anything he could feed and perhaps satisfy him. "Oh! And there *is* something I overheard Pierce say the other day," Jack said.

"What's that?"

"He said that once they finish construction of the bridge, he plans on bringing some heavy equipment over to the island. He mentioned something about a backhoe. Not sure what he plans to do with it because the foundation has already been dug and set on the island house. But that's what I heard anyway," Jack lied.

"Oh yeah?" Groat said cutting an eye toward Jimmy Greer. Well, there ya go! That's the kind of information I need to know about. You stay on that, Tagger. Now don't let the door hit you on the ass on your way out."

The screen door slammed. Greer looked at Groat and said, "Who the hell is that?"

"Somebody I've got working on another job," Groat said. "Why?"

"Because I've seen him before, I think. Something about him's familiar," Greer said.

"I doubt it. His job is out on the beach . . . over on Bird Island. Yours isn't. And he don't live out in your crossroad community. I'm sure Grissettown ain't on his list of Friday night hangouts," Groat said.

"Yeah, but . . ."

"But nothing. Ain't you got a flatbed loaded with slash pines that need to get to the turpentine mill in Tabor City? *Sometime today,* maybe?" Groat said.

"Yeah, I do," Greer said.

"I'd much appreciate it," Groat said.

Reaching for the door handle, Greer turned and said, "But I swear I've seen that boy somewhere."

"It don't matter. What *does* matter is that you get that pine to the mill. Once that's done, I wanna talk to ya back here," Groat said.

"What about?" Greer said.

"Pierce is gonna be gone for the weekend. I can use that bit of information. Now get your ass to Tabor City!" Groat said.

THE GREENSBORO SKYLINE GLIMMERED in the early evening dusk. Richardson Pierce was on edge. A bit shaky. He was eager to put the three-hour trip behind him and find resolve in knowing his son was home and well. Still, this wasn't like Rich. He'd always had his own mind, but he was a good boy. Never caused him any trouble to speak of. Pierce always loved seeing him coming. Even as a little boy, Rich Jr. would come running when he saw his daddy . . . running with arms out and an ear-to-ear smile as he jumped into this father's arms. Pierce recalled the sweet, sweaty smell when he buried his face in his little boy's neck.

The driveway to Rich Jr's. house in College Hill was empty. The garage doors were shut, igniting a spark of optimism in Pierce. He pulled into the drive, stopped his car, but remained under the steering wheel looking at his son's two-story house. No lights were on, but then again, they wouldn't be if he was on his trip. However, it wasn't like Rich to leave his home looking dark and deserted without a single interior light on. Richardson had always told his son to leave a light or two on and perhaps a radio when leaving on a trip to discourage burglars, even though gardeners and workers would sometimes be around.

Pierce got out of his car, studied the front of the house for a moment more, and walked up the sidewalk to his son's front door. The mail was stuffed into the mailbox beside the door. Pierce riffled through the mail looking at the dates stamped on the outside of the envelopes. *There's mail here since he left Sunset,* he thought. *He should have been by here and taken this mail-in before he left for Greece. Unless he never planned on coming home before he went to the airport.*

Pierce looked around the neighborhood just as a neighbor came out of his house heading for his car parked in the driveway. Pierce recalled meeting him and his wife once when he was at Rich's house. *Bransons,* he thought.

"Excuse me! I'm Richardson Pierce. Rich Junior . . . ahh . . . my son Rich lives here and . . ."

"Oh yeah, Mr. Pierce. I'm Pete Branson. My wife and I met you last Christmas when you were visiting Rich. We haven't seen him in a while, and his mail is piling up. I knew he was planning a trip to Greece this spring. We were wondering if he had already left and forgot to cancel his mail."

Richardson Pierce's mouth went dry. "That's why I'm here. His mother is expecting him in Greece, and he hasn't arrived. I came to town to see if any of his neighbors knew anything of his intentions or whereabouts."

"I'm sorry, Mr. Pierce. I'm afraid I can't help you. My wife and I have been home all spring, but we haven't seen him in over a month, I'd say."

"Well, this is certainly perplexing. Not like Rich at all. I guess there's no need to bother any more of your neighbors. It's obvious he hasn't been here after leaving the beach. I've never had a situation like this arise. I really don't know what to do now," he said more to himself than to the neighbors. "Well, thank you. Didn't mean to bother you. But if he *does* show up, would you mind . . . ," he said pulling a business card from his wallet and handing it to Mr. Branson.

"Not at all, Mr. Pierce. I'll call you as soon as I know something. In the meantime, have you thought of calling the police? Or the state highway patrol?"

The neighbor's statement caught him. No, he had not thought to do that. He'd never had to call the authorities for problems. Problems were always worked out in the corporation or within the family. There'd never been any need to call the police.

THE GREENSBORO POLICE CAPTAIN looked over at the dignified white-haired man standing outside the glass partition. The man seemed nervous . . . fidgeting . . . out of place.

"Sir, may I help you?" the captain asked through the round opening in the glass.

"Yes . . . I guess. My . . . my son is missing and I.. "

"You need to go to *Missing Persons.* Go right through those doors there and go to the end of the hall. Make another left, and it's the second door on the left. They'll have you fill out a missing person report."

"Thank you, officer."

"You're welcome," the captain said, watching him disappear through the swinging doors.

Pierce followed the Captain's directions. His leather soles made a loud, slapping sound on the marble hallway. The sound seemed to reverberate off the ceiling and walls, announcing him and his *situation.* He wished his traipse to *Missing Persons* could be more discreet.

Missing person report. The words sounded very strange and unfamiliar. He swallowed hard, but his dry mouth passed no saliva.

The room was a long, narrow one with a counter that ran the length of it. Behind it was rows of file cabinets. On this side of the counter were desks, each accompanied by a chair, where the person filing out the missing report sat to complete the report. An overweight officer, his belly protruding over and covering where it could be assumed his belt would have been, soon emerged from behind the counter.

"Can I help you, sir?"

"Yes . . . my name is . . . ahh . . . I think I need to fill out a . . . a missing person's report," Pierce said.

The officer opened a drawer where he stood, pulled out a sheet of paper, and slid it across the counter to Pierce. "Go over there," he indicated to one of the desks. "Fill this out, and then get it back to me," the officer said.

"Yes . . . I will . . . thank you."

"Who you got missing?" the officer asked.

The question hit Pierce in the chest. He paused at the question and then answered, "My *son*." The sound of that word seemed to reverberate within the room. That was the first time he had said it aloud. His knees buckled as he turned and headed for the nearest desk. He slid the chair out and sat, heavily.

Pierce squared the paper on the desk and took a deep breath. The paper blurred. He wiped the mist in his eyes and focused on the first question. The questions began at *A.* and ended at *K.* Some were generic questions. But at question B., he paused and took a deep breath. *Give a complete description of the missing person including height, weight, the color of hair, age, complexion, clothing at the last time seen.* His son's image began to evaporate from his memory.

"God, this is so difficult . . . what is he . . . about . . ."

He started to write. Three feet, five inches tall, approximately forty pounds, sandy color hair. The pencil dropped from his grasp as he realized he was describing his son as a little *boy.* He covered his face with his hands and moaned . . . "This is too hard. I can't do this."

The officer asked from across the desk, "Are you all right over there?"

Pierce muffled into his hands. "I'm okay." He then turned to the officer, red-eyed, and apologized. "I didn't expect this to be this hard. I don't know what I was thinking."

The officer softened. "We see this a lot. It becomes a little more real at this point. Fill out the report as best you can. This is preliminary . . . to get things started. A detective will follow up and be in touch with you in seventy-two hours."

"Seventy-two . . . three days?"

"It's a requirement. A person has to be missing for three days before they can be considered missing. Many a search has been initiated only to find the missing person return home after a cooling down period."

Pierce returned to the missing person report and read the remaining questions. Question C., *Describe the Circumstances Surrounding the incident.* The word caused him problems. *Incident!* What incident? There was no incident as far as he knew. Not yet. The questions continued. . . . *What is the missing person's probable destination and why?* And *Has the missing person ever left before?*"

He wrote, in answer to the last two questions, "Greece, to visit with his mother." And . . . "No."

CHAPTER 29

IT WAS LATE WHEN HE ARRIVED AT THE BRIDGE. He couldn't stay in Greensboro. It wasn't home, anymore. He'd divorced himself from that city, as his wife had done to *him*. Bird Island was now his love.

Richardson Pierce rolled down his window as he stopped for the raised pontoon bridge. He looked at his watch . . . three o'clock . . . Saturday morning. Even at this late hour with no boats in site on the waterway, the bridge was obligated to open on the hour, boats or not.

With his window down, he smelled wood smoke. It was weird, he thought, that anyone would have a fire tonight, as mild as it was. Pierce looked out toward the ocean, where the two rows of cottages dotted the beachfront's main road. He could see the pier lights, the lights from the Sunset Beach Motel, and a cottage light here and there.

The cables moaned as they taughtened and began pulling the pontoon back in. When the bridge was back in place and secured, the wooden stop arm raised, allowing Pierce to move across. On the long causeway over to the beach, the smell of wood smoke became stronger. He looked at the oceanfront again and followed the line of beachfront cottages to the right. At the western end of the beach toward Madd Inlet and Bird Island, he saw the lights. Garish red lights swirling up into the night sky in chaotic patterns. His thoughts went immediately to the guest house.

Pierce gunned his car and turned right onto North Shore Drive, the only other street that traversed the island other than Main Street, a sandy lane that served as a road that cut across the backside of the island leading to and intersecting with the last street on the island . . . 40th Street at the guest house. The ruts in the sandy road bounced the Cadillac up and down, fish-tailing as it gained speed. When he neared the end of the road and approached 40th Street, he saw the fire trucks blocking the road ahead of him.

He stopped his car behind the last truck and got out. He ran by several stopped trucks looking for a fireman, confused as to why the trucks were stopped in the roadway. Then he saw it . . . the sickening amber glow of his wooden bridge on fire. He stopped in shock and watched the lowering fire flickering across the expanse, all the way to the near side of Bird Island. It appeared the fire had run its course and was now in the dying stages.

A fireman approached the last truck in line and grabbed a water pump off the back of the truck. He strapped the canister on his back. He checked the nozzle to make certain it worked by spraying a small stream of water onto the road in front of him and then ran back by Pierce towards the burning bridge. Pierce grabbed his upper arm as he passed and swung the fireman back around.

"What good is that going to do now?" Pierce asked the fireman. "And why are your trucks parked out here on the road and not over there at the bridge?"

The fireman looked at Pierce and said, "Look at the tires on our trucks! Every damned one of them flattened. Whoever set this fire—and this ain't official, but they didn't want this fire to be put out. They had to know the shortest distance from the mainland to this fire would be North Shore Drive, and they lined the road with roofing tacks and nails . . . flattened every damned one of our tires!"

Observing the flat tires on the trucks nearest him, he released the young fire fighter's arm and watched as he continued towards what was left of the bridge . . . the pathetic water canister on his back. Pierce walked to 40th Street and stopped in the middle of the street. He looked to his right, down towards the guest house. Its large, canopied roof and the body of the house stood in a dark silhouette against the night sky. He felt a sense of relief. It *looked* intact.

The Sunset Beach Police Chief approached Pierce and said, "Sorry about your bridge, Pierce. A lot of good lumber up in flames. You have any idea who may have started this, *if*, in fact, it was intentionally started?"

Pierce looked at the chief and said, "Do *I* have any idea? How bout *you*, chief? Do *you* have any idea who may have started the fire? *Who* may have wanted to see the bridge burn?"

At that moment, a terrible crash caused Pierce and the chief to jump back. The section of the bridge that straddled the water closest to the mainland gave up. The girders groaned as they fell into the water, showering sparks up into the night air.

Both men instinctively backed away a few steps. The fire's glow reflected the anger in Pierce's face.

"Come on Chief. You really don't have anyone in mind regarding this arson? Because you know as well as I do this was arson. There sits the empty gas can right there at what's left of the bulkhead," Pierce said.

The Chief looked at Pierce with disdain.

"Not yet. Haven't begun my investigation. Have you?" he said sarcastically.

"I won't dignify that question with an answer," Pierce said. "You know as well as I do who's responsible for this."

"Well, If I was you, I'd stop right there. You don't want to cross that line and start making false accusations. I hear people can get sued for such," the chief said.

"Well, let it be known, to whomever, that is not going to dissuade me in any way. My son is as much a part of this project as I am. And I dread what his attitude is going to be when he gets back. He'll have *his* opinion as to who's responsible, as well."

"You're an intelligent man, Mr. Pierce. Let that intelligence guide you through this, and don't start something you'll be sorry for later," the chief said.

"I *always* think things through before I act, chief."

CHAPTER 30

LIEUTENANT BERGER TOOK THE EARLY Piedmont Airlines flight out of Greensboro to Atlanta where he caught a connecting flight to Caribou, Maine on Friday morning. He glanced at the in-flight magazine but retained nothing. His mind was on what he was going to find at 23 Garden Circle in Caribou, Maine. He had placed a call before coming to the Caribou PD and explained the situation. He was concerned that this lady who was occupying the house now may be up to no good and may have something to do with the deceased. Lt. Berger's counterpart with the PD was going to accompany him to the residence, along with three other uniformed officers.

Berger did not have a lot to go on, so his thoughts were simple, as was his plan. He would go to the front door along with the Caribou Lieutenant. A uniformed officer would stand guard behind them, and the two other officers would secure the back door.

The Lieutenant was waiting at the Caribou PD, along with his backup. After introductions, the two Lieutenants drove together in an unmarked car . . . the three uniform officers followed in a marked city police car.

The ride to 23 Garden Circle took about ten minutes. The International Harvester with North Carolina tags was in the driveway when they arrived. The unmarked car pulled to the curb. The marked car let the one officer out and then parked on a street that ran beside the house. The two Lieutenants went up the front steps, across the porch, and rang the doorbell. The one uniformed officer remained out in the yard behind them, the strap on his holster un-snapped, with his right arm bowed out and his hand shadowing the pistol's handle. Several tense seconds passed. The first two rings went unanswered. The officer out in the yard moved to the side for a better view of the door. The Lieutenant from Caribou stepped forward again, this time rapping the door knocker loudly, such that the neighbors should have heard it. Again, tense seconds passed before they heard footsteps inside, as if coming down a staircase.

"Hold on, I'm coming . . . I'm coming," came a female voice from inside.

The officers heard the dead bolt knob turn, and both stepped back from the door, hands on their pistols. The Caribou Lieutenant motioned to the officer in the yard to move closer.

The door opened part way, and an attractive young woman peered from the opening. "Yes? May I help you?" she asked.

"Ma'am, would you mind stepping out here? We need to ask you a few questions," Lieutenant Berger said.

The young lady looked at their hands resting on the holstered guns and then at the uniformed officer out in the yard. "Are you a police officer?" she asked.

"I'm Lieutenant Berger from the North Carolina Highway Patrol."

"Oh my," she said putting her hand over her mouth. "I hope nothing is . . . is anything wrong down there, officer?"

"Well, that's what we are trying to find out. Step out so we can talk, please," Berger said.

The woman exited the screen door and stepped onto the front porch. "What is it you need to speak to me about?" she asked.

"For starters, would you mind telling us your name?" Berger asked.

"Well, yes . . . I mean no, I don't mind. My name is Cassie . . . uh . . . ah . . . that's Cassandra Cavanaugh. And *why*, may I ask?"

"I'll get to that in a minute. But first, who is Sarah M. Prebscott, the supposed owner of this house? Do you know her? And why are *you* living in Ms. Prebscott's house?"

"Sarah M. Prebscott is . . . *was* my mother. She is deceased."

"Sorry, Ma'am. My condolences. Is Cavanaugh your *married* name?" Berger asked.

"No. That is my last name. My mother and father divorced when I was young. I kept my last name. Mother went back to her maiden name . . . Prebscott," Cassie said.

"I see. Well, I have to ask you . . . I need to confirm you are who you say you are. Can I see your driver's license?" Berger asked.

Cassie rolled her eyes and disappeared into the darkness of the house. The Lieutenant peered into the darkened house behind her. Seconds later, she was back at the door with a license in hand. "Will this satisfy you?" she asked.

The Lieutenant took it from her hand and examined it. "So, you're from North Carolina?"

"I am," she said. "Went to college there and fell in love with the state and stayed."

"Well then, what are you doing in Caribou?"

"I came up to spend the summer. I'm taking some time off, you might say."

"And by that you mean . . .?"

"Just that. I'm an artist. I came back up here to get away for a while. To clean the palate, so to speak."

"And why, may I ask?"

"And *why*, may *I* ask are you asking me all these questions? Am I suspected of doing something wrong?"

"At this point, no."

"At this *point*?" she reiterated.

"We're investigating an incident that happened back in North Carolina several weeks ago," the Lieutenant said.

"Incident? What kind of incident?"

"A motor vehicle accident."

"And what would that have to do with me?"

"Well, maybe not with you, specifically. But perhaps with your mother."

"How can that be? She's been gone for nearly a year."

The trooper was confused at this point, as to which way to proceed. He didn't want to alarm the woman any more than he already had. Still, he had to pursue. "Ms. Cavanaugh, the car involved was a Lincoln Continental. The vehicle identification number came back as belonging to your mother. Did your mother own a Continental?"

At this, he could see Cassie starting to wilt as she wrapped her arms around her mid-section and leaned against the door frame. "Do . . . do you think . . . could the car have been stolen?" she asked.

"We don't have any reason to think that; although, all possibilities are still open at this point."

"Well, what about the driver? *Who* was driving my mother's car?" she asked, more desperate, now.

"That's the problem. The car caught on fire, and everything was destroyed, including the driver," the trooper said.

"Oh My God! Rich!" she sobbed.

"Ma'am?" Berger said.

"My boyfriend. Rich. I need to make a telephone call," Cassie said, arms still around her waist as she slid around the door frame and back into the house.

"We'll wait out here," Lieutenant Berger said.

———•———

CASSIE WENT BACK INTO THE HOUSE and used the phone on the wall in the kitchen for privacy. Her fingers trembled as she dialed the 910 area code for Sunset Beach. At that, she stopped.

"What *is* the number for the guest house? 621 . . . 621 . . . what the hell is the number . . . 621-4789! That's it," she said as her finger poked circular holes that corresponded with each number. It took her two tries to get it right.

Each ring . . . slow . . . agonizing. She so desired, deep in the pit of her stomach, to hear Rich's smooth voice on the line.

Finally, she heard Richardson Pierce's voice filled the earpiece. "Hello?" he said, simply.

"Mr. Pierce! This is Cassie."

"Cassie! It's so good to hear your voice," he said.

"I'm glad to hear yours too, Mr. Pierce. Hope everything is good down there . . .with the house and all," she said.

"Well . . . things have been better, I'd have to say. We've had a little setback . . ."

She interrupted, her voice choking. "I ahh . . . I need to speak with . . . Is Rich there?"

"No Cassie. He's . . ."

She so hoped his next words that would follow were, "He's out surfing," or "He's over at the house on the island."

". . . not here."

Cassie slid to the floor.

"He left for Greece, but his mother has not heard from him. I was going to call you to see if he might be up there with you. Have you seen or heard from him?"

Silence between the two phones.

"Cassie? Are you still there?"

"Yes."

"Are you all right?"

"No. I mean . . . I'm not sure. What car was he driving when he left?"

"Your . . . I mean . . . your mother's Continental."

"Oh my God," she whispered into the dark room.

"What? What, Cassie?"

"Mr. Pierce. Please don't tell me that."

"Tell you what, Cassie? What's going on?" Pierce asked frantically.

"There's a North Carolina State Trooper standing on my front porch right this moment. He's investigating an accident that happened down there involving my mother's Continental," she said.

"Cassie! Who was driving the car? Was it Rich? Is he all right?"

"They don't know. There was a fire," she said.

"Well for God's sake! Can't they get any ID off the driver? Anything to identify . . ."

"They said everything was destroyed—even the driver," she said through a sob.

"Oh my God! Do they think it was him?"

"They don't know . . . aren't saying. Mr. Pierce, I can't stay here. I'm coming down there. What's the best airport for me to fly into? Would you be able to come get me?"

"Of course. See if you can get something into Raleigh. If not, Raleigh, try Charlotte. I doubt Greensboro has a direct flight. But I need you to get the officers to call me. Maybe I can find out some more information."

"Okay. I'll give them your number, and I'll get there as soon as possible . . . hopefully by tomorrow. And please, let me know if you hear something."

"I will, Cassie. And you do the same."

Cassie hung up the phone and went back onto the porch. The two Lieutenants were in conference when she stepped through the door.

"Anything?" Berger enquired looking up at Cassie.

"Well, no. My boyfriend's father says that he's missing." Tears filled her eyes. "He wants you to call him. I'm going back down to North Carolina—that is if I'm allowed. Am I under arrest or something?" she asked.

"No Ma'am. You're free to go," Berger said. "I'm sorry. I hope this isn't the person you suspect that was operating the vehicle."

"Me too," Cassie said.

"Ms. Cavanaugh. Where in North Carolina will you be going? Berger asked.

"Sunset Beach. I'll be staying with my boyfriend's father, Richardson Pierce."

"Okay. Can you give me the number?" He handed her his ledger notebook and a pen.

She wrote the number down and turned to go back into the house.

"Stay in touch. If you find anything out, please call me," Berger said, handing her his card.

CHAPTER 31

VERY LITTLE WAS SAID ON THE SUNDAY morning ride back to Sunset Beach. Little was known. There was nothing to say, and chit-chat was not an option.

"Does Mrs. Pierce know?" Cassie asked.

"Yes. She blames me for not knowing his whereabouts. Said Sunset was not a '*fit*' for Rich. Said he was wasting his life down here." Silence again rode in the car with them for a-ways before he said, "Maybe she's right."

"No, she's not!" Cassie said. "She always told him that, but he resisted. *This* is where he wanted to be . . . it gave him a reason. Greensboro or the university didn't!"

The two moved back into silence as the Cadillac passed a burnt-out spot in a field to their right on NC 904, of which, neither noticed.

———◆———

THE GRAY AND BLACK NORTH CAROLINA State Trooper cruiser was parked in the drive at the guest house when the Cadillac pulled in. A short, slim trooper in a smoky bear hat was talking with Roy James who was pointing to the charred remains of the bridge.

"Oh my God! That's him," Cassie said.

"Who?"

"The trooper. That's the trooper that came to my house. I can't believe he's already here. I hope it's not bad news traveling fast," Cassie said.

The Cadillac turned in, and the trooper walked over to the driver's door.

"Let's see what he has to say," Richardson said. "Maybe he has some positive information for us."

Richardson opened the car door and exited as the trooper arrived at his door. "I'm Richardson Pierce," he said extending his arm

"Lieutenant Stu Berger, Mr. Pierce. We spoke on the phone. I'm the investigating officer in this case."

"You have anything more on the driver of the Continental? Doesn't sound like, at this point, you have much to go on," Pierce said, somewhat hopeful.

"Well, I'm afraid I do now, Mr. Pierce," Berger said. "Can we go to the house and talk?"

"What you have to tell me, you can tell me here," Pierce said.

Berger looked at Pierce and then at Cassie who had now exited the car and was by Pierce's side. "All right. But it's not good. That's why I wanted to go up to . . . ."

"What do you have, trooper? What is it that's not good?" Pierce asked.

"Well, initially we didn't think the body in the car had any means of identification remaining. It was a very hot fire. The fuel tank blew. It looked as if the impact took away most if not all of the occupant's face. But the coroner's office in Chapel Hill did find one tooth . . . a molar in the back of the jaw. I received the information on my teletype when I got back to the office last night. According to the dental record, Mr. Pierce, I'm afraid it is your son, Rich."

"Oh, God!" Cassie sobbed as she slumped to the ground beside the Cadillac.

Both Pierce and the trooper were helping her up as Roy James approached the Trooper's cruiser.

"Roy," Pierce said, giving him a look with a motioning of his head back toward the guest house. Roy understood.

"Sure," he said taking Cassie's arm and putting it around his shoulder. "Come on, Ms. Cavanaugh. Let me help you up to the house."

Pierce turned his attention back to the trooper. "Lieutenant. Are you absolutely sure it was him? What happened?"

"Yes, we're certain it was your son. We're *not* certain of how it happened. We think that when Rich's car crossed the ditch, the berm on the other side must have ruptured the gas tank, and that's the reason for such a hot fire. As to why, we can't say. Perhaps he fell asleep. Or an on-coming car may have crossed the lane and forced him over into the ditch and ended up in the field. But there was no evidence of contact with another vehicle. No paint transference that we could make out. There *was* deformity to the front of the car, but that came from it going airborne across the ditch and landing in the field on its front end."

"This just can't be," Pierce said, walking around his car, running his hands back through his hair. "Are you certain it was him?"

The trooper put his hands on Pierce's shoulder and said, "I'm afraid the coroner's office has made a positive ID. It was your son."

Pierce leaned back against his car, covered his face with his hands, and emitted a guttural noise. Then he dropped his arms and stared red-eyed out across the inlet to Bird Island.

"How the hell did this happen?" he asked the trooper again. "An oncoming car forcing him off the road into the field? Have you investigated *that* possibility? If so, I want the son of a bitch prosecuted to the fullest!"

"We have, but there are just so many residents out there, and no one we interviewed saw what happened."

"No one saw a car on that day and in that area driving recklessly or at a high rate of speed? Or a blue Lincoln Continental westbound on 904? That wouldn't be a car often seen along that stretch of road this time of year, I wouldn't think," Pierce said.

"No, not that we found. And we canvassed all the farms and houses around there." Berger said, "Up and down the road where it happened. And all the side roads. We just came up empty. I wish I had something for you. I really do. But at this point, I'm empty-handed."

"I know you do, Lieutenant," Pierce said, folding his arms and leaning against his car. And I . . . I appreciate all you've done, finding who owned the car in Maine . . . locating Cassie . . . my son's Harvester. I'm . . . I'm just so empty right now. I feel like I've been kicked in the stomach, and I don't know which way to go . . . what I'm going to do without him. He was my biggest supporter, especially with my house over there," Pierce said with a nod of his head. "We were doing this thing together. Now, I don't know . . ."

ROY JAMES WAS SITTING BESIDE CASSIE, holding one of her hands, a box of Kleenex in his lap. The scene touched Pierce. He walked over to the couch.

"Roy, how about meeting the crew in the morning when they come in and give them the day off. Do it with pay. You can tell them what's happened. They have a right to know, I suppose," Pierce said.

The foreman gently patted the hand he was holding before putting it on the couch. He stood and gave his boss a squeeze on his shoulder on his way to the door.

"Cassie . . . Cassie," Pierce said as he sat on the couch beside her. "I just don't . . . I don't know what we're going to do. Do you?" He felt foolish just as soon as he said it.

Cassie's swollen face looked up at Richardson Pierce. "You're going to finish the house. Aren't you?" she said.

"Lord, I just don't know at this point," he said.

"You *have* to. You know how important this house is . . . *was* . . . to him," she said.

"I've got to think about it, Cassie. There is quite a bit of opposition to my building over on Bird. My bridge . . . or what *was* my bridge over to the island is an example of that."

"Yes, but you can't give in. You and he wanted this so badly!"

"We just need to deal with his death. I can't think about Bird Island right now," Pierce said.

CHAPTER 32

JACK ARRIVED EARLY MONDAY MORNING, hungover from the weekend. He didn't feel like walking three-quarters of a mile down 40th Street to the guest house, so he drove. As he pulled into the compound's driveway, the sight of the burned-out bridge didn't register in his dulled mind. He parked and sat taking the last couple of draws of his cigarette. Then, he exited the Jeep, crushing the butt with the heel of his boot, and proceeded toward the dock. He saw Roy James exit the house and start down towards him. Jack waved, but James didn't return the gesture. His mind cleared, and he became aware of the permeating odor of burnt wood. Out of the corner of his eye, he saw the image of the black, sharp erratic form of pilings and dangling wood. He looked at Roy James, then back at the bridge.

"What the . . . what the hell happened, Roy?"

"Bridge caught fire sometime Saturday night while Mr. Pierce was away in Greensboro. We think it was arson . . .we're thinking Groat."

"Saturday night? Why didn't I hear the fire trucks? They would've come right by my house," Jack said.

"No, they didn't. They came down North Shore Drive. But somebody, most likely the arsonist, lined the road with roofing nails and tacks. The trucks couldn't make it to 40th Street. They had to stop on North Shore Drive. Every damned one of the tankers' tires was flattened," Roy said.

Saturday night. When Mr. Pierce was out of town. Oh shit! Jack's mouth went dry.

"This, on top of losing his son. Damn if life can really be . . ."

"Losing his son? What are you talking about, Roy?" Jack asked.

"Rich. I'm sorry to have to tell you this way. I was coming down to tell you and the rest of the crew. Mr. Pierce just found out yesterday that his son, Rich, was killed in an automobile accident after he left here several weeks ago when he was on his way to the airport to see his mother in Greece. Pierce wanted me to tell you guys what happened and give you the day off. With pay," Roy said.

Jack stood motionless . . . his hands in his pockets. He didn't know what to say or do. Was he an indirect accomplice to this fire since he had relayed the information to Groat that Pierce was going to be away in Greensboro for the weekend? *And* the lie he'd told him about Pierce planning on using the bridge to bring over heavy-duty equipment after the bridge was finished? A wave of nausea rose in him. Everything associated with Groat was becoming tainted and foul. He needed to get out from under Horace Groat's tentacles. He feared Groat but just didn't know how to go about doing it.

The other crew members were arriving and getting out of their cars.

"What the fuck happened?" Hugh Wyrick asked Jack.

Jack said nothing, his hands still in his pockets. Finally, he said, "Roy has something to tell y'all."

"About who torched our bridge?" Hugh asked.

"That. And more," Jack said.

"What?"

"Go talk to Roy. He'll tell you," Jack said.

Jack left the parking lot as the other crew members were arriving. He turned right onto 40th Street, drove to the end, and parked on Main Street. He got out of his Jeep and crested the dunes. The breeze was blowing straight in off the ocean at a crisp pace.

Probably gonna storm later today, he thought.

He crossed his legs and sat down. He ran both his hands back through his hair then pulled out a pack of Winstons from his shirt pocket. He lit up and looked down towards Bird Island. There was not a person on the beach except one lone figure on the far side of Madd Inlet.

How the hell did it come to this? Rich was dead, the bridge destroyed. And Jack was working for Horace Groat.

He tried to convince himself the information he gave Groat about Mr. Pierce leaving the beach for a few days or the lie about the backhoe didn't have anything to do with the bridge being burned. But in his gut, he wasn't so sure. And something else was bothering him. Rich had died in a car wreck while driving back from the beach? *He* had seen a car traveling east . . . from the coast . . . involved in an accident. And the driver didn't have a face! He needed to talk with Roy. Get some more particulars.

He picked up a stick and started drawing a circle in the sand beneath his up-bent knees. Maybe he should get out of Sunset. Weird shit's been happening ever since he got there, and it wasn't showing any signs of getting more normal. But where could he go? Not back to Greensboro, where the draft would catch up with him, for sure. Maybe

Canada. Uncle Sam couldn't touch him there. Maybe buy a little farm, grow a little weed, and get back to the land.

He looked back over to Bird Island and saw that the man on the beach was getting closer, now just on the other side of Madd Inlet. He recognized the gait. *And* the man, he thought.

Jack continued writing in the sand waiting for him to come closer, but he stopped at the edge of the inlet. The tide was out, and he would be able to cross, so that was not the reason he stopped. Jack tossed the stick, left the dune, and started walking at a brisk pace in the man's direction. He was going to get an answer as to who this guy was and why he was stalking him.

The man watched Jack's advance, and then he turned and walked up the spit of sand that ended at a tall sand dune that overlooked Madd Inlet. Arriving at the top of the dune, the man turned back around in Jack's direction.

Jack, waded into the inlet, cupped both hands over his mouth, and hollered, "Who *are* you?"

The man stood still and said nothing.

"Who *are* you," he yelled again.

Jack stumbled up the inlet's far bank and started running towards the dune. When he was about halfway between the inlet and the dune, the man turned and disappeared down the other side.

Jack arrived at the top, ready to confront him, but there was nothing below him but heat, scrub pine, and sand. He looked across the flatness of the back side of the island and saw him again through the pine trees. He was at the front of the island house as if waiting to go in. Jack leaped off the dune, but his feet could not keep pace, and he stumbled, rolling down the back side of the dune. He stood and began running again, brushing himself off as he went. Limbs and briars stung his face, legs, and arms as he rushed through the thicket. He broke through the brush and was in the clearing, expecting to see the man, but he was not there.

Jack entered the ground floor of the house and walked through the framed-out rooms but found nothing or heard nothing of the man. Only the dry sound of crickets and cicadas outside in the heat. He walked to the back, sound-side of the house. A wooden walkway ran from the far side of the yard, through the scrub pines and yaupon trees, down to the dock at the sound. Jack's attention was drawn to the walkway. He stepped over the brick foundation and crossed the yard to the walkway that was framed by trees on both sides. He started down the walkway, and the man suddenly appeared between him and the dock. The man held out his right arm, as if signaling Jack to stop where he was. The man was far enough away that his face remained a blur . . . a mass. Without a word, the man pointed back over Jack's head. Jack turned and followed the direction he was pointing . . . the house.

"What? What're you pointing at? The house?"

The man nodded.

Suddenly, a random thought popped into Jack's mind, and as a shiver ran up his spine, he couldn't contain his query.

"Rich? You're Rich Pierce, aren't you?" Jack asked, looking back at the house. "What're you trying to tell me?" Jack asked as he turned, looking back towards the man. But the man had vanished.

Jack ran down the boardwalk to where he had been standing. He looked left and right, before hopping over the railing and cautiously, entering the tree line. He walked the area looking for any sign of the faceless man but found only silence. No sound of crickets or cicadas. He thought that strange. Had the man's passing through here silenced the insects?

Jack cupped his hands around his mouth and hollered, "Hey! You in here?"

He waited in the silence, but there was no answer.

Again, he stood still and waited, but no answer came.

"He's not in here," he said to himself. He jumped the railing back onto the walkway, walked down to the dock, and looked out over the water. Leaning with both arms on the railing, he lowered his head between his arms and said, "This shit's starting to get on my nerves. Is this for real? Or am I cracking up? The faceless man. And now, Rich Jr. dead? This isn't just a coincidence. It just can't be."

———•———

JACK WAS BOTHERED AND had no place to go. He wanted some answers, so he rode back over to 40th Street. Careful to avoid the guest house, he turned into Roy's driveway, one down from the guest house. He parked, walked up the back stairs to Roy James' cottage, and knocked on the screen door.

Jack heard footsteps, and Roy James appeared. "Yeah, Jack?" Roy James said.

"Roy, can I talk to you? Things that have been happening . . . I . . . ahh . . . I've got some bad feelings about all this."

"I do too, Jack. Yeah, come on in."

Jack took a seat at the kitchen bar.

"What's on your mind?"

"Well, those tacks and nails that were put in the road to cause the firetrucks tires to go flat . . . *and* the fire. It was done when the Pierce's were away from the beach. That just sounds a little . . . a little . . . I don't know how to say it . . ."

"It *does*," Roy said looking directly at Jack. "It seems very coincidental. Is that what you were thinking?"

"Well, yeah. I guess that's it," Jack said.

Roy looked deeply at Jack and said, "That's why I told you we were thinking Groat. But it seems to bother you. I mean, it bothers all of us. But you seem to be . . . I don't mean to sound rude or crass, but you really don't have a dog in this fight, do you? I mean . . . you're employed by Mr. Pierce, but so are all the others. And you're the only one sitting here with a burr up your ass. So, to speak," James said with a smile.

Jack swallowed hard but managed, "I like Mr. Pierce. He's a *good* man. Although I never met his son, his loss affects me more than I thought it would."

"I know it does, Jack. You're a sensitive fellow. So is Mr. Pierce. He knows that and likes that about you."

Jack sat with his hands folded in his lap. Neither man said a word until Jack asked, "How come it took so long to find out he was killed in a car accident?"

"Well, there were some complications," James said.

"Like what?"

"Like identifying the owner of the car. The car was so destroyed, it was hard to run a make on it. The license plate was melted, and there was only a partial VIN left. But the Highway Patrol was finally able to ID the car. The body was so badly destroyed from the fire and the impact, IDing the body took time as well. The face was destroyed, but the coroner found one tooth in the back of the head . . . a molar, and from that, they were able to ID the body as Rich Junior."

Jack looked confused.

"The Lincoln Continental Rich Junior was in belonged to his girlfriend's deceased mother up in Maine," Roy said.

Jack removed his hands from his lap and placed them on his thighs, rubbing them back and forth. "A Continental?" Jack said. "What color?" he asked.

"Don't know what it originally was. The car was burnt so bad, the final color was black." Roy said. "Why?" he asked suspiciously.

"I . . . ahh . . . when and where did this happen?" Jack asked.

"Happened about a month ago, I guess. Seems like a little before you came on board with us."

"Where?" Jack asked, rubbing his thighs faster.

"Out on NC 904, near Fair Bluff. His car ran off the road into a field and exploded."

Jack stopped the rubbing and sat staring at the floor in front of his feet and said, "And you say the face was destroyed?"

"Yes. Are you okay, Jack?"

"Oh, shit. Oh, shit, Roy. I saw it happen," Jack said just above a whisper.

"You what?"

"I think I saw it happen. Or just after it happened," Jack said.

"What are you talking about Jack? Settle down. Take a deep breath and tell me, from the beginning what you saw, or think you saw."

Jack took a couple of deep breaths trying to regain composure and asked Roy, "Could I have a glass of water? My throat's so dry."

"Sure," Roy said as he walked to the sink and poured Jack a glass of water. He slid it across the bar and walked back around and took his seat again. Jack took a big drink and tried to relax.

"Tell me about what you saw," Roy said.

"Okay. My buddy and I were on our way down here back in April. I was moving here, and my bud was on his way to hook up with some friends at Ocean Drive. He was gonna drop me off at Sunset and keep on rolling. Well, we were traveling along 904 . . . on the other side of Fair Bluff . . . just shooting the shit, and all of a sudden I saw it coming directly at us."

"Saw what?"

"The Continental. It looked big as a boat, and it was coming directly at us. It had already started crossing the center line, and this is the thing, Roy. The damage had already been done."

"What do you mean, 'the damage had already been done'?"

"I saw that car coming, and the front windshield was blown out. It had a hole in it the size of a basketball. And I could see him. I'll never forget that vision. The driver . . . ah . . . Rich, I guess, was behind the steering wheel, and I could clearly see his face . . . nothing but red pulp where a nose and a mouth should have been . . . staring right at me through that open hole in the window. And Roy, the strangest thing. I could see the hair on the top of his head blowing straight back from the wind coming through that open windshield. I don't know why, but that really bothered me. It was like he was just a regular guy with the wind in his hair. But he wasn't there. He was already dead. Something had already happened to him before he even got to us."

"You sure about this, Jack? What you're saying is serious. It takes this thing to another level."

"Yes," Jack said.

The room started to spin. Jack gripped the edge of the stool to steady the room.

Roy finally said, "This could explain why the car crossed the road and ended up in the field. We need to talk to Lieutenant Berger about this before we tell Mr. Pierce, I guess. God, I hate telling him about this. Him thinking his son just fell asleep would have been so much easier on him. Now, something else must have happened. Damn! Mr. Pierce has had enough put on his plate. Now just one more raw-ass thing for him to try and digest."

———•———

LIEUTENANT BERGER, JACK, ROY JAMES, and Richardson Pierce sat in the living room of the guest house. The four were being quiet in their effort of not waking Cassie, who was asleep in one of the back bedrooms.

Pierce looked at Berger. "What do you think, Lieutenant?"

Berger gave him a questioning look, uncertain as to what he meant.

"What happened to my son that caused this accident?"

"I . . . I don't know yet . . .what transpired, if anything, prior to your son's accident. I don't have . . . ."

"Jack," Pierce said, his tired, red eyes shifting over to Jack. "Did you see anything . . . any vehicle in the vicinity at the time?"

"No, I didn't. In all the confusion, a car *could* have come by, but I don't recall seeing one," Jack said.

"There was not a vehicle in front of you that may have caused Rich to cross the center line? Or perhaps one that was behind him that may have passed him and maybe sideswiped him and pushed him over into your lane and into the field?"

"No sir. I didn't see one. And I don't think that happened. Rich . . . your son . . . in my opinion, had already been injured *before* we saw him."

"Tell me about that, Jack. I know you told Roy and the Lieutenant here, but you haven't told me. What, exactly, did you see? Why do you say that, in your opinion, Rich had already been injured before you met him?"

"Well . . . there . . . there *was* no face. Where the face should have been, there was nothing . . . but red pulp."

Richardson Pierce jerked backward and grimaced.

"I'm sorry, Mr. Pierce. I didn't mean to . . ."

"No! I need to do this. I need to know. Go ahead."

"I saw him, and then I saw his car cross the embankment and go airborne. It landed towards the front end, and then it disappeared from view because it was covered up in field dirt. Huff pulled our car back onto the road, and that's when we saw the car go up in flames. It actually exploded."

"What did you do afterward? After he wrecked."

"We stopped and looked back at the car. It was in the field burning. It erupted into a ball of fire."

"Did you get out? Did you try and help in any way?"

"The car was totally engulfed in flames. There was nothing we could do."

"*But*, did you *think* about seeing if you could have done something?"

Jack's mind replayed the exchange between him and Huff . . . *we gotta go back and check on him. What the hell are you talking about Jack? I'm sitting here with a cooler of beer, not to mention the beer on my breath. The last thing I want to see or talk to is a State Trooper. No way I want to get involved in this. Pull that damn door shut, and let's get the hell out of here.*

"I ahh . . . we . . . yeah, we did discuss going back to check on him, but we decided against it," Jack said.

"Why didn't you try? I'm sorry, Jack. But that was my son in there."

Resentment rose in Jack. Why couldn't they have at least gotten out of the car and maybe walked over to check on him like Jack wanted? At least, as Mr. Pierce said, they could have tried. Huff's nonchalance had put Jack in the predicament of having to tell a man who had just lost his son that he didn't make the effort to see if his son was still alive. He was pissed at Huff, and just now, he didn't give a damn what light he was about to cast Huff in.

"I *did* want to go back and check on Rich. I told Huff we needed to do that. But he wouldn't hear of it. He had a cooler of beer in the car and beer on his breath from one he had drunk a little earlier. Plus, he had lost his license because of a DUI, and the last thing he wanted was to talk to a State Trooper with beer on his breath."

Richardson Pierce and Lieutenant Berger looked at each other.

Lt. Berger then asked Jack, "Did Huff's car make contact with the Continental?"

"I . . . I don't believe we did," Jack said.

"Did the Continental cross in front of or behind the car you were in?" Berger asked.

"It passed behind us."

Pierce followed, "Then if it passed *behind* you, why did your car end up going to the *right,* straddling the ditch?"

"I don't . . . I don't really know. That wouldn't make sense, I know. But I think that was just Huff's reaction. He whipped it to the right, perhaps thinking that if he went out into the field, he would avoid the Continental before it ever got to us," Jack said. "But I don't know that." Jack sat on the couch, bent from the waist with his legs open, his hands folded between them, looking at the three men across from him. No one said anything more until Jack asked, "Am I some kind of suspect or something?"

"Since we don't really know what happened, Mr. Tagger, we're just starting to look at all the possibilities. This is the first we've heard about the possibility that Mr. Pierce may have been injured before the accident happening. This opens a whole new perspective. Is that something you made up to cover your involvement? That something had already happened to him *before* he arrived at where you were on 904? And, the fact that you said the driver of your vehicle . . . what was his name . . . Huff? That Mr. Huff had consumed alcohol earlier. Did he cross the center line, forcing the Continental over into your lane, trying to avoid the accident? That opens, in my mind, the possibility that your car may have been the perpetrator that caused the accident," Berger said.

"I can say and will testify, if necessary, that Huff was not intoxicated. He'd consumed *one* beer, and that was back before we got to Laurinburg. He was *not* intoxicated," Jack said.

"Well, your testimony would possibly be tainted by the fact that he's a friend of yours. The fact that he was drinking, *prior to the accident*, has to be looked into," Berger said.

"It's not against the law to have an open beer in the car, is it?" Jack said.

"No, it's not. Your friend could have had a beer in his hand, waving at an officer as he went by, and not be breaking the law. But I can assure you that the officer would have turned on his red lights and pulled him to check to see if he was intoxicated. It's not against the law to have an open beer in the car or even to be consuming a beer while driving in this state. But operating a motor vehicle while intoxicated is another matter, as your friend, by your own admission, has obviously found out," Berger said.

Jack felt sick. A few minutes ago, he was pissed at Huff for putting him in this situation. Now, he'd turned the table, and *Huff* was in a situation. Maybe Jack, as well.

"Jack, I apologize for the interrogation," Pierce said looking at Berger. "What I know of you, I don't think you had anything to do with this or with Rich suffering a pre-existing injury. *But,* if he *was* injured or killed before approaching you two, I . . . *we're* gonna turn over every stone to find out what happened and who did it. Isn't that right, Lieutenant Berger? But as I just said, until I'm proven wrong, I don't think . . . *feel* you had anything to do with that," Pierce said.

"But, Mr. Tagger, this is now an ongoing investigation. And like Mr. Pierce just said, we're gonna be all over it. And until we conclude it, I don't want you leaving the county. You understand?" Berger added.

"Yes, sir. I hadn't planned to," Jack said.

"What is your friend's first name?"

"Bobby, Bob . . . ah . . . Robert."

"And, I'm gonna need his address. Is he back in Greensboro? We'll need to have the Guilford County District check for damage to the front end of the vehicle you were in. I don't recall you saying, but what type of car was it?"

"I assume he's back. He was just visiting some friends in Ocean Drive. The car . . . it was a Chevrolet . . . an Impala. Not sure of the year, though," Jack said.

———•———

"PERSON TO PERSON, collect call from Jack Tagger for a Mister Robert Huff," the operator said.

"Yeah, this is him," said the voice at the other end of the phone.

"Will you accept the charges?"

"I reckon so."

"Go ahead sir," the operator said.

"Huff! I need to tell ya, there's gonna be a Highway Patrol officer stopping by your . . ."

"Hell! He already did. First thing this morning. What are you trying to do to me, Jack?"

"I'm sorry, Huff. I should've called you yesterday, but it was late when I was finished meeting with Mr. Pierce and the Trooper. I didn't think they'd have gotten to you this quick."

"What the hell is going on down there, Jack? The trooper came by and looked at the front of my car. Then he took some pictures."

"I'm sorry, man. Pierce confronted me about his son. He asked why didn't we go down and see if there was anything we could've done for him. And I remembered our conversation in the car, and I just got pissed at you. I was thinking you should've been the one sitting there telling him why we didn't do anything. That's when I told them about you—that you were driving and it was your car."

"Well thanks a lot, buddy! I really need that attention from the North Carolina Highway Patrol. You asshole!"

"Huff! One question. *Is* there any damage to the front end of your car? Did you look?"

"Well, that's *one* thing going in our favor," Huff said.

"What's that?"

"That's about the *only* place that old Chevy doesn't have a ding on it."

"The front of the car. Really?"

"Yep."

"Holly shit, Huff! Thank, God. Last night, all I could think about was the front of your car. I couldn't recall any dings, but I couldn't be sure. And if there was some front-end damage, that Lieutenant would have been all over us, I'm afraid."

"You think so?"

"I do. I don't think he likes long-haired boys."

"Well, do me a favor. When it comes to '*tha man*,' forget my name. Like to scared the shit out of me this morning when I answered the knock at my front door and there stood Smokey the Bear," Huff said.

"I'm sorry, Huff. I really am. This shit that's going on down here is getting pretty heavy. Now, *this*!"

"What else's been going on?"

"That faceless man we saw on the beach that day?"

"Yeah?" Huff said.

"He keeps showing up. Yesterday, when Roy James told me Rich Jr. was dead, I went out on the beach and sat down on a dune to do some thinking. When I looked down toward Bird Island, there he was, standing on the other side of Madd Inlet."

"No shit?"

"No shit! And listen to this. When Mr. Pierce, Roy, and the state trooper were grilling me about what I saw, I told them about the damage to the driver's face and that it appeared that it had already been done by the time it got to us. Then it hit me!"

"What?"

"That the man on the beach and the driver of the car had no face. Coincidence? I don't think so."

"That's pretty far out, Jack. What'd you say?"

"I just kept my mouth shut. I didn't tell them about the faceless man on the beach."

"You know, I never thought about that. Oh hell! Listen to me! Now here *I* go," Huff said.

"And . . . oh yeah . . . I didn't tell ya. The bridge over to Bird was burned. They think Groat may have had his hand in it." Jack said.

"Your sugar daddy? Boss number one burns boss number two's bridge? Holy shit, Jack. Things *are* heating up, and it seems to be all around *you*. What kind of karma you spreading down there?"

"Seems that way! But hey . . . this dime is on you, and this call is getting kinda lengthy."

"Yeah, thanks for reminding me. You *did* call *me* . . . *collect*. But hey. I think I'm gonna be coming down next month."

You know when, next month, you're coming down?"

"Yeah! Beach Weekend . . . at Ocean Drive!"

"I can never remember the date. Which weekend it is?"

"Second weekend in May. Mother's Day weekend, Jack!"

"Yeah. That's it."

"We gonna hook up and raise some hell that weekend?" Huff asked.

"Hell yeah! I look forward to it! With all that's been going on here, I need to get away for a while. Even if it's just fifteen miles away, it'll seem like a world away."

CHAPTER 33

MONDAY MORNING, JACK SPOTTED Cricket's MG in the parking lot of the Vesta pier. He grabbed his board out of the back of his Jeep and ran over the dunes. On the beach, he waxed his board with one hand, while cupping his eyes with the other, looking out past the shore break for her. He saw her take off on a medium-size wave, fly past the breaking part of the face, and cruise up onto the smooth shoulder of the building wave. At the apex, she dug her rear rail into the face, turned, and careened back down into the trough.

Jack appreciated the move and ran into the surf to meet her at the end of her ride. "Nice!" Jack yelled, smiling.

Cricket shook the water out of her face and smiled back. "You like?"

"Oh, hell yeah. Smooth move!" He pushed his board out and flopped his torso on the deck, paddling out in almost the same motion, and said, "Let's get some!"

Sitting out in the lineup, straddling their boards, Jack and Cricket high-fived each other, smiling. "We need to do this more often, Jack."

"Yeah, I know. Been too long between sets," he said with a grin.

"You know it, Jack Tagger," she said, slapping his arm. "What's been going on?"

"Geez! Where do I begin?" he said.

Sitting on their boards drifting over incoming sets, he told her about what had transpired after he left on their last evening at Ocean Isle, including his paranormal experience in the mist at Bonaparte's Landing. He didn't mention the faceless man.

"Sounds like you may need to be smudged!" she said.

"That sounds like fun! Right now? Out here? I've don't believe I've ever done it on a surfboard," he said with a smile.

"Seriously! We need to burn sage over and around you. Smudge you. Get rid of the bad ju-ju."

"I'm just shitting you. I know what smudging is. But go on."

"It's a Native American ritual. You burn sage in someone's house or around them to get rid of bad spirits," she said.

"I don't know. I don't want to piss off any more of the spirit world than I obviously have."

"I'm serious, Jack. Burning sage really does work for some people. Can't hurt."

"You believe in that, Cricket? The spirit world and all?"

"It's a big wide universe out there, Jack. UFOs, the spirit world, who am I to doubt those things don't exist?"

"I'm there, Cricket."

"Really though. It's an old, ancient ritual. We could go down to Bonaparte's Landing one night where this experience happened and burn the sage around you and around the space where you saw the apparition."

"I'm down with it. Hell, I know what I saw . . . I think. You think it works? Smudging?"

"All I'll say is that I've seen it work. I have a friend, Lisa, who was having a bad time. Everything was going wrong for her. Everything! Her car broke down, her furnace in her house blew, and all this other shit. And she didn't have the money to fix them. So, my friend called on a shaman that I told her about, and the shaman smudged her house, and I swear, the bad energy left."

"You know someone who is a shaman?"

"Yes, Sarah. She's a friend of mine. She's my gal—a Lumbee Indian. Want me to set it up?"

"Yeah. Go ahead."

"When? Where? At the landing?"

"Yeah. Let's plan to meet at the end of the road there on Thursday, if she's available, at the landing."

"Yeah. Okay. I'll get in touch with her."

"Listen, Cricket. Do this for me. Don't give her any specifics about what happened. I'm not trying to trick her or anything, but I want to trust her, believe in her stuff."

"I won't. She doesn't work like that. She comes into a situation cold and picks up on energy without any prompting or direction. She's the real deal."

"Sounds good to me. Let's do it," Jack said.

———————⚫———————

CRICKET MET SARAH at the pier at Ocean Isle.

"What's up, girl," Cricket said as she Hugged Sarah Locklear.

"Nothing but the deep blue sky. How bout with you?"

"*You,*"Cricket said. "Question. How'd it all turn out for Lisa? Did the smudging work? Did her bad juju stay gone?" Cricket asked.

"It did. And is. I was able to clear her. It was a good cleansing. Now, what's going on with this friend of yours?"

"This guy, my surfing buddy. He's got some powerful shit going on, sounds like. He encountered something at Bonaparte's Landing that he doesn't understand. I told him about you and the possibility of a smudging," Cricket said.

"Oh, okay. Your surfing buddy," Sarah said.

"Yeah. He's wanting to do this," Cricket said.

So, he's open?"

"He is."

"Okay. So, Bonaparte's Landing," Sarah said knowingly.

"You got it, girl," Cricket said.

"Okay. That's all I need to know. I'll be there," Sarah said.

———●———

THREE DAYS AFTER THEIR CONVERSATION, just before sunset, Cricket and Jack stood on the sand at the end of the road overlooking the Intracoastal Waterway at Bonaparte's Landing.

"Does she know where the landing is?" Jack asked Cricket.

"Yeah. She knows about this place. She was emphatic we meet at this time of day," Cricket said.

Just then a Toyota Corolla in need of paint pulled up beside Cricket's MG.

"Here she is," Cricket said to Jack.

A short woman with a dark complexion who looked to be about Jack's age exited the car and walked toward them, turning her head left and right and cocked at a slight angle as if listening for something. She met Cricket with a smile and a hug.

"Jack, I want you to meet Sarah Locklear. Sarah, this is Jack Tagger."

Sarah held out her hand. "Good to meet you, Jack."

"Same here, Sarah," Jack said.

Sarah's attention immediately went elsewhere as she took in the lay of the land . . . the abandoned building, the sandy lane that ran out from them along water's edge, and the sandy bottom in the shallows of the Intracoastal Waterway. She looked up into the sky then closed her eyes, seeming to be in a momentary trance. She opened them, looked at Jack and Cricket, and said, "There *is* an energy here, Jack. It feels as if things are not the way they should be. But before we proceed, let me tell you a little about myself and my people. I am Lumbee Indian. It is not certain where my tribe originated or came from, but it is thought that we've always lived near the ocean. We may be descendants of the Croatan Indians that disappeared from the Outer Banks during the Lost Colony period. But that has never been proven.

"We were early believers in the immortality of the soul. Our people designated worthy members in our tribe to high positions. One was priests, who were wise beyond most. The other was conjurors or shamans who were chosen for their magical abilities. It was thought that the conjurers received their power from personal contact with a supernatural being. My grandfather was a conjurer. My power came from him. And so, that is why I am here this evening. Why Cricket asked me to come on your behalf. To delve into whatever may be happening in your world *and* on the other side of your world. Something that you probably don't understand."

"That may well be, Sarah."

"Okay. So, if we are going to proceed, you *must* open yourself and *trust* whatever happens here. If a spirit comes through tonight, its message will be specific and intentional. Any time you are calling spirits into an interaction, you need to be careful. The intent must be specific. And its intent must be pure. So, Jack, this is totally up to you. It's *your* decision."

Jack gave her words thought and then said, "I'm ready. Let's do it."

The sun was now a ball sinking below the tree-line behind them, sending its last rays upward, connecting with the clouds above, creating a magnificent bounce of color.

Sarah walked back over to her car and removed a blanket. She came back and walked around in circles as if looking to find a place to spread it. She stopped, closed her eyes for a moment, and then said, "This is it. This is where I feel the energy."

She then proceeded to pop the blanket out and let it alight on the sand. She looked out toward the ocean to the back of Bird Island. She lowered herself onto the center of the blanket and motioned for Jack to sit at the left front corner of the blanket, Cricket on the right corner.

"One of the most basic beliefs of shamanism is the belief that the tentacles of power run through all things," Sarah said. "So now that the sun is about to finish its day, let us sit in quiet and wait on that which is to come. This is Sandalwood, the divine," she said taking the incense and incense holder and a wrapped bundle of sage out of her bag and placing them on the blanket in front of her. "It is a good incense to burn to open the spirit world. I may or may not use the sage. It depends on who comes and what they want. If I feel a nuisance energy, I will use it to clear you. And now, I am ready to begin. But first, I must ask you two questions. First, how much do you want to know?"

"Everything," Jack said.

"*And*, may I enter your vibration?"

"You may," Jack said.

The three sat on the blanket in silence as the light began to merge with the dark, creating that in-between time when it's neither day nor night. Time passed into darkness and became irrelevant. Jack didn't have any idea how long they had been sitting there when he felt Sarah suddenly stiffen and make an unfamiliar noise. He looked at her from his corner of the blanket and saw her—head raised, mouth wide open, the strange guttural noise sounding as if being born and emitted from deep within her. Jack and Cricket exchanged glances.

"What the . . . ?" he whispered to her.

"Be damned if I know," she whispered back.

Sarah remained rigid for a period more until her shoulders and head dropped, indicating to Jack and Cricket that she had returned.

"Sarah . . ." Cricket whispered. "You okay?"

Sarah maintained her vision straight ahead but slowly nodded that she was.

Moments passed until she said, "Do you see the entity, Jack?"

"See what?" Jack said softly.

Sarah pointed straight ahead to the sandy path along the water. "That. Him," she said.

Jack followed the direction she pointed in.

"*There*," she said. "In the mist. On the path beside the water."

Jack and Cricket were staring into the nothingness, when suddenly Jack said, "Oh my God! He's back. He's in the fog."

Sarah raised her arm again and pointed to the apparition, saying, "You can come . . . come into our circle. We welcome you. We are here for you."

Cricket reached over and took Jack's arm. "What is it, Jack? What do you see?"

Jack pointed in front of him and said, "In the fog. The mist . . . right there. He's right out there."

Cricket followed where he pointed but said, "I don't see it."

"It's up to the entity. If it wants to let you in, it will. If not, it's nothing you did wrong," Sarah said.

Jack and Sarah watched the swirling mist move towards them. Jack was aware Cricket's gaze had shifted from the trail ahead and was upon him. He took her hand, and she responded, covering his hand with both of hers, comforting. Jack turned his head, slightly, towards her. Cricket started to slide over to him, but Sarah intervened.

"No," she whispered. "Maintain the space. It's important."

Cricket remained on her corner of the blanket. Jack focused back on the vision that was now coming more distinguishable.

The humidity left, and the temperature dropped.

"Oh, God! Do you feel that? I'm cold," Cricket said, wrapping her arms around her torso.

"Come," Sarah said again to the image. "Reveal yourself."

The image began to shape itself.

"Yes," Sarah said. "We are starting to see you more clearly. Pay attention," Sarah said softly to Jack. "It's working very hard. It's expending . . . oh . . . it's using so much energy trying to manifest itself."

The image Jack had seen before was now taking shape . . . starting to reveal itself in form. But still, it retained the qualities of a liquid-like, slightly moving illusion.

"Oh jeez," Cricket whispered. "I'm starting to see it now!"

Sarah put her arm out toward Cricket and issued a soft, "Shhh." Then, she continued. "We can see that you are with us now. Tell us why you remain here and choose not to cross over?"

The image began to speak to Sarah in a watery, gurgling manner.

Cricket said, softly, "Oh, Jesus, I'm seeing a mist now. And oh shit, *now* I see a . . . ."

Sarah held out her hand to silence Cricket.

The three sat in silence as the mist took the form of a man in a modern-day dress. The face remained watery, bleary.

Sarah started to translate the bubbling message. *"The one that is coming forward is having . . . . it is difficult for him to speak. He has recently crossed over, and he is confused . . . not certain of his state. He passes back and forth into both worlds. He feels he cannot communicate because he has no face."*

"Oh my God," Jack said as the apparition finally came through. "That's *him*."

"He wants to communicate with this one," she said, pointing at Jack.

"Jesus!" Jack said, putting his head between his knees.

"He worries for the father. The evil one is active and on the move, but the father's head is turned and does not see. This one," she said,

again pointing to Jack, "*must intercede on behalf of this one . . . the one that has crossed over.*"

Jack was listening, but his head remained between his knees.

"*This one,*" she said again, pointing to Jack, "*and the one named Cassandra.*"

Jack raised his head. He looked over at Cricket and she at him. He then looked back at Sarah.

"I've seen him before. It's him," Jack said, pointing at the apparition.

"What? Where?" Cricket whispered.

"On the beach. Over at Bird Island. And . . . on Highway 904. I think it's Rich. Mr. Pierce's son," he said.

Are you allowed to talk to him? To ask him questions?" he asked Sarah.

"I am," she whispered. "But *you* may ask him what you want, *through* me. I am the medium," she said. "Pose your questions as if you are asking *me* the question."

"Okay," Jack said and cleared his throat. He paused and then asked, "I think I know, but who are you?"

"*This is the father's son.*"

"It *is* him," he said. "What happened to your face? How did that happen?" Jack asked, turning back to Sarah.

"*He does not know. He saw a brilliant light and then found himself on this side, uncertain. That is all he knows.*"

"*Who* is the evil one?"

"*The name eludes him. It is all too confusing. But he says it's the one that wants to destroy and take from the father what is rightfully the father's.*"

"Groat," Jack said to himself. "What do you want me to do? How do I intercede?"

"He feels the father's intent waning. But it must not. His work on the land is too important to the father . . . to his peace. You must fill the void. Make him continue with his dream."

"Have you . . . do you know me? Have we met?" Jack asked.

"He has felt your presence before. Just after the brilliance . . . he felt you close by."

The spirit's image started to go static, like a bad television connection.

Again pointing to Jack, Sarah said, *"This one must be careful. The evil one is a danger to you as well. He and his minions . . . one of which knows of you.* The energy is getting weak. This is very hard for him . . . very taxing," Sarah said.

The image started to waver.

"The son needs to pass the words . . . tell him . . . so he knows . . . " And then a garbled sound followed that was undistinguishable to the three.

"Tell who . . . *what?*" Jack asked.

Again, weak and garbled. *"Tell the father . . . ."*

"Tell him what?" Jack said.

The faceless entity remained and looked in Jack's direction, pointing out toward Bird Island. It remained for several seconds before it started to dissolve. Then it was gone, and the humidity of the night rushed back in and took its place.

Sarah fell back onto the blanket, spent.

Jack looked at Cricket, bewildered. "What just happened? I don't believe this. I'm so glad you were here to experience this with me. That way, I know I'm not going insane. You *did* experience what just took place! Right?"

Cricket had her arms wrapped around her knees and was looking out into the black space. She remained silent.

"Cricket!" Did you hear me? Did you see what just happened here?"

"I did, Jack, and I wish I hadn't. I think the world as I knew it *is* no longer," Cricket said.

"Same here. It's gonna take some time to get my mind around this. Maybe never," Jack said.

"I'm going to smudge you," Sarah said, now sitting up on her blanket, taking a bundle of sage out of her hobo bag. "It's clear to me this one means you no harm. But that the evil one and his minions are a danger to you, too. I don't know what that is about, but a good cleansing might well be to protect you for whatever is to come," she said lighting the sage. "And who is *Cassandra*?" she asked, moving the smoking sage bundle over and around Jack.

"I don't know," Jack said. "I wish it would have answered that before it disappeared. Sounds like she . . . or whoever . . . is gonna play a part in all this before it's over."

"What did you tell me Rich's girlfriend's name was? Cathy? Cristy? Something beginning with a C," Cricket asked.

"Yeah. I never met her but heard Mr. Pierce mention her a time or two. But it wasn't Cassandra. Cissy . . . Carrie . . . *Cassie* . . . CASSIE!" Jack said.

"That's *it*, Jack! *Cassie* . . . Cassie is short for Cassandra!" Cricket said.

"Looks like you and this Cassie person have a future date," Sarah said, laughing as she got up from her blanket and brushed off her jeans.

"Sarah, thank you. And *you* too, Cricket, for being here," Jack said.

"How about a beer, Jack? I really could use one right about now," Cricket said. "Wanna come with us, Sarah?"

"I'll pass but thank you! I'm exhausted," she said.

"I am too. That's why I need a drink," Jack said.

———•———

JACK OPENED THE REFRIGERATOR DOOR, extracted two Michelob's, and set them down on the bar in the kitchen. He popped the top on both and slid Cricket's beer across the bar. "Hell of a night, huh?" he said.

"One *hell* of a night!" she said. "Like I said, I don't know *how* I feel about what I experienced tonight."

"Me neither. I'm sorry for getting you involved in this," he said.

"No, I got myself involved. *I'm* the one who solicited Sarah's help," Cricket said.

Both gulped a swallow of beer, put the bottle back on the bar, and were silent for a few moments, thinking over the events of the night.

"I mean, I have always been open to this kind of stuff . . . the possibility of the spirit world and all. And, I'm disappointed in my reactions tonight. It frightened me," she said.

"I know what you're saying because I'm going through the same thing, emotionally and mentally. In some ways, I wish tonight never happened. Then again, part of me is mesmerized, blown away," Jack said.

"I know, Jack, but still . . ."

"But still, my involvement in this thing isn't over. I know. Lieutenant Berger has his eye on me, so does Mr. Pierce, I think. Now, I have to explain to them what happened to Rich Jr., and by *who*, of which I don't know. *And,* how I came to know this. This ain't gonna be good," Jack said.

Cricket laid her head on the bar. "Do *they* think you had something to do with his death?"

"I get that feeling. Especially with Berger. He told me not to leave the county because this case is currently under investigation."

"What are you going to do, Jack?"

"What do you mean, what I am going to do?"

"I mean, it all seems that so much is coming down on you right now. Lieutenant Berger, Pierce, and now this command from the headless horseman. And to top it off, Uncle Sam's looking for you to send you to fight in his damned war."

"He's not headless, Cricket."

"I know, but that's the first thing that came to mind."

"Yeah, I know. And I came down here to lose myself and find some peace. From the draft and . . . *her*."

"Your old girlfriend?" Cricket said.

"Yeah. And there's one more problem I haven't told you about Cricket," Jack said.

"Oh great!" Cricket said "Just one more? As if you don't already have enough on your plate!"

Jack leaned against the bar. Cricket lifted her head from the bar.

"And please, let this be it. No more to come later, okay?" she said.

"Cricket, soon after I got down here, I landed a construction job with Horace Groat. Very soon after I started, he approached me and made me another offer—an offer that I couldn't refuse."

"Lord, what?"

"Groat doesn't like Pierce."

"No doubt. He's trying to stop Pierce from building his home on Bird Island. I *do* know about that," Cricket said.

"He wanted me to get on with Pierce's crew and be an insider. To basically spy on Pierce and relay back to him what Pierce was doing over there, what his intentions were . . . . whether or not he is going to develop the island. From what I'm getting, he definitely wants to stop Pierce from doing that, if that's his intention. And to do that, he was going to match whatever Pierce was paying me so I'd make double."

"I guess that would be hard to turn down. What exactly does Groat want with the island?"

"That's not fully clear to me. But it *is* clear that Groat wants to expand his holdings on the beach, and to do that, he would have to dredge the water and marsh behind the beach on the Bird Island end. But Pierce has a lifetime right-of-way across the marsh to his island. So Groat thinks Pierce, with his money and connections, has a thing going with the state. And Groat thinks he pretty much owns this beach and has grandfathered rights to it. So, he's hot as a hornet at Pierce. That's what the ghost meant by the evil one wanting to take or destroy what is rightfully his father's. That, I get. But to answer your question, I don't really know yet what Groat would want or intend to do with the island if he owned it. Maybe it's just the fact that Pierce owns Bird Island that is enough for Groat to detest him. Because it's out there and he can't have it."

"What are you going to do?"

"I'm not sure. Well, I *am*, actually. I can't do Groat's work anymore, but I don't know how to get out of it. Mr. Pierce has been through enough. He's been good to me and, he's a good man, plain and simple. I can't add to his hurt or betray him any longer."

"How are you going to tell Groat you're through with him?"

"I don't know. I thought about stringing him along, maybe for the summer. Just feed him tidbits or make up stuff. Collect the spare change until I had saved up some money over the summer. I just wanted to finally get my share. I'm tired of being on the losing end. But now . . . ." Jack said.

"I don't think you can do it that way, Jack. My daddy used to say, 'Cricket, take only what you need and leave the rest for the person that comes behind you.' I'm not preaching, Jack. Lord knows I've taken more than I needed at times, but it always came back to haunt me."

"I know. And now, I've got to do some payback. I gotta get out of this thing with Groat, and I don't know how. He scares me."

"Really?"

"He does. There was one of Pierce's laborers who fell from the bridge and died just the day before I applied for work with Pierce. Groat had told me to try and get on. I told him that might not happen if Pierce had a full crew and there was no room for me. He said something to the effect that laborers come and go. The next day, a laborer was dead, and lo and behold, there was a vacant position on his crew. I took that dead man's place."

"Do you think Groat had anything to do with that?"

"I really don't know. I confronted him about it. I had my

suspicions. He assured me he wasn't a killer and had nothing to do with it—that it was a total coincidence."

"Now *I'm* worried," Cricket said.

"Yeah. I've got to think about how I'm gonna do this."

"Are you going to tell Pierce?"

"No! I don't want to hurt him any more than he already is. Remember, I've got to be the one that keeps him on course with this project. Me and Cassandra . . . ahh . . . Cassie. She's down here now, staying over at the guest house. I've got to tell her and convince her that her ex-boyfriend paid me a visit . . . *us* a visit. And that he has a message for her. Will you help me? Will you go with me to talk to her? And then, once we've convinced her, maybe we can all three approach Pierce not to give up on the house on the island."

"Don't you think I'm kinda an outsider here?"

"No more than I am. I've never met her. And my meeting her will be me telling her I met her deceased ex-boyfriend in the spirit world and that he had a message for her and his father. That's gonna make a real impression on her," he said.

"When do you want to do it?" Cricket asked.

"The sooner the better. How bout the day after tomorrow. Saturday?"

"I'll be here after my lunch shift at the restaurant. Say about three?"

"That'll do. And thank you, Cricket. I owe you."

"Yes, you do, and the IOUs are adding up."

CHAPTER 34

CRICKET ARRIVED AT 40ᵀᴴ STREET AROUND two on Saturday, an hour earlier than planned. Her knock on the door was met by Jack, covered in a towel from the waist down, his long hair dripping from his shower.

"This is a surprise," Jack said. "I thought we said around three."

"We did. I was hoping I would surprise you and walk in on you, sans the towel."

"You almost did!"

"No, really, my shift ended early, so I thought I'd come on down."

"Well, have a seat, and let me get dressed. You need anything? A Coke, water, a beer?"

"No, I'm good. Get dressed."

Jack had just gone back to his bedroom when Cricket heard another knock on the door. "You expecting anybody?" Cricket asked.

"No. How bout seeing who that is."

Cricket opened the door, and a girl with dark hair and eyes set in a lovely olive complexion face stood at the door dressed in a white peasant dress. "I'm sorry to bother you. I thought I was at the right house. Obviously, I'm not," she said.

"This isn't my house. I'm visiting. Who were you looking for?" Cricket asked.

"I was looking for a Jack Tagger. I'm sorry . . ."

"No! Wait!" Cricket said. "You're right. I mean this is Jack's apartment. Hang on, and I'll get him. Who should I say is calling?"

"He doesn't know me, but my name is Cassie, and I'm a friend of . . . was a friend of Rich Pierce," she said.

"Oh yes! God! I'm so sorry about Rich. And for you! Please. Sit down, and I'll go get Jack."

"Thank you. I don't mean to intrude," Cassie said.

"You're not. Believe it or not, we were just about to pay *you* a visit. Hang on."

Cricket entered Jack's bedroom. Jack was dressed but had a perplexed look on his face. "Is that her?" he whispered?

"Yes. Poor thing. She looks so lost," Cricket said.

"Geez. I guess this makes our day a little easier, doesn't it," Jack said.

He left the bedroom and walked out into the living room where Cassie was standing.

"Cassie, I'm Jack Tagger. I'm so sorry . . ."

"Thank you, Jack. I don't mean to intrude, but Rich Sr. told me where you live and that you were probably the last to see Rich Jr. I wanted to come here to talk to you. He explained what you saw, the car veering toward you, almost hitting you before ending up out in a field. Right now, I feel so alone. It's as if my world has suddenly been pulled out from under me. I don't know if he was still alive when you saw him, but for some reason, I needed to be with the last person to be near him in his last moments on Earth. Does that make any sense at all?"

"Yes, it does. I believe, in an indescribable way, I understand your feelings, and I probably would feel that way as well."

"Thank you for understanding. I have something to ask you. A huge favor, actually."

"What's that?"

"Well, in sort of the same vein, I want to go to where this all happened. To be near . . . *at* the place, where he was last alive. I need to feel that . . . to be *at* that place. I know you're thinking I'm a real case by now, but I have to be honest and that's *all* I'm feeling right now. Would you . . . could you take me there? I don't have a car, but I could give you gas money."

"I'd be glad to take you, Cassie, but I'm not supposed to leave the county."

"I know about that. I told Mr. Pierce I was going to ask you, and he told me what the Lieutenant said, but Mr. Pierce's feelings are that you and your friend weren't responsible. He said, under these circumstances, and if we were back by this evening before dark, he thought it would be fine. The fact that we're together, it would be obvious that you're not on the lam, as it were," she said, managing a little laugh.

"When did you want to go?"

"Today. Now! I need to go there! I really do."

Jack looked at this watch . . .

"I know I'm intruding, and I'm sorry! But other than Rich Sr., I have no one to turn to. He's dealing with his own hurt and loss. We really can't console each other right now. I think our hurts are mirror images of each other. We magnify the loss both of us are feeling."

"No, I was just looking at my watch to see what time it is . . . if we had enough time to get there and back before dark. And I think we do. It's about an hour or so away, and it's two fifteen now. Are you ready to go?"

"I am."

"Okay, let me get my wallet and my sunglasses. Cricket, do you want to come with us?"

"No, you and she need to talk. Y'all go ahead and call me when you get back. Maybe I can come over, and we *all* can talk," Cricket said, raising her eyebrows and cocking her head to let him know she would come over and back up his story about the visit with Rich Jr.

"I'm sorry! I don't want to intrude," Cassie said to Cricket.

"Oh no, you're not, really. I had just stopped by. I really need to get back to Ocean Isle to get ready for my evening shift," she lied.

"Oh, you're from Ocean Isle?" Cassie said.

"I am. My family has a place there, and I waitress at a restaurant. You guys drive carefully. I'll see y'all later," Cricket said.

Cassie and Jack left Sunset Beach right away. He was a bit apprehensive as to what they would talk about during the drive. He didn't know if she knew about Rich's physical damage before the accident. If not, should he tell her?

Jack started the small talk. "So, you're from New England?"

"Yes. I grew up in Caribu, Maine," she said.

"Your family still there?"

"Not anymore. My dad died when I was in Junior High. Mom, within the last year."

"Man! Tough year."

"It has been," she said.

"Any Cavanaughs left up there?"

"Well, no. My dad was a Cavanaugh. They were from Tennessee. My mom's side was Prebscott, and they were the ones from Maine. The Prebscotts were, as the name sounds, a very *fine*, old New England family. As you can imagine, Tennessee Mountain folks and Maine aristocracy are like oil and water. They don't mix well. And neither did my mother and father. They divorced when I was young. I kept the name Cavanaugh. Mother took back her *fine* family name."

"You sound like you're more like your daddy," Jack said.

"Well, I am. And I'm proud of the Cavanaugh's salt-of-the-earth heritage. I wear it well, I think. But I don't mean to cast any aspersions on my mother. She was good to Dad. The divorce was amicable, just two people coming from two different worlds trying to mesh. I loved Mother! She was kind and gentle. I admired both of my parents. But there came a time, and I had to leave. I had to get away from Caribou and strike out on my own. So, I left and came South. The nature of the people down here appeals to who I am, I think. There, again, the Cavanaugh, perhaps. How bout you, Jack?"

"Nothing interesting. Just the regular run-of-the-mill garden variety southern family," Jack said.

"Not that it matters, but where are you in school? Are you just off for the summer?" she asked.

"No, not in school. I dropped out. Several times, actually. School's just not for me right now."

"How are you avoiding the draft?"

"I'm down here."

"What do you mean?"

"I'm resisting, in my own way. I'm laying low down here, you might say. If they can't find me, they can't draft me."

"Isn't that kind of risky? Wouldn't it be safer to get back in school and get your school deferment?"

"Yes. For most guys, but not for me," Jack said.

"Why? Why not for you?"

"I dropped out before I flunked out. I mean . . . really. I'm not a good student."

"That's so sad."

"Sorry. I'm just not."

"No! Not *you*. The times we're living in. There's no place for a guy like you to go. College isn't in you right now. So, what's a guy like you to do? Get drafted, go to that nasty war or, *hide out*. That's no option. It's either-or."

"And that about sums it up. Hopefully, our generation's gonna change some things. End this war, protect and clean up the environment, racial equality . . ."

"*And* . . . gender equality," she said.

"Sorry. That too. Power to the people and all that . . . leave it all a little better than we found it."

Quiet took a seat in the Willys. Cassie leaned her head against the window, her thoughts obviously projecting down the road ahead of them. Jack let her have the silence.

They arrived at the stretch of highway on 904 where it happened. Jack veered his vehicle over to the side of the road and did a U-turn back in the direction he and Huff had been traveling and pulled over onto the side of the road where they had almost collided with Rich's car.

"We're here," Jack said.

She said, "Tell me what you saw, Jack. Don't soft-pedal it. Tell me *all* of what you saw. I need to know, now that we're here. I need to see it. See *him*."

Jack looked straight ahead, unsure where to go with her request. "I don't know what to say. I think Mr. Pierce has told you about all . . ."

"No. Act as if he hasn't. Start from the moment you saw my mother's car and tell me everything that happened."

"Okay. We, my buddy Huff and I, were traveling in the direction we are now. Rich was coming in this direction towards us," he said pointing down the road. "We were shooting the bull, and suddenly, I see this big blue Lincoln. At first, I wasn't sure what kind of car it was, but it was big and it was blue. The car suddenly crossed the center line and was making a line drive right for us. I yelled out to Huff, and he swerved to the right. And the car—your mother's car, passed behind, just barely missing us. We swerved over and rode the ditch for a ways until Huff was able to bring it back over onto the shoulder.

"He and I went down the road a short distance and stopped. We sat there for a moment trying to settle our nerves, and then we heard the explosion and turned around and saw the car go up in flames. I have to tell you. I wanted to go down and check on him to see if there was anything we could do for him. But Huff, because of some previous trouble with the law, didn't want to down there and get involved. So, we left."

"Tell me. Did you see him? As he was coming towards you? I mean, you were so close to each other."

"Well yeah, I could see him. I saw him through his windshield."

"What did you see? I mean . . ."

Jack sat looking straight ahead, recalling the faceless figure behind the steering wheel.

"I *need* to know. Was he dead? Was he *gone* at that point? Mr. Pierce said he may have already been . . ."

"I just don't know how that is going to help you," Jack said.

"There's a reason."

He sat, pondering his response, and then it came out. "There was no face. He didn't have a face by the time he got to us!" Jack said.

Cassie let out a gasp and put her hands to her face.

"I'm sorry, Cassie. I shouldn't have . . ."

"No. It's okay," she said, her eyes red-rimmed and brimming over. "I needed to know because . . . I just needed to know because . . . I've been seeing him! Mostly in my dreams, but then they aren't dreams. Not in the usual sense. And . . . my dream-like contacts with him are sometimes accompanied by a loud, disturbing noise . . . like a BOOM or an explosion! It's happened more than once. And when it happens, it seems real. Like I really heard it. I think he's trying to contact me, Jack. But every time he comes to me, I can't see his face. I call out to him, but he doesn't answer."

Jack remained quiet, relating to what she's just said.

She continued, "And sometimes I feel him when I'm awake. There have been times I thought I saw him in a crowd. I'll see the back of him and the hair is just like his. It's *his* hair . . . wavy in the back and breaking over the back of his collar, just like his. And I run and try to catch him, but he's not there. It's like he has something to tell me, but he can't."

Jack stared out the front windshield. *Is this the time?* Jack thought to himself. *Should I tell her that he may be trying to contact me as well?* But he remained silent.

"Thank you for telling me, Jack. And thank you for bringing me here. His silence makes sense now, I guess. He *can't* tell me. Let's go home," she said.

Jack started the Jeep and eased out, eastward on 904.

She asked. "But there were no other vehicles that you saw? Not before him or after you saw him?"

"None. And I'm certain of that. None, except for one pickup truck that was parked and backed up in a sandy dirt road that leads up into a field down here on the left."

"Where?" Cassie followed.

"Right down here," he said pointing down the road.

As they approached, Jack slowed and pointed up the drive where the pickup was parked.

"Up there," he said as the Willys slowly coasted by.

"Turn around, Jack!"

"What? Why?" Jack answered.

"Just do it!" she replied.

Jack made a U-turn in the road and drove back and turned up into the sandy lane.

"I'm sorry. This is one of those things . . . I just feel a compulsion . . . a *need* to go up here. It's like I'm being pulled to this place," she said.

"It's okay, not a problem," he said.

The driveway made a looping left turn at the top and opened up onto a field. At the far edge of the field, Cassie told Jack to stop, and she got out. Jack watched as she walked around the ground above Highway 904. She studied the roadway below and remained in thought for a moment. Then she turned, walked back, and got in.

"Are you okay?" Jack asked.

"No. Not really. I feel a darkness in this place. I can't explain it, but I don't like it here. I feel somewhat nauseous."

"Let's get out of here then," Jack said putting the gears in reverse.

"Hold it, Jack! What is that?" she said.

"What?" Jack replied.

"That shiny thing there on the ground. What is it? Stop the car!" she said, opening the door and landing on the ground, trotting to keep from falling.

Cassie walked out in front and stopped, looking down at the ground. She bent over and picked something up. Jack put the Willys in park and walked to her as she stood, gingerly holding something between her finger and thumb.

"I'm *very* nauseous now," she said as she dropped it in the palm of his hand.

He looked at the object in his hand—a spent shotgun shell, the casing still a bright copper. He turned and looked at the distance from where the shell was found on the top of the hill, down to the road. He estimated it to be roughly fifty yards from the crest down to the roadway. He knew, from his limited experience and knowledge of shotguns, that a regular shotgun shell would not travel that distance and be fatal. The pattern would spread out too much. However, a single shotgun *slug* would have made what he estimated to be about fifty yards and probably be fatal.

"I don't know if this means anything or not, Cassie. Maybe just some hunter's spent shotgun shell."

But he knew dove season was over last fall, and this shell looked too fresh to have been out in the elements that long.

"I'll take it back with us, anyway. Let's be careful not to get any more of our fingerprints on it," he said as he reached down and picked up a twig onto which he slid the empty, hollow shell.

———◆———

JACK AND CASSIE HAD JUST crossed the Brunswick County line when he pulled into a filling station. "I need to make a quick phone call. You need anything from inside?" he asked as he exited the Willys.

"No, I'm fine," she said.

Jack stepped into the phone booth, inserted a dime, and made his call. Cricket answered on the second ring.

"Hello?"

"Cricket."

"Jack. Where are you?"

"I'm in Grissettown. I still have Cassie with me."

"I've been waiting to hear from you! How was your day?"

"Long, and emotional. I'll tell you about it. Listen, I'm about thirty minutes away. Do you think you could meet me at my house? I didn't tell Cassie about our experience the day before yesterday because I wanted you to be there to back me up."

"Yeah. I can leave now and beat you there."

"Good. On second thought, it would be nice to have Sarah with us, but by the time you got up with her and . . ."

"No, Jack. She's right here. She came over to talk about last night. This works! We'll be there by the time you get home. But drive slow."

"I will. Thanks! I really need to get *this* part over with."

"See you there, Jack!"

He hung up the phone and exited the phone booth. As he walked toward his vehicle and Cassie, he observed a red pickup drive by slowly in the late afternoon light. The driver seemed to be studying Jack as it passed. Jack instinctively threw up his hand in greeting, but his gesture was not met. The driver had a ball cap pulled low across his forehead.

———•———

JACK AND CASSIE PULLED IN at Jack's house. Cricket's MG was parked in the driveway.

"Why are we stopping here, Jack?"

He cut the engine. "Listen, Cassie. There's more to this than what I told you out there today. I have something to tell you, but I wanted . . . you know the girl that was here when you got here earlier today?"

"Yes, Cricket?"

"Yeah. Well, we both experienced something, and it relates to Rich. There was another person with us, and she experienced the same thing. They're waiting inside. I hated to be dishonest with you, but I believe this is the best way."

"I don't understand. You're frightening me."

Jack turned to her and took her hand in his. "I don't mean to.

Trust me. What we have to tell you might give you some relief, some peace. You've been through a lot. I hope it will, anyway."

Cassie looked frightened.

Jack let go of her hand and patted her on the thigh. "Come on. Let's go in," he said, smiling a kind smile.

She smiled back at him.

The two entered Jack's living room where Cricket and Sarah were sitting in the middle of the floor around a wooden cable spool table, a glass of red wine in front of each of them. Candles lit the tabletop. Neil Young's album *Everybody Knows This is Nowhere* played on the stereo. A bottle of Taylor Lake Country Red with two empty glasses stood waiting. Jack filled one of the two empty glasses and handed it to Cassie.

"Thanks! I need this," she said crossing her legs and lowering herself to a sitting position.

"You met Cricket earlier today. This," he said gesturing, "is Sarah."

Cassie acknowledged Sarah with a smile. Jack poured himself a glass of red and sat beside her, across from Sarah and Cricket on the other side of the table.

"Where do I start," Jack said, sighing. "Cassie, Sarah is a medium."

Cassie gave Jack a confused, lost look.

"For lack of a better word, she's a soothsayer—a mystic—someone who can connect with the other side, the spirit world"

Sarah let out a laugh and said, "That'll work, I guess." She looked at Cassie and said, "I'm a shaman. I am Lumbee Indian, and shamanism's been in our culture for many years. And being a mystic or soothsayer, as he described, I *can* and *do*, sometimes, connect with the other side."

"So, this is what happened, Cassie," Jack said, picking up the conversation. "I was coming back from Ocean Isle one night and missed the turn into Sunset and ended up at the end of the road at Bonaparte's Landing. Do you know where that is?" Jack asked.

"Yes. Rich took me there once. We went crabbing. Strange place!"

"It *is*." Jack re-told the story of that evening, of the appearance of the apparition. Cassie watched Jack tell the story with her hand over her mouth as Jack continued.

"I told Cricket what had happened, and she's the one who suggested bringing in Sarah to see if she could connect to the other side—to this entity that had appeared to me, to find out what it wanted from me. A few nights later, we three met at the landing. And now, I'll let Sarah tell what happened that night."

"Cassie, please just keep an open mind. That's all I ask," Sarah said.

"I'll try," she said.

"Good. Stay open," Sarah said. "So, the three of us sat down at a spot that seemed appropriate, in an energy field. I began channeling, opening myself to the universe. I don't know how long we were there before the spirit manifested itself, initially to Jack and me, and then to Cricket. It came through just like Jack saw the first time. We learned that it was a man, and he asked that I communicate for him because he couldn't speak for himself. He said his soul had recently crossed over, and he felt that he couldn't communicate because they took away his face."

"Oh my God!" Cassie cried out. "Was it Rich?"

Sarah nodded her head and continued. "Yes. Rich said he wanted to communicate with Jack."

" *Who* took away his face?" Cassie asked.

"He didn't know. He said he only saw an intense flash, and then he found himself on the other side, confused."

Cassie put her head in her hands and sobbed, "Oh poor thing . . . the poor, poor thing . . . that beautiful face of his."

Sarah resumed, "Rich is concerned for his father because a person whom he calls 'the evil one' is on the move. Jack thinks the evil one *could* be a man named Horace Groat because this Groat person has very bad feelings for Mr. Pierce. Rich said he wants you and Jack to 'take the place of the void.'

"What does he mean by that?" Cassie asked.

"I assume he means that he wants the two of you to fill the void that has been left and to support and encourage his father to continue and complete his dream on the island."

"Did he really mention me by name?" Cassie asked.

"Well, he said Cassandra," Sarah answered.

"That's my given name," she said softly.

"And he said that you two are to intercede on his behalf because he cannot—that he feels his father's will is waning because of what has transpired. And that was the last message because then the energy started to leave, and it receded back into the other side."

Quiet surrounded Cassie's soft crying. It was as if the air had been sucked out of the room. Everyone was spent. Finally, Sarah broke the vacuum.

"Cassie, there may be something comforting in all this."

"What?" Cassie asked.

Consider this. Rich *is* still here. He remains with you, but in another form—another dimension. And he has asked something of you—and Jack. You now have a quest, a mission. And it came from *him*. He wants you to love and support his father, to take care of him, nurture him and his dream."

"Cassie, I'm supposed to be with you in this, so you're not going through this alone," Jack said.

"Thank you, Jack, but you don't know Mr. Pierce. He's a good man. A kind man. But he still has some of that businessman mind in him, and he can be hardheaded. When he gets his head around something, it takes a lot to make him change his mind. The burning of his bridge and now this. Rich was right. His spirit has been damaged. He's hurt and wounded right now. I don't blame him. I'm devastated too, but I'm not sure if he'll ever come out of it," Cassie said.

"I understand what you are saying. But still, we have to try. Just know I'm in it with you, and I'll follow your lead," Jack said.

"I have no idea how to broach this with him. Should we tell him about Rich coming to you with a message for both of us?" Cassie asked.

"You know him better than I do. What do *you* think? Would he be receptive to this—the idea that Rich came to us in spirit form? Gonna sound kinda crazy. It does to me, if I was on the listening end," Jack said.

"I don't know. Do we leave that part out and just try and support and coax him?" Cassie asked.

Jack thought for a moment and then said, "How bout this? Let's first do what you just said. We'll talk to him and encourage him to continue. Then, if he balks or doesn't go along . . ."

"That sounds reasonable, but if Mr. Pierce comes off negative, then *you* be the one to tell him how Rich's spirit came to you. Maybe we should have Cricket there to back your story up if he's skeptical," Cassie said. Cassie turned to Cricket and asked, "Would you come?"

"I guess so. If you really think it would be a good idea and you need me to," Cricket said.

"Okay. Let's approach him tomorrow. You tell him we're coming by to talk with him about something. Don't tell him what. Cricket and I will come to the guest house at about eleven in the morning. You start the conversation by telling him we think he should pursue the house and his plans. If we meet or detect resistance, then I'll step in and tell him that we're going to level with him, as ludicrous as it sounds, and I'll tell him the whole story and just hope he doesn't run me and Cricket off."

"Sounds good," Cassie said. "But I have a thought."

"What?" Jack asked.

"You said that Rich didn't know what happened to him, but if he doesn't have a face, then somebody did this to him intentionally, right?"

Jack ran his hands through his hair. "I don't know. I mean, yeah. That's what I'd assume."

"So, if Rich is talking about 'the evil one,' does that mean that this person is the one who killed him?"

Jack thought about Groat, and once again, he wondered if he was capable of something so horrific. "I don't know, Cassie. I really don't. I just know that Rich seemed to be more focused on his daddy and the house than anything."

"You're right. That's Rich's wishes, so we gotta do this for him," Cassie said.

CHAPTER 35

"MR. PIERCE, JACK TAGGER AND A FRIEND of his are coming over to talk with you this morning," Cassie said removing the breakfast dishes from the table and putting them in the sink.

"What do they need to talk with me about?" Richardson Pierce asked.

"I'm really not sure," she said. "Jack asked if you were going to be here this morning. I told him I thought you would. He said he'd be by around eleven," she said, her back turned to him on purpose as she fidgeted over the sink.

"Well, I can't imagine what he wants to talk to me about," Pierce said with a worried tone in his voice. "Lieutenant Berger may have caused Jack some concern, but I told him that I didn't feel like he was or is culpable in any way in this."

At that moment two figures appeared at the front screen door and knocked.

"Mr. Pierce?" Jack asked peering through the front door with the flat of his hand, shielding his eyes from the brightness outside.

Pierce walked to the door and opened it. "Yes, Jack. Come in."

"Oh, sorry," Jack said as he backed away from the opening door. "I didn't mean to be peering into your living room. The door was open, and I couldn't see in because of the brightness out here," Jack said.

"No need to apologize. Come in."

Jack and Cricket entered the living room.

"Have a seat," he said, ushering them towards the couch. "Can I get you something? Coffee? I just made some sweet tea," Pierce said.

"I think I'll have some tea, if it's not a problem," Jack said.

"How bout you, miss?" Pierce asked, looking at Cricket.

"Oh, I'm sorry. This is my friend, Cricket Williams. Her folks have a place down at Ocean Isle."

"Any relation to Orthel Williams?" Pierce asked.

"He's my grandfather."

"Well then I guess you *do* have a place at Ocean Isle," Pierce said, smiling.

Jack looked at Pierce, then Cricket, a confused look on his face.

Pierce picked up on Jack's look and explained, "Orthel Williams owns . . . or at one time, *owned* pretty much all of Ocean Isle Beach. Williams was or is the equivalent of what the Groats were to Sunset. Only much more principled," Pierce said.

"Yeah, my granddaddy isn't anything like Groat. And he and Groat don't get along. As he described it, Groat is oil, and granddaddy is water. And thank you, but I'm fine on the coffee and tea," she said.

"I've known your grandfather for a long time. And no, he's nothing like Horace Groat."

Jack looked at Cricket with a surprised look and mouthed, *I didn't know that.*

"Now what is it you wanted to talk to me about, Jack?" he said setting the iced tea on the coffee table. Cassie came over from doing the dishes in the kitchen and joined them on the couch.

Jack looked at Cassie and gestured with a nod of his head toward Mr. Pierce.

"Mr. Pierce. I wasn't being completely honest with you a few minutes ago. We . . . Jack and I . . . we're here to . . . we want to talk to you . . . ah . . . we want to encourage you to continue with your plans . . . your dream over on Bird Island. I know that's what Rich would have wanted for you . . . to go on with it," Cassie said.

Pierce sighed, then said, "That's very thoughtful of you *and* Jack. But Rich was such a big part of this dream of mine—of *ours*. With him gone, it's lost its luster for me."

"We understand, Mr. Pierce. But think of Rich. This was his dream as well. I didn't know him, but from what I've heard and gathered from Cassie, Roy, and you, he was a special guy."

"He really *was*, Mr. Pierce. Maybe think of finishing it in his honor," Cassie said.

Pierce gave both Jack and Cassie a kind smile. "One thing I don't think you two are thinking of or envisioning, and being the young people that you are, I wouldn't expect you to, but once the house is finished, I'm in there alone. And when the quiet afternoons settle in and the late day sun comes creeping its way through the windows, well that's a depressing time of day for me—always has been.

"But this scenario makes me all the more depressed. I've been lonely for some time now, but when Rich was around, it wasn't as lonely and dark. But with him gone and me sitting in that house that time of day by myself . . . I don't want to go through *that* type of loneliness. I just can't face that. I'm afraid my mind's made up."

"Maybe you *won't* be in that house all alone," Jack said.

"I beg your pardon?" Pierce responded, unamused.

Jack took a good-size gulp of sweet tea and then set it back on the table. "Well, this is gonna be hard, but please bear with me Mr. Pierce."

"I'm sure it can't be anything harder to hear than the news I've received here recently," he said.

"Well, it's closely related," Jack said.

Pierce looked at Jack with a look of concern. Jack began by telling him about his initial spirit encounter that night at Bonaparte's Landing.

Richardson Pierce remained quiet sitting on the couch, his hands in his lap, a blank expression on his face.

"After that experience, Cricket told me about a friend of hers who is a shaman and could contact the other side."

Cricket nodded her head in agreement.

Pierce then interjected. "Okay, Jack. I see where you're going here, and I don't think I appreciate . . ."

"Mr. Pierce. Please! I know it's far-fetched, but I *have* to do this. I'm obligated to tell you about what happened."

"Obligated? To who?" Pierce responded curtly.

"To Rich."

"Okay, that's it, Mr. Tagger! I've heard just about all I care to hear."

"Please!" Cassie blurted out. "Let him say what he has to say. Then, if you don't believe him, you can tell him to leave and then walk away from that dream of yours over on the island. This is why he and Cricket came—to try and persuade you to continue your work, at Rich's request. *And* to tell you about what they experienced at Bonaparte's Landing. Cricket was there and experienced the same thing Jack and the shaman saw."

Pierce's attention left Jack and moved to Cassie and Cricket. "Have you already heard this, Cassie?"

"Yes, I have," she said.

"And you believe this?"

"*I do.* It's hard to believe, but my gut—my instincts tell me they are honest in what they experienced," Cassie said.

"I trust your instincts," Pierce said. He turned his face away from her and addressed Jack. "Okay. Go ahead, Jack."

"Before this happened, I was like you. I didn't really believe in that world. But I had heard about shamans and soothsayers, and so the more I listened to Cricket, the more I relaxed, so I heard her out. I *knew* I'd seen an apparition, something I'd never experienced before. But the spirit that came through was one that I recognized from a previous experience."

"And that experience was . . . ."

"Out on Highway 904. Near Fair Bluff," Jack said.

He paused a few seconds, and then Richardson Pierce asked, "You're saying that you . . . that it was . . ." His voice quivering, Pierce implored Jack with his eyes.

Jack cleared his throat again before saying, "I saw the person I had seen in the blue Continental. It was *Rich*."

Richardson Pierce took a deep breath that sounded like something between an inhale and a sob. Jack wasn't sure.

"It . . . ah . . . *Rich*, couldn't speak to us because of damage to its . . . to his face. He had to come through Sarah," Jack said.

"What did my son say?" Pierce asked.

"Well, this is where it comes back around to what Cassie and I were talking to you about a few minutes ago. He said, again through Sarah, that he's worried about you—that you're losing the interest—that your spirit is waning, I believe, is how he said it. But then he said that it must not wane—that he really wants you to pursue your dream—to continue," Jack said.

"You stand by this, young lady? Did you experience what Jack just said?" Pierce asked Cricket.

"I do, Mr. Pierce," Cricket said. "I believe this has changed *my* life, in some way. It was an experience, to say the least. I know now that there *is* another side."

Pierce looked defeated. Like the fight and his denial had hit a wall.

"He also said for you to be wary of *the evil one*," Jack added. "He said that the evil one is on the move and is moving towards you, but that your head is turned. He didn't know the name of the evil one, but he knows that the evil one *does* want to destroy you and take from you what is yours."

"Groat," Pierce said quietly to himself.

"That's what I was thinking too," Jack said.

"What do you know about Groat?" he asked.

Jack wanted to come clean with him about being Groat's plant, but now was not the time to do it.

He added, "I've just heard from some of the men talking about him—that he's a scoundrel and can't be trusted." Then he quickly added, "And I've heard he doesn't want you to build your house because he thinks you're gonna develop the island. Plus, he wants to expand the beachfront that he owns towards Bird Island but that the state won't let him fill in the back side of the beach. And he blames you for that."

"I didn't know the entire crew was privy to all that information about Groat and me."

"*I* knew that," Cassie said. "Rich told me all about Groat. He hated him! And he worried for you. That's why he came to us, I guess. He doesn't want Groat to win out. And if you give up, he wins. Mr. Pierce, will you at least keep the door open? Don't give up yet. Continue with the construction and see if it eventually feels right again. With what we've told you today, consider Rich's desire."

The room was silent.

Finally, Pierce said, "I don't know what to say, at this point. I'm numb."

Cassie put her arms around Pierce's shoulder. He responded by wrapping his arm around her waist. "This is all so hard," she said putting her head on his shoulder. "I wish . . . I wish . . . I don't know what I wish. I guess I wish this was all a bad dream—that all this never happened—that Rich really isn't on the other side, alone."

Her voice broke, and both she and Pierce let go of a sob that filled the room. They reached out for each other, attempting to console the other.

CHAPTER 36

A WEEK AFTER THE MEETING, ROY JAMES received word from Pierce that he wanted the crew to go back to work out on the house. The charred remains of the bridge would have to be torn down and removed, but Pierce would hire another, less experienced group of laborers for that chore. Everyone had been in limbo waiting to find out if they had a job or not. The news they received from James was like a collective exhale.

As instructed, the crew gathered Monday morning at the dock below the guest house. Roy waited until all had gathered on the deck of the dock before he came down.

"Fellows, Mr. Pierce, *and I* appreciate your concern and devotion. This has been, to say the least, a shock and a very trying time. Mrs. Pierce is back from Greece, and Mr. Pierce is with her in Greensboro, working out the funeral arrangements. With that, we can assume his stress is not leveling off. So, what I would like for each of you to do, if it's in you, is to give him something personal . . . give him something of yourself. And that is, to start today anew in our efforts. I don't want this to sound corny, but I, for one, am going to rededicate myself to this project and work as good, as hard, and fast as I can, but still retain the quality of work Mr. Pierce expects. I want to give him that. And I hope you guys have that in you as well."

They all responded with nods of their heads. Some responded with balled fists held high, interspersed with shouts of "Hell yeah" and "Damned right" and "Right on!"

Other than nodding his head in the affirmative, Jack said nothing. He was in thought as to what he was doing by aiding and abetting Horace Groat. He felt like a traitor. Hell, he *had* been a traitor. But the situation that had presented itself early on when Groat approached him was . . . well different then. But Jack was a different guy now. And that guy needed to tell Groat of his intention to leave his employ.

———•———

JACK PULLED UP TO THE VISTA PIER for a beer and to check the surf. It had been a long, hot day. All the guys, Jack included, had taken what Roy had said to heart and busted ass.

He stopped the Willys, put the gear in neutral, and then pulled up on the brake. Big Tom and Little Tom sat on the front steps of the pier. Though it was good to see them because Jack liked them, he also felt a twinge of anxiety. After all, they *were* Groat's men. They were staring into their BPR cans and had not seen him yet. He reached for the key still in the ignition and thought about leaving before they saw him, but it was too late. Big Tom looked up from the top of his beer can, spotted Jack, and responded with a big friendly smile and a meaty wave of his hand.

"Come on over and let me buy you a beer," Big Tom said. Little Tom was smiling. Jack felt better. He jumped out of the Willys.

"How you guys doin?" Jack asked as he approached the two, his flip-flops popping the heel of his feet as he walked across the hot sand to the steps.

"We've been doing all right, Jack. And you? Haven't seen you in some time. Pierce keeping you busy on that big house, I guess?" Big Tom responded.

"Yeah, I know. It's been a while. Been busy. You guys?" Jack said.

"Same here," Big Tom said. "Groat don't give us no slack."

"You doing okay, Jack?" Little Tom asked in his low, more serious voice.

"I am, I reckon. You boys hear about Mr. Pierce's son, Rich?"

"Hell yeah! Didn't know him, but yeah, we heard about that," Big Tom said.

"What's Groat been up to?" Jack asked.

The two looked at each other but said nothing.

"You guys got salt water in your ears? What's he been up to?"

"You know . . . same ole, same ole. A dollar here, a dollar there," Little Tom said.

Both men looked at each other and became silent.

"What? What's up you guys?" Jack said.

"What'd you do to piss Groat off?" Little Tom asked.

"What do you mean?" Jack asked.

"We're actually not as dumb as we look, Jack. You started off this spring working with us on these cottages. Then you and Groat have that pow-wow in his car, and after that, we don't see you on the job anymore. We know you went to work for Pierce, and that probably wasn't a bad idea, seeing as how we've pretty much caught up on repairing Groat's cottages. What you do is none of our business. And

I don't delve in Groat's business . . . we know better'n that. But yesterday, he asked us both if we'd seen you in a while. When we said we hadn't, he let out a stream of cuss words I've yet and probably won't ever hear again in one sentence."

"What else did he say, besides cuss words?"

"He just said that if we see you, to let him know. So . . . I guess now we gotta let him know we've seen you," Little Tom replied.

Jack looked out at the parking lot, thinking about what he'd say to Groat when suddenly he spotted a red truck. *Oh shit*, he thought. *I've seen that truck. That's the truck that was backed into that drive the day Rich died.*

"Y'all know whose truck that is?" Jack asked.

"Yeah," Big Tom replied. "That's Jimmy's truck. Jimmy Greer. You haven't met him?"

Jack suddenly remembered Groat introducing him to Greer, and he remembered Greer's smile when Jack told Groat about Rich being missing. He gulped.

"Oh yeah. I met him," Jack said.

"Well, it looks like we won't hafta worry about telling Groat that we saw you. He just pulled up," Big Tom said.

The three men turned their heads towards the parking lot in unison. There, peering out the front window of his car, behind aviator glasses, sat Groat.

"Guess you're gonna find out sooner than later why he's pissed at you, Jack," Big Tom said.

"Guess so," Jack said as he turned and walked over to where Groat sat in his car. "Afternoon, Mr. Groat," Jack said standing beside his car. Jack glanced in the back seat and saw Jimmy Greer sitting in the back, silent.

"Get in," Groat said through the open passenger's window.

Jack ratcheted open the door handle and took a seat beside him. The two Toms got up from the steps and walked out onto the pier. Both Jack and Groat sat silently for a moment before Groat spoke.

"Where you been? I ain't heard shit from you. How come?"

"Mr. Groat, I don't have any information for you, and I didn't want to come to you just to say that. I know how mad that made you before," Jack said.

"Hell boy! You ain't *seen* mad, yet!" Groat said.

Jack looked into Groat's face. Flustered, he blurted out, "I don't want to do this anymore."

"You what?" Groat responded.

"I just can't! I can't spy on Pierce anymore. He's not doing anything wrong or anything he doesn't have the right to do! He's . . . he's a good man who has just suffered a terrible loss, and I don't want to do anything that would hurt him even more!"

Groat looked at Jack incredulously and said, "Boy, you don't know it yet, but you just fucked up. I told you early on, don't mess with me. It ain't no game that I play. It's serious. Deadly serious. You hear me?"

"I hear you. But intimidation can only go so far," Jack said.

"You think so? We'll just see how far it can go. I'll bet some government folks'd love to know where you are, right about now. And if they don't get you, I will. You better know I can make people disappear from here. Kinda like Rich Jr. did. Not that I know anything about that . . . but you catch my drift? Now get out of my car, you draft-dodging, long-haired, hippie freak."

As Jack got out, he mumbled under his breath, "Asshole."

Just as he was about to close the door, Groat leaned across the front seat and said, "You better watch your back, Tagger. You've stepped out of the safety of the boat and into dark swamp waters. And it ain't safe in the swamp. You hear me," he said.

Jack ignored him and slammed the door, and Groat sped away leaving a cloud of dust in the parking lot.

Jack saluted Groat's leaving with his middle finger. "Fuck you, Groat! I've had it with you!" Jack said as the dust started to settle.

CHAPTER 37

THE DRIVE OUT TO THE HIGHWAY PATROL DIVISION headquarters in Shallotte took Jack fifteen minutes after work.

Lieutenant Berger had put in a transfer from Sampson County to the Brunswick County Highway Patrol division. Because the Pierce case had focused on Sunset Beach and Berger was having to spend so much time there investigating the case, the transfer was approved.

The dispatcher had told Jack that Lieutenant Berger came on duty at 4:00 and that he felt Jack would have enough time to get there before the Lieutenant checked in, went through roll-call, and hit the highways for his shift.

Jack pulled into the parking lot and walked up to the front screen door and entered an area where a roomful of people were sitting in folding chairs waiting to re-new their driver's license. Jack was told to go to take a seat in another adjoining room. The dispatcher would let him know when the trooper was there.

About ten minutes, later the trooper entered the area where Jack was sitting, looking down, while adjusting his hat, a group of papers under his arm.

"Lieutenant Berger," Jack said standing.

The Lieutenant looked up at Jack and frowned. "Yeah, Tagger. What can I do for you?"

"Well, I wanted to show you . . . ahhh . . . look. I know you told me not to leave the county, but Cassie wanted to see where Rich went off the road and was killed. So, I took her and . . . ."

"You left the county after I told you not to?"

"I did. I'm sorry, Lieutenant, but I didn't know what to do. It was important to her, and I knew we would be back before dark. I wasn't gonna be gone overnight. She had told Mr. Pierce about her desire to go to the accident site, and he told her that under these circumstances and as long as we were back in one day, he didn't suppose there'd be anything wrong with me taking her."

"And why are you telling me this?"

"Because of this," Jack said, pulling the empty shell encased in a clear plastic bag from his jean pocket. He handed the shell and plastic bag to the trooper.

The Lieutenant took the bag and looked at the spent shell. "What is this? I mean, I know what it is, but why are you giving it to me?"

"Because I don't know if this means anything or not, but when Huff and I were coming down to the beach on Highway 904 that day, well, right after Rich's car almost hit us, we stopped. And then, while we were trying to decide what to do, I saw a pickup truck backed up and parked in a driveway that led up into a field there, just off 904. This was just up the road from where this all took place."

"Why didn't you tell me about this before now?"

"I guess I just forgot. I mean, I really didn't remember seeing the truck til me and Cassie went out there."

"Go ahead," Berger said.

"So, anyway, I told Cassie about seeing the truck, and she insisted I drive up the driveway. She said she just felt the need to go up there. Well, when we got up there, there's a little perch—a knoll up there that looked down on 904. And as we were leaving, Cassie saw something shiny on the ground and told me to stop. She got out and went over and picked this empty shell off the ground. She gave it to me, and I put it in the console of my Jeep. When I got home, I put it in this plastic bag. It looks like a fresh-spent shell."

"I see. Are you prepared for this?"

"Prepared for what?" Jack asked.

"Well, let's say the State Bureau of Investigation runs the prints off this shell and finds your prints all over it. Are you prepared for what comes next?" the trooper asked.

"My prints shouldn't be *all over it*. Maybe Cassie's. She dropped it in the palm of my hand, and I picked up a twig and put the opening of the shell on the twig. Based on that, I'd be surprised if my fingerprints were on it at all."

The trooper cut Jack a look just under the bill of his hat and asked, "You say Cassie is the one who found this shell?"

"Yes, sir. My head was turned cause I had just started backing out when she yelled for me to stop cause she saw what turned out to be this shell. She got out and picked it up and handed it to . . .Oh shit!"

"Oh Shit, what?" Berger said.

"She put the shell in the palm of my hand, but then I grabbed it with my thumb and finger before putting it on a twig. Some of my prints might be on that shell," Jack said.

"I thought you just told me your prints wouldn't be . . . ."

"It just dawned on me! I *did* touch it. Oh, Christ! I *did* touch the shell! But not much. Just briefly with my palm, and my thumb and my pointing finger."

"Son, you know which digits are usually used to insert a shotgun shell into a chamber?" Berger said.

"No sir," Jack said.

"The index finger and the thumb," Berger said, looking suspiciously at Jack.

Jack paled. "You think I may have been the one who . . . ? How could I have done that? How could I have fired a gun from the top of the knoll and have been in the car on 904 at the same time? And why would I bring this down here to you if I had anything to do with this?" Jack said.

"At this point, we're not ruling anything out. How do I know you were in that car like you say you were? No witness can put you in the car."

"Yeah, there is. My buddy, Huff."

"Your buddy," the trooper said. "Your buddy who supposedly was drinking and driving? I wouldn't say he's a very reliable witness."

Jack shook his head. "Damn. I was just trying to help, and now . . ."

"Look. I'm gonna send this to the SBI in Raleigh and put a rush on it. In the meantime, don't you leave the county, period. And I mean it this time," the trooper said.

"Yes sir," Jack said.

The trooper turned back to Jack. "Anything else?"

"Yes, sir. The reason I came down here is that I saw that truck again, and I asked around and found out who owns it."

He pulled a notepad out of his shirt pocket. "Alright. What's the name?"

"Greer. Jimmy Greer," Jack said. "He works for Horace Groat."

Trooper Berger wrote the names on his pad. "Alright. I'll look into it. Remember. You are *not* to leave the county. Understood?" Berger said.

"Yeah. I understand. I won't," Jack said.

CHAPTER 38

JACK STEPPED FROM HIS APARTMENT DOOR and into the morning light. After locking the door, he put the key in his jean pocket, turned, and came face to face with trooper Berger.

"Morning, Jack."

"Trooper Berger!"

The site of the trooper gave him heart palpitations.

"I have some information back regarding that empty shell Cassie found when you two took your *unauthorized* trip out of the county," Berger said.

Jack's mouth went dry. "Yes sir?"

"I don't have the print results back yet, but what I *do* have is somewhat interesting, and I thought I'd drop by and tell you."

Jack waited, saying nothing.

"It turns out the shell she found contained a slug. You ever been a hunter? You know what that means . . . a slug?"

"I think I know . . . I'm not sure."

"Well, let me explain. Normal shotgun shell packings are usually arranged by shot size and the amount of packing, that being gunpowder. The majority of shells are bird, duck, or rabbit shot. Those being like four, six, and eight-shot. Shot sizes are packed with bb-size pellets. Relatively small shot. But the most damaging shotgun shell is a *slug*. A slug is *one* steel pellet, and it's very destructive. It is used to kill larger animals like deer or bears. Perhaps, in this case, it could have been used to kill a human being."

"You mean . . . are you saying the shell she found is . . ."

"Now, I'm not saying *anything* at this point, but here's what we have. We have a dead man who was driving his vehicle that suddenly crossed the road and came at the car you were a passenger in, so you say. And the driver, as *you* say, had no face. That is, it was a pulpy mess. *And,* you supposedly saw a hole in his windshield the size of a basketball. And this was *before* he crashed and burned in the field. And, as you and your buddy were leaving, you saw a pickup truck backed up into a driveway that led up into the field where you and your friend later found a spent shotgun shell, which, according to the remaining gunpowder residue, contained a slug and not normal bird shot. That's where we are, Mr. Tagger, and that's all that I'm saying at *this* point."

"Jesus! Do you think I may have seen a possible shooter in that pickup truck?"

"Again, I'm not saying. But by the way, you told me who you thought owned the pickup, but do you know the make or model?"

"No. As I said, I saw it again in town. It's a small, red pickup. But I met Jimmy Greer when I first got here, and I don't think that's who I saw in the driver's seat that day. It looked like a kid behind the wheel, and he was wearing a ball cap."

"I see. Okay. Well, given the particulars that I just mentioned, I find it curious that a spent shell containing a slug was found up on the crest of a hill overlooking Highway 904. *And* the looks of it . . . the relative newness and the shininess gets my attention. I appreciate you bringing it in, so I thought I'd give you an update. We'll know more when the prints come back, though," Berger said as he turned to walk back to his vehicle.

"Lieutenant Berger, will you let me know as soon as they come in? The fingerprints?" Jack asked.

Berger remained, facing him, curious. "Why Jack? Why is it important I let you know as soon as they come in?"

"To be honest, I'm kinda nervous about all this. I'll just feel better when the results are in."

Berger studied Jack for a moment and then said, "Okay. I'll let you know. Actually, you'll probably be the *first* to know."

Berger's answer and inflection of that last sentence did nothing to ease Jack's concern.

CHAPTER 39

THE SEA WAS ANGRY, ROILING UNDER A foreboding gray sky. The wind was on-shore, causing the waves to break as whitecaps farther out at sea. Jack stood on the deck of the Vesta pier looking down into the undulating sea. Earlier, he had thought about going out for a session, but now he was glad he wasn't down in the cold grayness that spread out in front of him.

Groat's last words came to him. '*You've stepped out of the safety of the boat and into dark swamp waters. And it ain't safe in the swamp.*' Looking out at the rolling, gloomy sea and the dark, heavy knotted sky sent a shiver through him. He buttoned up his jean jacket and leaned his forearms against the railing of the pier. The vision of sea and sky mirrored his mood.

How the hell did this happen? he thought. *My world's coming apart. Groat, Berger. Hell, I don't even know where I stand with Pierce. And on top of all that, I've been visited by a ghost! And, I'm in hiding from Uncle Sam! I'm probably a gnat's ass away from spending five years in prison—or the rest of my life in Canada. Groat could see to that, now. You can't make this shit up!*

He shook a cigarette from the pack, cupped both hands to block the wind, and lit-up with his Zippo lighter. He took a drag and looked down into the water below. A dorsal fin broke the surface. In the pier light casting down on the water, he watched a large, gray figure rise to the surface. He could clearly see the striped shape of a big Tiger Shark directly below him. The creature thrashed one massive stroke of his tail fin and rolled over on its side. Then, its cold dark, eyes looked up at him. Jack held the stare. Whitewater from broken waves covered the beast, but once the wave had passed, the shark resurfaced, still on its side looking up at him.

"What are you doing? You trying to tell me something?" he yelled down to the shark. He took another drag off the cigarette and flicked what was left down at the creature in the churning water below. "Fuck you! You don't scare me. I've already got sharks circling around me."

Jack looked over his right shoulder toward the pier house. Bruce Kinnard was walking toward him, his long, white hair and beard blowing back from his face in the on-shore wind, his tan face, a palate on which the whitest of teeth were exposed through a smile.

"What are ya looking at Jack?" Kinnard asked as he took a place beside Jack and looked down into the sea below the pier.

"A shark. Looks like a big ole Tiger," Jack answered.

"You're probably right. There's been a big Tiger lurking around the pier. He's showed up bout every day ever since this weather turned so warm. Too damned hot for this early in May."

"I wonder if it's a sign," Jack said absently.

"Sign for what? You look worried, Jack. Something on your mind?"

Jack blurted out, "What do you know about Horace Groat?"

"Why do you ask?"

"Is he dangerous?"

"I don't know if dangerous is the right word. But I can tell you he ain't someone to be trifled with. I don't fear him. Don't have any reason to. He wants to buy my pier, and I'll probably end up selling it to him in the end. Why? What's up?" Kinnard asked.

"Just wondering," Jack said.

"Naw, son. You're not just wondering. Why'd you want to know if he's dangerous?"

"I don't know . . . I just . . ."

Jack looked into Kinnard's tan face and saw that in his 'Old Man and the Sea-ness,' there was a comforting, wise nature about him. It was as if he saw right through you and knew your inner thoughts and fears.

"You don't have to talk to me about it, Jack, but I can see that you're struggling, son."

Jack looked back at the swirling water, and he knew that Kinnard was right. The churning breakers matched his inner turmoil.

"Well, is it Jack?" Kinnard asked, his voice startling Jack out of his revelry.

"What? Is it what?" Jack asked.

"That shark down there. You wonder if it's a sign. Maybe it *is* a sign meant for you. And he's around *my* pier, so that gives me some authority to ask this question, I would think," Kinnard said, smiling.

"I didn't think you were into that kind of stuff, Mr. Kinnard. Signs and things," Jack said.

"I'm not. I just pay attention." Kinnard smiled.

"That's good to hear." Jack smiled back.

"You know, I remember when you were down here as a kid, with that buddy of yours—when you were young salty dogs, down here surfing. Seems like y'all were down here all the time in the summer."

"Almost," Jack said.

"I used to get a kick outta watching you boys. Both of you getting darker by the days . . . two Little Black Sambos riding the waves for hours."

"You were an enigma to us, Mr. Kinnard."

"An enigma? How's that?"

"You were a puzzle. A mystery. We always called you the old Man of the Sea."

Kinnard chuckled through his Ipana smile, his tan, weathered face framing his twinkling blue, mischievous eyes.

"You had your long, white hair and beard. You were ahead of our generation. You were the wise wizard. Merlin. Still are," Jack said.

"Me thinks you over estimate me. I'm just an old man who's seen too many storms come in over the years. I'm not wise. I'm just an observer that's getting older with the passing of each season."

"You didn't know, did you?"

"Didn't know what?" Kinnard asked.

"That I'm an observer, too. And I've been watching you all these years."

"Naw," Kinnard said, chuckling, pulling down on the front of his beard. "Don't reckon I did. But I'd figure you'd have picked someone or something more interesting to observe."

"You *are* the spirit of Sunset Beach, as far as I'm concerned," Jack said.

Kinnard's eyes moistened. "Well, thanks, Jack. I appreciate those kind words. I really do. This place has always meant a lot to me."

"Yeah. It used to mean a lot to me, too. Now, I just don't know."

"Well, because I'm an observer, I know that Horace Groat is an issue for you right now. And like I said, Groat isn't someone to toy with. Now you wanna tell me what this is all about? You don't wanna proceed in delving too far into something with him all by yourself. You need to be armed, and I don't mean with a gun or knife. You need to be armed with knowledge—and a plan, if necessary."

Jack leaned against the pier railing looking out over the angry sea, covered with froth and waves, concealing what lay beneath. He backed off the railing and turned to face Kinnard. "You got a few minutes?"

"Of course."

Jack confided in Kinnard what he had gotten himself into ever since his arrival at Sunset Beach—how he'd become employed by both Groat and Pierce but had come to like and respect Richardson Pierce. "When I told Groat I was done, well, he was angry, and he told me to watch my back. Then he said I've stepped out of the boat into the dark swamp or something like that," Jack said.

"Well, I *do* believe you've got yourself between a rock and a hard place—between two powerful men, one good, the other not so much. But I *do* think you've come down on the side of a good man in Richardson Pierce. However, you gotta be aware of what Groat said. When he threatened you about stepping out of the boat into the swamp, I think he was referring to things that you don't know about. Kinda like a metaphor. It's hard to see beneath a swamp's dark water," Kinnard said.

"Yeah. I agree. And I'm scared," Jack said.

Kinnard rubbed his hand through his beard again while looking back out at the grayness and turbulent sea. "I think I'd keep a low profile if I was you. For a while, anyway. Maybe this will all blow over. Give him time to settle down and cool off," Kinnard said.

"I will. It's Beach Weekend coming up, and my buddy's coming down from Greensboro, and we're gonna spend the weekend down at Ocean Drive. I won't be around here this weekend."

"Sounds like a good idea, whatever Beach Weekend is," Kinnard said.

"It's a Greensboro thing—a gathering of the tribe, so to speak."

"Well, be careful. I hear those O.D. cops can be pretty tough."

"They *are*. And I *will*. Thank you."

CHAPTER 40

"DAMN HUFF! IT'S BEACH WEEKEND DOWN at Ocean Drive. I told Bruce Kinnard all about Groat's threat, and he said I need to lay low and get out of Sunset for a few days. That's why I was so stoked to get away from here and spend the weekend at O.D. I swear! I came down here to avoid a war, but it seems I've ended up in one, anyway," Jack said into the pay phone at the pier.

Jack listened to the voice at the other end of the line.

"I'm sorry about your mom. I understand, and you need to stay in town to see this through. How long do they say she'll be in the hospital?" Jack asked.

He listened again to Huff's reply.

"Well, tell your mom I'll be thinking about her and that I wish her the best."

After hanging up the phone, he opened the glass doors, eased out of the phone booth, lit up a Winston cigarette, and looked both ways up and down Main Street, hoping not to spot Groat's Cadillac. He left the phone booth and walked across the parking lot to his Jeep.

"Jack! Hey, Jack!"

He instinctively hunched his shoulders forward, ducked his head, and then looked back over his shoulder to see who had called his name. Relief flooded him when he saw Cassie behind the wheel of Pierce's car.

"Cassie! Jesus Christ! You scared the shit outta me," Jack said.

"I'm sorry. Why?" she asked leaning across the seat, opening the passenger door. "Get in!"

Jack slid in all the way across the leather seat, ending up shoulder to shoulder to Cassie.

"Well! I'm glad to see you too, Jack." Cassie laughed.

"Sorry. I'm not used to leather seats. Slippery as owl shit," Jack said as he slid back over to the passenger's seat. "Drive!" he said slumping down in the seat.

"*Okay*! What's wrong with you, Jack?"

"Just drive," he said.

"Where to?" Cassie asked.

"Is Mr. Pierce still in Greensboro?"

"Yeah. He said he still had some things to tie up and would be staying the weekend and come back the first of the week," Cassie said.

"So that's why you're driving his car?"

"Yep. He flew back to Greensboro from the Wilmington airport. I'll have to pick him up there when he decides to come back."

"Then let's go back to the guest house," Jack said.

"I saw you guys working over on the island. I'm so glad he's decided to continue. At least for the time being," Cassie said.

"Time being?" Jack said.

"That's what he said. But I figure when he gets back into the project, it'll consume him. Hopefully, it'll bring him closer to Rich," Cassie said.

Cassie and Jack pulled into the driveway at the guest house and cut the engine.

"Now, tell me what's going on," Cassie said. "Why were you acting so sketchy when you got in the car?" Cassie asked.

"I've got a problem with old man Groat. I just want to avoid him for now," Jack said.

"Why? How are you going to avoid someone like him on this island? It's only so big, you know."

"Yeah, that's the problem. That's why I gotta get away for a few days," Jack said.

"Where're you going?" Cassie asked.

"Down to Ocean Drive. Gonna go for the weekend. It's Beach Weekend."

"Beach Weekend. What's that?" Cassie asked.

"It's a hometown tradition. This coming weekend, every May, people from my old high school, from our cross-town rival, and kids from other North Carolina cities like Salisbury and Charlotte converge on Ocean Drive for a weekend of debauchery. It's like the opening of beach season. Although Easter weekend is a biggie, Beach Weekend is it. A huge beach party weekend," Jack said.

"Sounds cool!" Cassie said.

"Why don't you go with me? It'll do us both some good to get away from here for the weekend," Jack said. Then, he looked over at Cassie, hopefully. But before Cassie could answer, he said, "Oh hell, Cassie. I'm sorry. What am I thinking! You haven't had time to deal with the loss of Rich, yet. What an ass I am! How're you doing?"

"I'm coming along. But no, Jack! You're not an ass! That was sweet.

And it *does* sound like fun! Like you said, it's something we may both need right about now."

"Are you sure? I don't want to force you into something you're not ready for," he said.

Cassie twisted a half-turn towards him and said, "You're not forcing me to do anything I don't want to do. Besides, Rich and I weren't together when he died. That's why I was back up north. We had mutually decided we needed some space. We didn't know if we were going to get back together or not. We were apart, physically, but we'd been apart emotionally for some time before we split. I still loved him, but he had become more like a brother to me."

"I didn't know you guys were apart," Jack said.

"Please don't think I'm mean or cruel. I'm not. I'm just a realist. I'm young and still have my life ahead of me. If I'm lucky, I'll fall in love again. I hope so."

"No, I don't think you're cruel. I like that you're a realist. I could use a little more of that trait myself."

"What do you mean?" she said.

"I don't know. I guess I'm a dreamer. I'm not a linear thinker. I'm too right-brained. There are no road signs out in the distance or in the past for me. It's all spatial. Like a wide-open field. And I'm terrible with dates," he said smiling.

Cassie laughed and said, "That's good . . . so clear! I get it. You ought to be a writer, Jack."

"I put words to paper sometimes! But, that aside, how bout the weekend at O.D.? I think you'd have a good time. You'll meet some of my old high school friends. Good folks. Free spirits. I think you'd like them. And I don't have a problem with separate bedrooms," he said.

"This is 1969, Jack. I can do the same room as long as there's a sofa I can put my sleeping bag on," she said.

"I'll do the couch, but I'll need to use your sleeping bag. I didn't bring mine down here," he said grinning at her.

"Okay. Yay. I'm excited. I definitely could use a little fun to take my mind off everything. Let me run up to the guest house and get some clothes. You wanna come in?"

"No, I'll wait here for you," he said.

"Okay. Be right back. Oh, but Jack. What about your car?"

"I'll leave it at the pier. No, on second thought, I better not. Groat knows my car. Can you drop me off there so I can get it? I'll get my car and follow you back, and you can leave Pierce's car at the house. We'll take my mine. Probably a better idea anyway," he said.

"Sure. Let me go pack a little bag. Be back in a sec," she said.

Jack watched Cassie run up the slope to the house. "Damn! She's cute," he said feeling a bit guilty. Rich Jr. hadn't been gone long, and his spirit, evidently, was still close by. Not to mention that Jack had noticed that his feelings for Cricket may have exceeded surfing pal.

Shit, Jack. You've got enough problems without trying to juggle two girls, he thought to himself.

"Oh shit," Jack said aloud, suddenly realizing that he'd be leaving the county, against Berger's warning.

Hell! I'll be leaving the state. Fuck it. I don't care. I need this—to get away from this crap.

He was still deep in thought when the driver's side door opened. Cassie threw a backpack into the back seat and slid it in the driver's side. "Let's go pick up your car, and I'll follow you back here," Cassie said.

"Let's roll," Jack said.

CHAPTER 41

MAIN STREET OCEAN DRIVE RUNS PERPENDICULAR to the beach, eventually dead-ending at the ocean, beside the O.D. Pavilion on the right and the famous, or infamous, "Spanish Galleon" bar on the left.

The legendary beach dance-bar mecca "The Pad" stood, as it had since the mid-1950s, across the street from the pavilion. The Ocean Drive and Cherry Grove beach lifeguards lived on the second floor. Southern soul and rhythm and blues bands, the likes of the Catalina's, Willie Tee, the Temptations, The Impressions, Little Anthony and the Imperials, and the Drifters supplied southern dance-shagging beach music.

Judy Clay and William Bell's "Private Number" wafted out over the ocean nightly from the juke box on the front side of the Ocean Drive Pavilion, encompassing young couples walking in the moonlight on the edge of the surf.

By the time Jack and Cassie arrived, it was late afternoon, and young people by the hundreds were milling in the streets throwing the peace sign, hand slapping, and high fiving acquaintances, new and old, from all parts of North and South Carolina, as if awakening from winter and coming together for a southern May fest.

"Oh my God, Jack! Look at this! The kids have taken to the streets. It looks like Fat Tuesday in N'awlins," Cassie said.

"In where?" Jack said, smiling.

"I guess you've never been. You know. N'awlins. The Big Easy."

"I was just bullshitting you," Jack said, still smiling. "But yeah. I guess this resembles Mardi Gras. A small one. But from what I hear about the cops down there, they don't have anything on the O.D. cops."

"What do you mean?"

"They're looking for reasons to lock you up down here. Step out of a bar and onto the sidewalk with a beer in your hand down here, and like the song says, 'Step outta line, tha man come and take you away.'"

"Who wrote that? I know that song," Cassie said.

"Sure, you do. Buffalo Springfield—*For What it's Worth.*"

"Oh, yeah. But they didn't write that song about down here, did they?" Cassie asked.

"No," Jack said. "Down here, they just lock you up and spoil your weekend. Make your friends hit the streets, spare changing to bail you out. Nobody ever comes back and stands trial. It's just a money-making thing for the cops. I've heard they split the take after Beach Weekend."

"Well thank God," Cassie said.

"For what?" Jack asked.

"For locking these kids up. At least they don't billy club them and spray them with fire hoses."

"No. But I *have* seen the street in front of the Pad filled with green smoke from smoke grenades fired by the cops when the partying got too wild. Speaking of, let's go check-in and then go get a cold one," Jack said.

"Yeah. I'd love to see the infamous Pad before they turn the air green," she said smiling.

"YOU STAY HERE. PABST BLUE RIBBON okay with you?" Jack asked, looking at Cassie as he wormed his way up to an already crowded bar.

"Well, I'd rather have a Blatz. But that'll do," she said smiling.

"Okay, stay right there. I'll be right back."

"What'll you have, brother?" the bartender asked, wiping his hands with a towel.

"Two PBR's," Jack said. "Make 'em tallboys."

"You got it," he said thrusting his hand back into the ice in the long metal cooler that ran the length of the wall. The beer was ice-cold as advertised on a sign that hung outside over the entrance to The Pad.

"There you go, my man. That'll be seventy cents," he said sliding the two tall boys across the bar to Jack.

Jack pulled out a dollar bill and tossed it in on the bar. "Keep the change, barkeep," Jack said with a smile.

"Thank ya brother! Just remember there's more where that came from."

"Will do," he said as he left the crowded bar.

He found Cassie standing at the edge of the wooden dancefloor, mesmerized, watching couples dancing in tandem, holding hands, and doing dances that mirrored each other's moves.

"Look at them," Cassie said. "What's that dance?"

"That's the Shag," Jack said, as *"Stay,"* by Maurice Williams and the Zodiacs drifted across the dance floor. Most of the couples mouthed the words as they danced.

"Look at them. They glide. *Literally*," Cassie said.

"They really do," Jack said.

"Can you do that?" Cassie asked, looking over her shoulder at Jack.

"I'm not really into dancing," he said. "But I do love to watch people Shagging. And I still love beach music. Always will, I guess. But the music has changed. Time has changed. It's more rock n roll . . . protest . . . folk music nowadays," Jack said.

"Yeah, you're right. But this is still cool," Cassie said.

"Always will be," Jack said.

The song on the jukebox ended, and the couples on the dance floor changed positions, embraced, and slow danced to "*For Your Precious Love*," by Jerry Butler.

"As it should be. You guys grew up on this. It's part of your Southern heritage. Right?" she said, now turned and looking up into Jack's eyes.

"I guess. Yeah! You're right. This stuff is deep in our souls forever."

"You *guess*?" she said softly.

"Forever," he said smiling back into her eyes. Jack moved closer. "I can dance to this. May I?" he asked, extending his arm to her and bowing at the waist.

"You may," she said feigning a Southern curtsey.

Jack took Cassie in his arms for the first time. Her cheek was warm and smelled of Patchouli. The two held each other, neither saying a word. The song built in intensity, and Jack pulled her closer, smelling her tangled hair. He felt her breasts and tucked her tighter to his chest.

The energy between them crescendoed with the music. Cassie lifted her cheek from his and looked up into his brown eyes. She smiled a warm, contented smile. He returned the smile, and they both gently gave their cheeks back to the other.

Jack whispered in her ear. "You wanna get away from here for a while?"

"And go where? You haven't even seen any of your friends yet."

"That can come later," he said. "There's a place up at Myrtle Beach I think you'd like."

"Myrtle Beach? I thought you hated that place!"

"Well, I do. Overall. But there's a section of the beach down there, a residential area called The Dunes Club where there are old, gracious ocean-front homes like you'd see like in California. And right in the middle of it is a grand old hotel called The Ocean Forest. It was built back in the '30s. It has a band shell on the ocean front. Sinatra, Crosby, and big-name bands played there. But it may not be there much longer. There's talk about them demolishing it and building condos in its place. I guess the grand old lady has outlived her use. Just tear her down, and all the moments and memories go with her. That's the way we do things here in the ole US of A. Come on. Let's finish these beers and go and maybe make our own memories," Jack said.

"Sounds nice," Cassie said.

———————●———————

BY THE TIME THEY ARRIVED, it was well past dark. The driveway to the Ocean Forest Hotel left Highway 17 and meandered through a neighborhood of fine, elegant homes tucked in a maritime forest. Spanish moss hung from the trees. Most looked occupied, as this was a year-round neighborhood, not amenable to the seasonal tourist trade. The tacky glitz of Myrtle Beach was south of here.

The lights of the ten-story structure blinked through the forest, the first indication of what was to be revealed.

"Oh my God. Is that it? Are those its lights I'm seeing?" Cassie said.

"That's her. You're gonna love it," he said.

The road emerged from the tunnel of overhanging limbs from the forest and traversed the circular drive-in front. The grand old lady stood before them in whitewashed majesty. With a ten-story center spire and five-story wings on either side, she looked like a white wedding cake glistening in the night.

"Jesus, Jack. It's magnificent! Like something you'd see in an old 1930's movie," she said.

"Come on. Let's go in," Jack said, sliding out of the Jeep.

"Should we? I mean, we aren't staying here," Cassie said.

"Yeah. It doesn't look crowded at all. Like I said, her best days are behind her. People are vacationing at other, more modern places. Like condos and sleek motels in Myrtle Beach proper."

Jack gazed at the top of one of the wings of the motel and then grabbed two beach towels from the Jeep. He took Cassie's hand as they started across the parking lot.

"What? Are we going swimming?" she asked.

"No, but I have an idea," he said, still looking up at the roof of the wing nearest to them.

When they entered the empty lobby, the night clerk glanced up and smiled, uninterested. Jack led Cassie down the hallway that led off to the left. It was empty, also. They stopped at the elevator and Jack pushed the "up" arrow. Inside, he pushed the button for the fifth floor.

"Where are we going? You didn't rent a room, did you?"

"No. We're just gonna go explore this grand old lady. Something I've always thought about doing, but in the past, it was always too busy. There's hardly anybody here now, so this may be the last chance."

The elevator door pinged and opened onto the hallway on the fifth floor. Jack and Cassie leaned out and looked both ways down the hall.

"Empty. Good," Jack said taking her hand. "Follow me."

"Geez! I don't know, Jack. This is kinda freaky! This place is deserted."

"Trust me," he said leading her down the empty hallway. At the end, a large window overlooked the band shell on the grounds below. Jack pulled on the bottom of the window. It was unlatched. He opened it and took her hand.

"Come on," he said stepping through the window onto a fire escape landing.

"Jack! Is this legal? Are we going to get in trouble for this?"

"You see anybody around that might care? I think we're okay," he said.

They stepped through the window onto the landing. Metal steps led up to the roof.

Jack stepped on the first rung and said, "Follow me."

"We're going up there?" she asked.

Jack smiled and continued up the ladder. At the top rung, he stepped out onto the roof and then turned to assist her. She joined him there on the flat rooftop. Then, they walked over closer to the edge and stopped. A full moon sat low over the ocean, spreading a path of light across the surface toward shore. The white froth of the breaking waves below created a surreal view.

"Oh, Jack! This is beautiful!"

"Yeah! More than I imagined," he said.

"You've never done this before?"

"No. I've come over and walked around, but I've always wanted to do this—to climb up here and take in the view."

"I *do* love this. It's breathtaking," she said.

Jack withdrew a bottle of red wine from the beach towels. "Voila," he said as he presented her with the bottle and two wine glasses.

"Oh, Jack! You're so chivalrous," she said smiling.

Jack handed her the bottle, spread the two beach towels, and asked, "Madam. Would this do? A beach towel for two?"

"Oh, yes. I should think so. And the view is quite lovely," she returned.

Jack spread the towels, and they both sat. After he poured the wine, he inhaled, held his breath, and then exhaled the night's salty air. "Ahh. This is nice," he said.

"It *is*," she said. "Thank you, Jack. I needed to get away. This is like a balm on a wound."

"I had a feeling you needed a break. You've been through a lot, here recently. The ocean can do wonders for a soul. Like a balm in Gilead," he said.

"A what? Where?"

"It's an old song. It's a spiritual we used to sing in church, back in my childhood. During Easter, I believe. 'There is a balm in Gilead that makes the wounded whole.'"

"That's nice. What does it mean?"

"Believe it or not, I remember this from Sunday School. It refers to spiritual 'medicine' that's able to heal the broken hearted."

"Wow," she said. "I didn't take you as the religious type."

He chuckled. "I'm more spiritual than religious."

"You keep surprising me, Jack."

Jack took Cassie's chin in his hand and looked into her face.

Cassie looked deeply into Jack's eyes, put both arms around his neck, and kissed his lips. She whispered in his ear, "Tell me about *you*, Jack. Cricket said you have some stuff going on, as well—that you're recently out of a serious relationship and that you came down here to heal yourself."

"Yeah. That was one of the reasons I came down here to get away. *She* went one way, and I went the other. No, actually, I didn't. I kept *my* course. I didn't, or couldn't, change."

"And what about Groat? You mentioned a problem you have with him."

"Oh yeah. That's a current issue," he said.

Jack explained to her the problem with his dual working relationship with Groat and Pierce.

"I've severed my relationship with Groat, but it was a ragged cut. He's out for me, now. From what I've heard, you don't betray Horace Groat. But I *had* to do it. I've come to really like Mr. Pierce. He's a good man. I know that now. And I can't hurt him anymore," he said.

"Jack, I'm not gonna sugar coat it. That was a serious fuck-up. But

I can understand the predicament you were in. Why don't you level with him? Tell him, like you just told me, the situation you were in and what you did to remedy it. I don't know how he'll take it, but you clearing the air will hopefully give you some peace," she said.

"I've thought about that," Jack said.

Jack laid back on the towel, both arms under his head. He purposely didn't tell her about the draft issue and Groat's veiled threat. Cassie remained sitting on the towel.

"Jack. You're a special guy. Thank you so much for tonight." Then she leaned over and kissed him again.

Chapter 42

"JACK LOOK. THE SUN'S JUST COMING UP on the horizon. It's beautiful," Cassie said.

He wiped the sleep from his eyes and pushed himself up onto his elbows. "God! That *is* beautiful," he said.

They watched the deep purple sky lighten as the sun rose and crested the ocean's surface. "Jack, this truly has been a balm for me. Thank you so much!

Jack smiled at her.

"So, what should we do now? I don't know if I'm in the mood for the Pad or the Spanish Galleon or learning to shag." She smiled. "Wanna head back to Sunset? And take this a little slower? We don't need to rush things."

"You read my mind," he said. "You hungry? I know this little place on the waterfront at Little River. We'll grab some breakfast there on our way back," he said.

"I'm famished," she said.

———————◆———————

JACK AND CASSIE PULLED into the guest house driveway.

"Doesn't look like he's back yet. I guess I'm still on call to pick him up in Wilmington when he returns," Cassie said as she retrieved her bag from the back seat.

"Want me to come up with you?" Jack asked.

"No, I don't think so. Actually, I need to go back to the place I was before this weekend. I just need to be with *him* and his memory right now," she said.

"I understand."

"Jack, please don't be hurt. I had a wonderful weekend, and the full moon and sunrise from the roof of the Ocean Forest Hotel—it was what I needed. But now we're back to the real world, and his passing is still so close. I need time with it," she said. "And you're fresh out of your relationship, too. Like we said, let's take it slow and see where it goes, okay?"

"Yeah. You're right. We both need some time and space, I guess. But don't be a stranger, okay?" he said as he reached across her lap and opened the passenger door.

"I won't." Cassie leaned across and gave him a peck on the cheek. "You're sweet, Jack. And I really had a blast this weekend. It was really a trip! Thank you. Please don't think I'm not interested. I *am*. I just want to take it slow because I don't want to ruin what we just experienced," she said.

"Same here. Last night was really special to me too," he said as she exited his car.

She started to walk up the drive, but she paused and turned around. "Oh, and Jack!"

"Yeah," Jack said leaning out the Jeep's side door.

"Stay safe!" she said.

Jack looked confused.

"Groat," she said.

"Oh yeah. I will," he said.

At the end of the driveway, he stopped before entering 40th Street. *Yeah, she's right. We're back in the real world now. And Groat lives in that real world too. I probably shouldn't have told her about my situation with him. She might go to Pierce about it, and I'm not ready for him to know what I've done. But what am I gonna do now? I'm in some deep shit."*

Canada was looking like a real possibility. He could leave Horace Groat to his greedy world. *Let him develop the western end of Sunset Beach all the way to Madd Inlet. Let him ruin this part of heaven. If and when I leave, I won't be coming back.*

CHAPTER 43

WHEN CASSIE PULLED UP AT THE Wilmington Airport, Richardson Pierce was waiting on the sidewalk, his bag at his feet, already retrieved from baggage claim.

"I'm so sorry I'm late, Mr. Pierce. There was a wreck on Highway 17 just this side of Winnabow, and traffic was blocked until they cleared it and could open one northbound lane," Cassie said.

"Yeah, they told us before we de-planed and advised us there may be some traffic delay due to the accident. Sounded pretty bad. I have a meeting with Roy James as soon as I get back, but I called him from the pay phones in the terminal. He's waiting for me at the house. So don't worry. You couldn't help being late. It's all going to work out."

Cassie looked straight ahead out the windshield and asked, "Is it?"

Pierce looked back at her with a sad smile and replied, "I think so."

"I hope so," she said.

"One way or another. It all works out. Eventually," he said.

——————•——————

"HAVE A SEAT, ROY. Just let me put my bag in the bedroom, and I'll be right back out," Richardson Pierce said to his foreman.

"Take your time."

Moments later, Pierce entered the living room, wiping his hands with a handkerchief. "You need anything to drink, Roy? Some tea? Water? A beer? With what we're going to talk about, perhaps a beer might be the ticket," Pierce said.

"I don't know if I like the sound of that," Roy James said.

Pierce didn't reply as he went to the refrigerator and extracted two Heinekens. He popped the tops with an opener and handed one to Roy as he took a seat on the couch beside him. "Roy, I'm gonna get right to it. This weekend, I thought a lot about this project, and I'm thinking it's time to pull out."

"But this is your dream."

"Roy, it *was* my dream—mine and Rich's. But now Rich is gone. And so is the bridge. The bridge is destroyed, and Rich can't come back. My heart's just not in it anymore. My ex-wife and my family have expressed the folly of going forward with this, and with what's transpired, I think they may be right."

Roy James rubbed his palms on both his thighs and said nothing. Finally, he said, "I'm gonna speak frankly with you, if I may. Cause there's a part of my heart out there as well," he said motioning out toward Bird Island.

"I know that, Roy. And yes, get it off your chest, and speak your mind."

"Mr. Pierce, I've thought about this, should this day come," Roy James said as he stood and walked over to the screen door. The sky was approaching that evening-time light. "Look out there," he said, again motioning out over the marsh, Madd Inlet and Bird Island. "That's Rich. I know what I'm about to say breaks with my fine, Southern-

Baptist upbringing. But I have a feeling about our souls. I don't think they leave and go to some place called heaven in the sky. I believe some souls remain and are close by us. Same with Rich. I don't think Rich's spirit will ever leave this place. He's out there."

"Roy, I appreciate your . . ."

"And one more thing. There's a lot of sweat, hard work, and attachment out there over the marsh and on the island. A man—Lucky—died out there. And Rich Junior had his heart in it all. This was his dream as much as it was yours. So how can you do this? How can you shut the door on all this? That berm out there—we dredged and built it just to get the bridge out over the marsh. And the bridge and the telephone poles that will carry power, light, and connection out to the island . . . well, if you stop now, what will remain of a dream, or *parts* of it, will be out there as a quiet reminder. A reminder that very few people will remember, or even know about. It's hurting me, as I speak. It hurts me to look out there and see it now. Even burnt, that bridge is still a work of pride. It's not ever gonna glow golden in the sun again, but there is memory and prideful work in those charred timbers. And if you stop, what are you going to do with the island?"

"I've already been in touch with the state. I'm looking into the possibility of donating it to them for preservation. Or I may just sell it all. I really don't know where I'm going with it. It's not what I wanted. It's what has presented itself. That burnt, charred bridge out there is representative of what the dream has become. But I guess, in the meantime, until I decide what exactly I'm going to do, I'll put the crew back to work. That'll give them some income until I reach a final conclusion."

Cassie, in the back bedroom, overheard the conversation and called Jack.

"Jack! I'm so glad I caught you in. I just overheard Roy James and Mr. Pierce talking out in the living room., and from the sound of it, Mr. Pierce thinks he's going to give it all up. Roy put up a great argument against it, but we need to try to persuade him like Rich asked us to do. Can you come down here?"

"I'm on my way."

"Thank you, Jack! Hurry."

———•———

"WE'VE ALREADY BEEN THROUGH THIS. I've come to a decision, and I'm afraid there's nothing . . ."

"Mr. Pierce," Cassie inserted. "Jack and I have to do this—to persuade you to continue—to not give up," Cassie said.

"Cassie, I . . ."

"I know. This all sounds so crazy, Mr. Pierce, and to a sophisticated, educated man like you to consider what we are saying, that your son is contacting us from the spirit world, must be very much beneath your way of understanding things. I get that. But all we're asking at this point is for you to meet with Sarah," Jack said.

"Who's Sarah?"

"Sarah, the medium we told you about. She's a shaman—one who connects with the other side. She's Lumbee Indian, and they've done this for generations. This is nothing new to the Native Americans," Jack said.

Pierce mulled the thought over and then turned to Cassie. "Have you met this person? This shaman?" Pierce asked.

"Yes. I have."

"And she's credible? You believe what she has to say?"

"I do. And you might too, once you meet and talk with her. Please do this for us. For *you*. For *Rich*!" Cassie said.

Pierce thought it over for a moment. "All right then. I'll go that far, at least. Set it up for this week, if possible. I need to move on one way or another," he said with a sad smile.

———•———

THE SUN HAD SET BELOW the tree line back over the mainland. Pierce mixed himself a gin and tonic and stepped through the screen door that opened to the deck. He walked to the edge and leaned against the railing, looking out over the marsh, inlet, and island. He took a deep breath and then let it out slowly.

"It can all look so different at various times of the day. It changes with its mood, I guess," he said to himself.

The fact that he'd agreed to meet Sarah bothered him. Was he losing his mind? This was not like him—pragmatic, cautious, sensible. But then again, he knew his was not the hard-driving mind of a businessman. He was just not cut from the same cloth, they had said. And in his being, he knew this. His thoughts and direction were too esoteric for the business world—and thus, his family.

He ventured off the main highway and took side roads in his approach to life. He opposed the war in Vietnam. Sending boys who were still boys to fight old men's wars was reprehensible. War, in itself, was reprehensible. He believed mankind and the Earth should be cared for and nurtured. Another point of contention and thus an embarrassment for the family.

Another sip from his gin and tonic loosened the screws, a bit. His mind started to relax. He felt himself let go and meld into the moment.

"Rich is out there," he said, quoting Roy James, as he turned his head and viewed the expanse, the breeze blowing back his hair. He felt his defense dissolve.

"Okay. If you're out there, Rich, don't go away," he said into the breeze.

SARAH SAT CROSS-LEGGED AT the spool table in Jack's house. Cricket sat next to her, and Jack was on the other side of her when Cassie and Richardson Pierce arrived. Pierce was obviously nervous.

Cassie preceded him in and gestured toward the three sitting around the table. "Mr. Pierce, I believe you know Cricket," she said moving her arm across the room. And Jack. This is Sarah," she said gesturing.

Sarah looked up at Pierce and held out her hand. Pierce's met hers, and both politely shook.

"I'm sorry about your son and what you've been through, Mr. Pierce. But if you come away with anything tonight, I hope that it's an opening or a realization of the possibility that life continues on the other side. In different forms, granted, but consciousness and awareness go on," she said.

"Well, you used a word that I used with myself in consideration of my coming here. That is, to be *open* to the possibilities of what you have to say about all this. I'm an open person and I'm here. I'm listening. So, proceed."

"Okay. I'll start by telling you something about what I do and how it comes to me. I am a shaman. There are various types of shamans. My shamanism is what's known as a shamanic medium. That is, I can connect and talk with people who have passed on. It *is* important though, before opening to a spirit, that I ascertain whether the spirit has passed on—whether they have evolved and gone on to the light and have reconnected with their higher knowing. If not, their advice can be suspect," Sarah said.

"I thought shamans were medicine men. People who dealt with animal spirits . . . totems . . ." Pierce began.

"Some are. But shamanism covers a wider range than that."

"The spirit that Jack said presented itself to you, my son. Had he gone to the light? Was his advice suspect, as you say?" Pierce asked.

"No, it was not suspect. And yes, he had gone to the light. But he was confused. He would cross over and then come back to this side. But his intentions were good. Therefore, I spoke for him. But we'll get to more into that later."

"How does all this come to you? How do you communicate or connect with the spirit world?" Pierce asked.

"It's all about energy. Our souls or spirits live on in another form. Energy. We are energy when we're alive, but once we pass, that energy is heightened, and we become total energy. Now, back to your son. He has not been on the other side long enough to totally connect with the light. He's still searching, and he's not really certain that he has passed on. But he had a desire to connect with this side."

"Okay, and I mean no offense, young lady, but Jack and Cassie have pretty much already told me all this," Pierce said.

"Well, Mr. Pierce, like I said before, I think Rich was dead by the time I saw him in the wreck," Jack said. "But after that, the first day I got here, my buddy and I went out surfing. At the end of the day, we were walking up from the surf, and when we were on the beach, we noticed a guy walking towards us. When he got to us, my friend said he was looking at *me*. But this guy's face was distorted. I thought he was a casualty from the war—that Napalm had melted his face. And that wasn't the only time. I have encountered this person several more times since then. Once again after surfing and another time over at the house on the island. And I just had a gut feeling that he had something to tell me—that he was trying to communicate with me," Jack said.

"So, you're saying that you saw my son before your séance, or whatever it was?" Pierce asked.

"Yes, sir, and as I told you before, he wanted me to tell you to beware of Groat and his intentions—and for you not to give up on your dream out there," Jack said pointing out towards Bird Island. For you to complete it because he knew how much that meant to you."

Richardson Pierce sat motionlessly. "Again, Jack, you've already told me all this, and it sounded crazy the first time I heard it. I didn't really believe it then, and I'm not sure I believe it now."

"I know this all sounds pretty preposterous, but this was real for me," Jack said.

"Anything else?" Pierce asked.

"What do you mean?" Jack said.

"Did he tell you anything else? Did he tell you what our verbal connecting message was?"

"What's that?"

"Well, we devised a code, a message for each other, if something happened to one of us. We came up with it because of my wealth so that if one of us were to ever get kidnapped or ransomed, it would let the other one know that we're okay or still alive. If you knew that, then I might believe all this nonsense."

Jack looked questioningly at Cricket and then at Sarah.

"Ahh . . . no. I don't think . . ." Jack began.

"Well, again, I mean no offense about what you think you experienced, but that's a very important matter for me. If you had been in Rich's presence, that is *one* thing he would have clearly asked you to tell me."

"Well, didn't you just say it would be used to indicate that the other one is okay? That he's alright? I mean, technically, he's not okay," Jack said.

At Jack's response, Sarah rolled her eyes at him and said, "But Jack. They *are* alright over there. It's as perfectly normal for them to be there as it is for us to be here on this side. As with Rich, the crossing can be confusing, but once the soul accepts and understands its new dimension, it understands it's the continuation into the next realm."

Pierce stood up. "I don't think this is helpful."

Sarah looked at Pierce and said, "I'm sorry, Mr. Pierce. Jack is new at this. But if I may say, this is not my first experience in summoning dear ones from the other side. This was, in fact, a very strong manifestation. And it was your son, Rich. I never knew him, but I felt his essence very strongly. His message was fervent."

Pierce said, "Thank you for your time and your interest. I mean that. I feel your sincerity. I really do. But this is all too much for me right now. And the absence of the message . . . I just can't. I'm sorry. Cassie? Are you coming, or do you want to stay for a while? I'll understand if you stay. I really will."

"I think I'll stay a talk a little while longer. I just don't think I could go to sleep right now. Don't stay up for me, though," Cassie said.

"I won't. I'll leave the hall light on for you, okay?"

"Okay. Thank you."

Jack walked over to the kitchen and brought out a bottle of Lake Country Red. He pulled the cork, took a swig, crossed his legs, and lowered himself into a sitting position at the cable spool table. He took another swig and then passed it to Cricket who did the same before passing the bottle around the table to the others. All four sat in silence for a moment before Cricket asked, "So what do we do now?"

"I don't know if there's anything more we can do, at this point," Cassie said. "Once Mr. Pierce's mind is made up, he stays with it. He usually doesn't *unmake* it." She laughed a sad, little laugh. "Rich used to say that. His dad wouldn't '*un-make* his mind, once it was set." Then she looked up at the ceiling and said, "Isn't that right, Rich?"

There was silence in the room until Sarah spoke.

"But, wait a minute. Didn't Rich say something else? I was so exhausted at that point, so I don't think I really picked up on it then, but didn't he start to say something there at the end? Just before he faded out?"

Cricket and Jack gave it some thought, and Jack said, "You know, it seems like he did say something, but I couldn't make it out before everything went quiet. Did you hear those last words, Cricket?"

"No. I can't say that I did," Cricket said. "But wait. Didn't he say something about 'tell the father' or 'pass the words'?"

"Well, shit. What do we do now?" Jack asked.

"Why don't we go over to the house right now and tell him that he tried to say something else like 'tell the father' or 'pass the words' before the energy faded out," Cricket said.

"Well, let's not bound over there right now, especially after we've had this session with him. It's been a pretty intense evening for him, I'm sure. Let's give him some time," Cassie said.

CHAPTER 44

THE CREW ARRIVED AT THE DOCK below the guest house. The faint smell of burnt wood and creosote still lingered in the air. Roy James came down to meet the men.

"We still have jobs, Roy?" one asked.

"I can't answer that, at this point. Mr. Pierce is still mulling over what he's going to do. With no bridge now or in the foreseeable future, we'll have to bring in supplies by boat from Little River to the dock on the back side of the island if we continue with this project. We've been doing some of that up til now, but doing it full time will be slow, not to mention expensive. But for now, today, yes, you still have a job. And I would ask you to stay the course with us until we know something definite. If you decide to leave and find work elsewhere, we wouldn't blame or fault you for that. But if you can stay around for a week or so, we should know something by then," Roy said. "Now, if you feel so inclined to hang around, how bout a show of hands. Like I said, if anyone decides to leave, it will be understood."

Hugh Wyrick turned and looked at the men. "How bout it guys?" he said as he raised his hand to stay. One by one, every hand in the group reached skyward.

"Thank you, men. Mr. Pierce will be grateful."

———•———

"WHAT ARE YOU GONNA DO, JACK?" Hugh Wyrick asked as they stepped up onto the guest house dock. "Wanna go grab a cold one somewhere?"

"When were you thinking about going? Jack asked.

"Hell, I was ready when I stepped off the island. Been kinda a shitty day," Hugh said.

"That, it has. But I've been thinking about going surfing ever since lunch. I think I need to clean out my pores with ocean water," Jack said.

"That sounds nice, even if I ain't a surfer. We'll do a raincheck on that beer," he said.

"You got it, Hugh," Jack said.

Jack swung into his jeep and headed up 40th St. to his cottage. He shed his t-shirt and khaki shorts in the hallway as he entered and pulled on his surf trunks. He grabbed two Heinekens, wrapped them in his beach towel, and headed out the door. He drove east on Main Street toward the Vesta pier. Along the way, he made several stops to check out the surf at normally good spots. With nothing really pumping, he headed for the pier.

He pulled into the pier parking lot but not before checking out the vehicles as he usually did nowadays wherever he went on the island. There was no sign of Groat's car. He got out, pulled his *Sunshine* surf board from the rear of the Jeep, and walked around the corner of the pier. At the ocean's edge, he stopped, waxed his board, and then skimmed the board and himself across the top of the water before duck diving beneath the first wave.

Situated out past the breakers and into the lineup, Jack turned his board around and faced the shore. Out even with the end of the pier, he waited for the first set to come in. As with the other spots he'd stopped and observed, the surf didn't look to be happening here either. But that didn't matter to him. Not right now. Just being in the ocean was soothing to him.

Just then, a set rose on the horizon, and Jack turned back around and paddled out to meet the wave. The timing was perfect, and both surfer and wave rose, heading for the shore. Jack worked the wave up top, then dropping into the trough, digging his right rail into the smooth surface, carving and leaving a trail of spray as he rose again up the wave's face. He rode the top of the wave for a distance, just in front of the breaking water behind him, and then he shot across the face and down into the trough again. As the wave started to close out, he rode it up and over the back. When the wave passed under him, he sat straddling his board. Jack shook his head side to side shake the salt water out of his hair and eyes.

"You ain't half-bad, Jack the surfer-boy!" came a voice from the pier.

Jack looked up to the end of the pier and saw aviator sunglasses reflecting the sun back out to where Jack sat on his board. He wiped the saltwater from his eyes and focused on the man resting his forearms on the pier railing.

"Groat," Jack said, in recognition.

"Or should I call you by your *real* name?" Groat asked.

Jack did not respond.

"Jack the *Draft Dodger*. Or *Coward*. Or *Chicken Shit*? Which is it, boy? Which one fits you best?" Groat asked. "But then I guess they all ring true! You'll answer to all of 'em, I guess. Ain't that right?"

Jack didn't answer He started to turn his board around back out to sea.

"You had any unexpected visitors lately, boy?"

"Groat, I don't have any quarrel with you. You hired me to do a job for you, and the way I see it, I was unable to perform that job. So, I resigned before you eventually fired me. Happens all the time," Jack hollered up.

"That's the way you see it, huh coward? You ran from the job like the coward that you are. You quit. You're a quitter in addition to being a draft dodger, a coward, and a chicken shit. But back to my question. You had any visitors come around looking for you lately?"

Jack felt Groat's intent and swallowed hard. His mouth went dry, and he tried to answer. "And who would that visitor be?"

"Oh, I dunno. Just someone who might be looking for you. Someone who might have an interest in contacting a lazy, long-haired, draft-dodging surfer boy."

Jack rubbed more water dripping from his hair into his eyes and looked back up at Groat and saw that another man had now joined him on the pier. Jack recognized the man. Jimmy Greer.

"So, what are you saying Groat?"

"I'm surprised you haven't made their acquaintance yet. But any day now, I'm sure. Any day."

Groat smiled, turned, and started walking back to the other end of the pier, grinning, taking intermittent looks back at Jack as he went. Jimmy Greer followed, but he turned and looked down at Jack. Then he formed the image of a gun with his thumb and forefinger and placed the imaginary gun to the side of his head and mouthed the word . . . 'BAM.'

"He's gonna report my ass to the draft board, sure as hell, if he hasn't already," Jack said out loud. "Shit! Shit! Shit!" he yelled as he beat the top of the water with the flat of both hands.

He turned and sat on his board, letting the swells rise and flow beneath him while looking out to sea in contemplation. *What's my next move? Short of Canada or prison. Or maybe he has plans to make me disappear. "I can make people go away, just like Rich Jr." Should I tell Berger of his threat, veiled as it was? Would he even believe me? If I run, I become more of a fugitive. Shit. I don't know what to do. Maybe Cassie's right. Maybe I should go tell Mr. Pierce what I've done—that I double-crossed him and that the bridge may have been set on fire on the night he went to Greensboro to look for his missing son because I told Groat he was gonna go. Damn! As if he didn't have enough on his mind, he comes back and his bridge to his lifelong dream has been torched. And now Groat's doing me in as well. Son of a bitch is gonna win this battle. And all because of me. You screw up everything you touch, Jack Tagger! Maybe you just ought to leave, quietly. Before you cause any more trouble.*

A few more sets came in and rolled under him.

Finally, Jack spoke aloud, "I've got to talk to Pierce. To level with him, like Cassie said. He deserves that. I'll do it before I leave Sunset Beach."

Jack laid out flat on his board and began paddling in. Another set rolled through. They were building, and the surf was getting better. But right now, he wasn't in the mood. In addition to leveling with Pierce, he needed to talk to Lieutenant Berger.

———•———

"JACK, COME IN," Richardson Pierce said. "But I must tell you, I haven't changed my mind on this."

"Thank you, Mr. Pierce," Jack said as he walked into Pierce's living room. "But I'm not really here about that."

"Oh? Well, have a seat. Can I get you something to drink? Water, Coke, a beer?"

"No, I'm fine," Jack said before thinking the better of it and said, "on second thought, I think I *will* have a beer, if you don't mind."

Pierce walked to the refrigerator and extracted two Heinekens. "I think I'll join you," he said. He handed the beer to Jack and sat on the couch beside him. "What can I do for you, Jack?"

"I don't think *you* can do anything for me," Jack said.

"What? Why's that?" Pierce said.

"I . . . uh . . . I don't think you can . . . it's about *me* . . . to you. I mean . . . it's about what *I* need to tell *you*."

"What is it, Jack?"

"Mr. Pierce, I haven't been totally honest with you."

"If it's about what you and Cassie and that shaman woman were telling me about, son . . . you were trying. I know you had my best interest at heart. I understood that," Pierce said.

"No! Not that. I wasn't lying about that. All that was true."

Pierce looked at Jack with consternation. "What part was *not* true, then?"

Jack took a swig of beer and looked nervously out the window over towards Bird Island.

"Jack? What part was *not* true?"

"Like I said, I haven't been totally honest with you. Hell, that's not true. I've been very dishonest with you."

"Get it out, Jack."

"When I came down here, I knew about you building your house over on the Bird. And I wanted in the worst way to get on with your crew. But I met two of Groat's men, right away. We got along pretty good. Had a couple of tall ones with them, and it wasn't long before they mentioned that they were short-handed trying to get Groat's cottages ready for the season. Long story short, I got on with their crew. I met Groat, and he told me the work would be temporary, just until they got caught up."

"Okay," Pierce said.

"So, I went to work, and it wasn't but a few days after that Groat made me an offer. Now, please understand, I was broke, and some things had happened back home that left me pretty low."

"What kind of offer?" Pierce asked.

"He offered to double my salary."

"That's not such a bad deal, Jack."

"No! It *was!* See, there was another side to the offer. My purpose and value to him was for me to get on with your crew—to keep an eye on you—and to report back to him."

"Go on."

"I'm afraid it gets worse. See, I really didn't have much to report back. You were honest. You were building your dream home over there. I knew that. But Groat didn't want to hear that. He wanted more. He was certain you were going to develop the island, and that would have ended his plan to fill in the back side of the beach and extend cottages all the way to Bird Island. So, when I heard you were going back to Greensboro to look for Rich, I relayed that to him. Not only that, but I made up a lie and threw that in. I told him I had heard once the bridge was finished, you were going to bring in some heavy, earth-moving equipment, like a backhoe. He was really interested in knowing if you were going to dig up or disturb any more of the island. So, I just threw that in to get him off my back. I didn't see how that information could help him or hurt *you* since it wasn't true. But then, he burned the bridge while you were gone! I never thought . . ."

"No, you didn't!" Pierce said.

"Didn't what?" Jack asked.

"Think! You didn't *think*. You really fooled me, Jack. Of all the men on the crew, I had you pegged as . . . well, Roy and I had you pegged as one of the smartest, most honest, hardest-working members of our crew. We had expectations."

"I know. I *felt* that, Mr. Pierce. And you don't know how this hurts, but this arrangement between him and me took place right at the beginning, before I got to know you and Roy and Hugh Wyrick and the rest of the guys. I was pretty broke. And my girl back in Greensboro had just left me for the big life because I didn't have enough to offer or keep her."

"That's no excuse, Jack," Pierce said.

"I know that, *now*. But I was torn about what to do. I thought I needed the money to support myself in finding a new life down here. And Uncle Sam was getting close. The draft was right on my tail. And again, I was torn. I don't believe in this unjust war. I'm sorry, Mr. Pierce, but they send the poor, uneducated boys who can't afford college or don't have rich daddies who have contacts and can get deferments by having their doctors write up phony physical conditions like bone spurs! I'm resisting, so I ran away. I came down to Sunset to hide because it was secluded and one of the most peaceful places I could think of. But I've screwed that all up, too. This all could end any day now. And not just because you are about to fire me."

"Yes. You've ended your employment with me. I cannot tolerate deceit or disloyalty. As much as I still like you, Jack, I have standards that I can't ignore."

"I understand, sir," Jack said, looking down.

"Why do you say it's about to end any day now?" Pierce asked.

"Groat. When he hired me, he asked why I wasn't in the military if I wasn't in school. I just told him I was laying low, didn't tell him I was resisting. But he caught on. And when I realized I could no longer do his work in good conscience, I quit working for him, and he doesn't take to being shunned. So, I'm fairly certain that he reported me to the authorities, the Selective Service, the draft board. He said I should, be seeing them any day now. And then he said something else that made me shiver."

"What was that?"

"He said if the authorities didn't get me, he would—that he could make people go away, just like Rich. Jr., and he was mad as hell, so I don't know if he meant it, or if he was just trying to scare me. But that's what he said. I wanted you to know that," Jack said.

Pierce looked thoughtfully at Jack for a moment before responding. "He said that? That's a serious allegation. You need to tell Lieutenant Berger what you just told me," Pierce said.

"If you wouldn't mind, I'd rather you tell him. I don't think he'd believe it coming from me. He'd think I made it up because he still thinks I may have had something to do with Rich's accident," Jack said.

"You're the one who heard Groat say it, so I think it'd be better if it came from you. Might be good for you, regarding your standing with Berger. I had a gut feeling about Groat's possible involvement in all this, but I have no way to prove it. Now, we may have probable cause. Thank you for telling me."

"Yes, sir," Jack said, standing.

Pierce started to walk away but then turned back around and faced Jack. "Look, I'm not changing my stance regarding your employment. You *are* fired. But I want to tell you something. You and I are somewhat alike, I think."

"How?" Jack asked. "What could we have in common?"

"A couple of things. I come from a very wealthy family. My father started a bank, and it grew and did very well. He passed away unexpectedly, and when he did, the board voted to turn the reigns over to me. I became the president—but only for a short time. After four years at the helm, the board of directors, which consisted largely of my family, replaced me with someone from outside the family. They said

I wasn't cut out to be the president of the company. This hurt me badly. It almost destroyed me.

"I mention this because of what you told me about your financial situation and your girlfriend finding you unworthy. We have that in common. It doesn't matter that it was your girlfriend and it was my family mine and a multi-million-dollar business. That experience of being told you aren't worthy cuts deep. We were both shunned by a mistress. I have all the money I'll ever need. You don't. But we have a commonality—we both *escaped* to Sunset to try and put our lives back together and heal our wounds," Pierce said.

"I didn't know about all that. You said we have *several* things in common," Jack said.

"Yes, I did. You're resisting. You don't believe in this war," Pierce said.

"I'm sorry for what I said about rich boys, but it's true. You probably don't understand or approve. People of your generation and social stature believe we should do our duty to fight the Commies and defend our country and freedom. I've heard all that before," Jack said.

"No, Jack. I don't believe that."

"You what?"

"No. I do not believe that. Not with *this* war. I respect your stance."

"You don't think I'm a coward dodging my patriotic duties?"

"As I just said, no. I do not. And yes. What you said is true, I'm afraid. There is a double standard in this country—one for the haves, one for the have-nots. I understand that," Pierce said.

"Well, I'll be damned . . ."

"This is the other thing that makes you and I alike, I think. You see, Jack, one reason I was replaced as president was that I wasn't like my father. I wasn't aggressive enough or astute enough, in their minds, to do the job that needed to be done. All my life, even during my youth, I've felt I was different. I marched to a different drummer, as your generation is fond of saying, just as, I think, *you* march to a different drummer," Pierce said.

"Yes," Jack said.

He continued. "And I *was* different. My difference was solidified that day they replaced me in the family business. That side of me was not accepted by the others in my family or within my social community. I have, for a long time, before and during my days at UNC, been drawn to things and ideas that were not, let's say, mainstream. I have always felt an obligation and connection to our planet," Pierce said.

"Does that have anything to do with that Earth decal on the back bumper of your car?" Jack asked.

"It does," Pierce said smiling. "*This*, was what I was meant to do. This is the life I should have lived—a more peaceful, contemplative life. Looking back, I spent so much time, wasted time, getting here— time spent listening to others decide my life, but not listening to myself. This is *you*, Jack. *Now*, is the time—*your* time. Life is like a rope, sliding through our open palms. Close your hands. Make a fist. Make that rope burn as it slides through your hands. Embrace and be passionate about what you are doing and feeling. Own it. Because it *is* you. I wish I'd done that a long time ago. I wish somebody had told me that years ago."

"We may well be alike in some ways," Jack said. "I didn't realize . . ."

"Listen, about the draft thing. I know a good lawyer down at Myrtle Beach. I'll call him and see what your options are."

"Thanks, but I can't afford a lawyer right now. I'm kinda out of work right now," Jack said.

"I will be the one talking to him, initially. Not you. But in the least, if you decide to go back to Greensboro, you might pay a visit to Guilford College. It's a Quaker school, and the Quaker religion is very much against war—*this* war, in particular. And I think they offer counseling to young men who are resisting. They might be able to help. I was, at one time, on the board there. There's a Quaker minister who also teaches religion on their staff. His name escapes me right now, but I'll make a phone call if you decide to go back there," Pierce said.

"Thank you! But why are you doing this, Mr. Pierce? After what I've done to you!"

"What you did was something you were not prepared for. You got into something you didn't fully grasp and had no good way to get out. I understand. But that wasn't *you*, Jack. *This* is who you are—an honest person at heart—and someone with a lot of courage."

"Honest? I don't think so. And *courage*? I'm a draft dodger. A coward who couldn't stand up to Groat," Jack said.

"No, Jack. You made a mistake—an error more likely born out of need and necessity. But you fessed up to what you did. That took the work of an honest man. And yes, you're courageous. You're taking a stand against a bigger and more powerful foe for what you feel is an unjust war. And within that war comes the loss of innocent civilians and American youth."

"I don't . . . ."

"And let me add, if I may. Much of that bravery is inherent with what lies within your stance and what's ahead for you wrapped in that commitment—the unknown. What's waiting for you out there, down this path you've chosen, well, I'm scared yet so enthralled by your generation and the young people in it, people like you," Pierce said.

"Damn," Jack whispered.

"What?" Pierce said.

"Damn! I wish we could have had this conversation sooner. Like before I got fired," Jack said.

"It wouldn't have mattered—wouldn't have changed things," Pierce said.

"I know, but . . ."

"No, I just mean that there still wouldn't have been a job for you here—not for you or any of the crew."

"What are you saying?"

"I'm saying I've decided to close down this project."

"But you can build the bridge back—or bring in supplies from Little River. You don't have to . . ."

"It's not the bridge, Jack. It's Rich's death. It's all of this—Rich, Groat's involvement with Sunset, and his indirect involvement with the island. I keep a knot in my stomach, and it won't go away. I came down here to get away from that type of aggressive, backstabbing life. Now I find myself back in the middle of it. I'm positive that Groat had a hand in the burning of the bridge—and possibly the other thing. I know I should stay and fight, but I'm just tired. Rich was my *only* supporter in my family, and now that he's gone, it's just lost its luster. I just don't have the desire, anymore," Pierce said.

"I'm sorry you feel that way. But we *did* make contact with Rich down at Bonaparte's Landing. I *do* believe that. *And* in that contact, it was his wish that you finish your dream, but I can see that the island is no longer your dream, and I have to say, under the circumstances, I can't blame you," Jack said.

Pierce smiled and said, "Thank you, Jack. I'm glad you understand what I feel. That gives me some validation in my decision. I'm gonna have Roy tell the guys in the morning."

Jack held out his hand to Pierce and said, "You're sure?"

They shook hands.

"I'm sure, Jack. And about the draft thing, if you decide to go back to Greensboro to decide what you're going to do, let me know, and I'll make a phone call to Guilford College. And I'll wait until I hear back from you before I make that call to that attorney in Myrtle Beach. In any event, don't leave without coming by and seeing me and saying goodbye."

"I won't. You've been good to me. I won't forget you, Mr. Pierce."

"And I you. Godspeed, Jack."

CHAPTER 45

LIEUTENANT BERGER WAS SITTING AT HIS DESK reviewing accident reports when his secretary buzzed him on the phone.

"Lieutenant, the crime analysis office is on line one," she said.

Berger threw the stack of reports on his desk and popped the receiver up from its cradle. "Lieutenant Berger here," he said into the mouthpiece.

"Lieutenant, this is Jeffries from CAO in Raleigh."

"Yeah Jeffries. What have ya got for me?"

"We've got information on that spent twelve-gauge shell you sent us. It was a Remington, originally a number-four shot that had been converted to a slug. But I think we already relayed that to you. Tests indicate it had been discharged fairly recently. That is, within the last three or four months," he said.

"Any prints?" Berger asked.

"Yeah. It appears to have been handled by several—maybe three individuals. But we were only able to make out two prints. One set belongs to an Easley Johnson, of Sunset Beach, NC. Looks like he's got quite a record."

Berger wrote down the name. "And the other?" Berger asked.

"The other print came back to a Jack Tagger of Greensboro, NC.

He's not as prolific as Johnson. Just a misdemeanor bust for possession about a year ago."

Berger's hand froze. "Jack Tagger?" he said.

"Yeah. Sounds like a name of interest to you!" Jeffries said.

"Yeah," Berger said. "You just confirmed my suspicions."

"Well, I'm glad I could . . ."

"And the third print, you couldn't make out?" Berger asked.

"No, we were able to lift a partial, but it didn't come up in print records . . . didn't match anything we have on file."

"I knew it!" Berger said to the ceiling.

"Knew what?" Jeffries asked.

"Nothing. I was just thinking out loud. Thank you, Jeffries. I think this'll do me." Berger hung up the phone. He took his Smokey the Bear hat from the hat rack and walked out into the outer office. "I'm going over to Sunset. Probably won't be back today," he said to his secretary as he walked out the door.

———————— ◆ ————————

LT. BERGER PARKED IN THE driveway of the cottage that Jack Tagger rented. He exited his cruiser and looked in the Willys parked in the driveway. Nothing of any interest caught his attention.

He proceeded to the back door and knocked several times, but to no avail. The trooper backed away and scanned the carport and the side of the cottage. Again, nothing of interest. Berger took one last look around and then got in his car. He backed out onto 40th Street and headed his car down the street to the Pierce guest house.

He pulled up into the yard and sat for a moment while he scanned the area. Pierce's car was tucked underneath the cottage under an overhang, out of the sun. Nothing looked amiss, except maybe the quiet and the stillness. He exited his car. The slight smell of burnt creosote lingered as he crossed the yard and climbed the steps to the second floor of the house and knocked. Several seconds passed until he saw a figure cross the living room and come to the door.

Richardson Pierce opened the door and asked, "Yes, trooper? Can I help you?"

"I was looking for . . . are you okay, Mr. Pierce?" Berger asked.

"Yeah. I've been a little under the weather the last few days," Pierce said.

Lt. Berger detected the odor of alcohol on him. It appeared he hadn't shaved in a few days, either.

"Sorry to hear that," Berger said, looking questioningly at Pierce. "I'm looking for Jack Tagger. Have you seen him around?"

"It's been a few days, I guess, since I've seen him. Something wrong, Lieutenant?"

"Well, this is all preliminary. But a shotgun shell was found on a hill overlooking Highway 904 near where your son's car crashed. There were two sets of fingerprints on it. You sure you haven't seen him? I know he's an employee of yours, and you seemed to take a liking to him, but if you're not leveling with me . . ." Berger said.

Pierce looked at the Lieutenant through bloodshot eyes. "I hope you're not insinuating I'm holding anything back or hiding him or anything like that, Lieutenant," Pierce said.

"I'm sorry. I didn't mean for it to come out that way, but I need to find him. I've been to his cottage, and no one answers, and his Jeep is in the driveway."

"Well maybe he's out surfing, but like I said, I haven't seen him in a while," Pierce said.

"Maybe so. But you have my card. Call me if you see him?"

"I will, Lieutenant," Pierce said as he started to close the door. "But ahh, Lieutenant," Pierce said.

"Yes?" Berger said turning back toward Pierce.

"You said there were *two* sets of prints?"

"That's correct," Berger said as he started to turn and walk away. Then, he stopped, turned back, and faced Pierce. "It's ironic. Both sets of prints have ties to this county. We haven't made contact with the second person, but we're looking for him, too. I'll let you know," Berger said.

"Please do," Pierce said. "Ahh, and, by the way, Lieutenant Berger, there's something I've been meaning to talk to you about, but admittedly, I've been in a distracted state lately," Pierce said.

"What's that?" Berger said.

"The last conversation I had with Jack, he said Horace Groat had threatened him over a business disagreement."

"Business disagreement? Interesting. What was the disagreement?"

"Did Jack not tell you about this? He was supposed to . . . the particulars of the disagreement are not important. But he told Jack that he could make people go away, just like Rich Junior," Pierce said.

This bit of news caught Berger's attention. "Oh? And this was . . . ?"

"Recently. Like I said, it's been a few days since I've seen Jack, and he indicated to me the threat was made in the not-so-distant past," Pierce said.

"Rest assured, I'm on it. This bit of information leads this investigation in a whole new direction and adds to the necessity for me to speak with him. It's imperative that I talk to him ASAP. You have my card. Call me immediately if Jack shows up or if you hear anything else," Berger said.

"Will do, Lieutenant," Pierce said.

CHAPTER 46

LIEUTENANT BERGER HELD THE STARE. "Ya see, Mr. Johnson, Mr. *Easley* Johnson. That *is* you, correct?"

"That's what my momma named me," Johnson said.

"Funny. But I got a problem," Trooper Berger said.

"What's that?"

"Not only am I dealing with a comedian, but I'm also dealing with a pretty damned infamous outlaw it looks like," Berger said.

"How's that?"

"Your criminal record is about as long as any I've seen lately."

"Why you runnin my criminal record? I ain't done nothing wrong," Johnson said.

"Because a certain spent shotgun shell has come to my attention—and that shell has your fingerprints on it. You have any business on Highway 904 this side of Fair Bluff? Say, within the last four or so months?" Berger asked.

Easley Johnson's face paled. "I don't know nobody up that way. Don't have any business there either," Johnson said. "So, I don't know what you're talking about."

"You don't know what I'm talking about? What about the name Richardson Pierce? They called him Rich Junior. That name mean anything to you?"

"Naw. Should it?"

"You tell me," Berger said. "Richardson Pierce Junior was shot and killed on that stretch of roadway that runs just below a high spot of land where the spent shell with your prints was found."

"Like I said, I don't know nothin' about that. I . . . I gotta go," Johnson said.

"Stick around, Johnson. We may have more to talk about, *real* soon," Berger said.

Johnson turned back around toward Lieutenant Berger. "You ain't got nothin' on me. If you did, you'd of put me in handcuffs already," he said as he walked off.

"Soon," Berger reiterated.

———•———

"YEAH, THAT CUR DOG sum bitch turned on me. Should'a never trusted that city boy. But he's gonna get his," Groat said to Jimmy Greer and three other of his workers who were sitting around the Formica table in Groat's office.

"Didn't he tell you Pierce was planning on bringing in some heavy equipment—a front-end loader to work the backside of the island? But then we don't know if we can trust what he said," Greer said.

"Well, I aim to find out. And find out before Pierce starts a'digging."

Just then the screen door flew open, and Easley Johnson entered the room. "You gotta do something, Mr. Groat," Johnson said as the screen door slammed behind him.

"I gotta do what, about what?" Groat said, looking up at Easley Johnson.

"A state trooper came to see me a little while ago."

"About what? You get another DUI? If you did, that's on your dime. That ain't in the benefits package I offer," Groat said, smiling at the three other men seated around the table.

Johnson looked at the others and said, "Can we have a minute? Alone?"

"Anything you gotta say can be said in front of these three here. I trust em. You can too," Groat said.

"Naw, boss. I'd feel better if . . . Jimmy Greer can stay. But with what I'm bout to tell you, I feel better if it was just us three," Johnson said.

Groat looked at the men seated around the table, excluding Jimmy Greer. "You boys wanna step outside? Looks like me and Johnson have some business to discuss."

The two slid their chairs back and rose from the table. Both exited out the screen door, eyeing Johnson as they left.

Groat gave it a minute, then said, "What is it I gotta do something about, Easley? It better be important, you coming in here busting up a meeting like you just did."

"It is, Mr. Groat."

"It is what? It better not be . . ."

"The trooper came and questioned me about Rich Pierce's death. Said they found my fingerprints on a spent shell that was on the ground out on 904," Johnson said.

"They did what! What the hell was the spent shell doing lying on the ground? You didn't have enough damn sense to pick it up after you ejected it? Why the hell did you even eject it? Why didn't you just leave it in the chamber? You got him with the first one, right? So, there was no need to fire off another one, "Groat said.

"We . . . uh . . . . we got nervous, Boss. A car was coming down 904 when it happened. We . . ." Johnson began.

"I thought you had that covered, Jimmy," Groat said turning his attention to Greer. "Wasn't your boy supposed to be running interference behind Pierce so that no other car would come up behind him and witness what went down?"

"He did. And the plan worked fine from that end. Easley's talking about this car coming in the opposite direction, traveling *east* on 904. That road is so deserted that time of year with it not being beach season yet, we didn't think about a car coming from the other way going *towards* the beach. We just didn't figure on *that* car coming. It got there right after Easley shot him. Pierce's car almost hit them. They came to a stop right after his car went into the field there," Jimmy Greer said. "We were afraid they'd see us. We wanted to get the hell off that knoll. I guess Easley didn't have time or didn't think to pick up the shell."

"Well, I'll be a son of a bitch! You didn't take into consideration a car could've been coming in the opposite direction? Exactly the type of situation I was trying to avoid! And I'm just hearing about this now? You know this is some serious shit, don't you!" Groat said looking at both men. "Get the fuck outta my office!" Groat said.

Johnson turned and started for the door. Greer pushed his chair back and started to stand.

"*You*, keep your damn seat," Groat said to Greer. Easley Johnson stopped and started to turn back when Groat yelled, "You, get the fuck out! Now! And don't say a damn word about this to anyone! You hear!"

"I won't, Boss," Johnson said as he exited the screen door.

Both Groat and Greer sat opposite of each other. Greer stared down at the yellow Formica tabletop. Groat broke the silence. "I always thought he was too damn dumb to be in on this. But you pushed for him to be involved," Groat said.

"I know, but I knew his aim is steady. He's a damn good shot. I wanted *him* to be the shooter," Greer said.

"Well, got-damned! There are plenty of good shooters around here. Bout everyone of 'em are hunters. You had to pick the dumbest outta the group," Groat said.

"Hell . . . I know it. I'm sorry, Boss. I . . ."

"*You* gotta take care of this. You hear me?"

"Yeah. I hear you, Boss. I hate it, but yeah . . . I hear ya," Greer said.

"Johnson is the only connection they have to this. Right *now,* that is. I don't want that dumbass to have a chance to spout off to that trooper while under the pressure that's bound to come," Groat said.

"What . . . ahh . . . what exactly did you have in mind, Boss?"

"That's up to you. But whatever you do, do it right! That's a mighty big ocean out there. Someone could disappear and never be found. You got man-eaters and other creatures out there that love the taste of human flesh. Just get it done. And fast!" Groat said.

CHAPTER 47

LIEUTENANT BERGER CLIMBED THE RICKETY STEPS at the front of the mobile home to a wooden landing that served as a front porch. His knock was answered with a weak, wobbly female voice. "Yes? Who's there?"

"Lieutenant Berger, North Carolina Highway Patrol. You called me yesterday."

A few moments passed before he finally heard the inside bolt slide from its nesting place. The door cracked open, but the darkness inside hid the face. "Are you the one I spoke to yesterday from the payphone?"

The smell of cat piss and stale cigarette smoke escaped through the crack.

"I am ma'am. Are you Miss Johnson?"

"Yes."

"You said you had something to show me, possibly about a death in the county?"

"Maybe two. Come on in, Officer," the woman said, opening the door, exposing a thin, sad face. "Pshaw! Get back," she said kicking at two mangy kittens underfoot.

"Two? Two what? Berger said.

"Two deaths. Murders," she said.

Berger looked questioningly as he entered, passing her.

"Have a seat," she said motioning to the warn, slip-covered couch. "I said get outta here!" she said swatting at one of the kittens who had escaped her notice and jumped on the couch in anticipation of human companionship.

Officer Berger bent down and brushed cat hair off the couch.

"Yeah, I shudda vacuumed that cat hair up before you got here. I'm sorry. I just plain forgot. Here. Sit on this," she said reaching for a pile of newspapers beside the couch. Cigarette stench rose as she pulled a section from the top of the pile, offering it to the Lieutenant.

"No thank you," he said, pulling his pant legs up by the crease before sitting. "Tell me about this information you have about a murder—or murders," he said.

She lit an L&M cigarette and crossed the room to a pine cupboard in the far corner of the room. Opening a drawer, she took out a piece of yellow legal pad paper. She unfolded it and handed it to the Lieutenant.

"Before you read that, let me tell you a little bit about it. What you have there in your hand is something my husband gave me. His name is Easley Johnson. He worked for a man up on the beach at Sunset named Groat. Horace Groat. A powerful man," she said, dabbing at the moist corner of her eyes with an obviously dirty handkerchief.

"I've known of Groat. I know who he is," Berger said. "I also know who your husband is."

"My husband and another man went on a job for Mr. Groat. It was out of the county, back in early spring. Well, he had a meeting with Groat a short while ago. Easley said it didn't go too good. He said Groat got really mad, cussed him, and ran him outta the office."

"Did Easley say why Groat was mad at him?" Berger asked.

"No. My husband don't tell me much, especially about his business with Groat," she said. "But he was worried about what Groat might do to him. He said it was a very serious job they'd been sent out on, and if anything went wrong, there'd be hell to pay. And he was afraid *that* hell to pay was just over the horizon cause something *did* go wrong. But what, he didn't say. He said that if anything happened to him or if he disappeared, for me to give that paper to you, that it would explain what had happened," she said, wiping a sniffle and then blowing her nose into the handkerchief.

Lieutenant Berger slowly opened the piece of paper while looking at Ms. Johnson. "And you're sure your husband wrote what I'm about to read?"

"I'm sure."

"Did you see him write this note?"

"I did. He called me into the bedroom and said he wanted me to witness him write it. He said if not, there may be some argument about the truthfulness of it down the road if I didn't see him write it with my own eyes."

The trooper unfolded the note.

> *To who it concerns and mainly to the state*
> *trooper who came to see me about the shotgun shell*
> *with my fingerprints on it I writing this is to say if*
> *something happens to me and someday I dispeer or*
> *come up dead I want you to know who did it or had*

*a hand in my dispeering. If your readn this I musta
already dispeered.*

*Me and Jimmy Greer was sent by Mr. Horace
Groat to do a job to take care of somebody in Mr.
Groats way. It was Rich Pierce Richardson Pierces
son. We did it, but it didn't end right and Mr. Groat
went wild mad at me for screwing it up.*

*I'm fraid that Mr. Groat may do something to me
to get rid of me. I'm writing this in front of my wife.
She'll witness me writing it and my signature. I really
wrote this.*

Very truly yours
Easley Junior Johnson

*PS. Don't look over Jimmy Greer either. He may
have a part in me dispeering too.*

Lieutenant Berger folded the paper back up, unbuttoned the flap
to his shirt pocket, and slid it in. "Who's Jimmy Greer?" he asked

"That's one of Easley's coworkers. Kinda like his foreman, but not
really. He was just over Easley and told him what to do."

"Who else has read or touched this statement?" Berger asked

"Just me. And now you" she said.

"And your husband?"

"Yeah. That'd be right," she said.

"You sure? No one else?"

"I'm sure," she said.

"How long has he been missing?" Berger asked.

"It's been a while now," she said.

"What's a while?" Berger said.

"Almost a week," she said.

"How do I know he's not hiding out down at Myrtle Beach? Or off on some binge?"

"Cause that ain't him to do something like that. In all the years we've been married, he's never taken off on me. And as far as being off on a binge, Easley ain't no saint, by no means. He likes his liquor, but he's always done most of his drinking right here in the trailer. I'm worried, sir. Real worried. This ain't like him. Something's gone wrong. I know it."

Lieutenant Berger remained on the couch, both hands rubbing the tops of his thighs, thinking. "Mrs. Johnson this is a very serious allegation. And in its form, it may present potential problems. It could be construed as hearsay because your husband is not here to testify that he wrote it and to prove that it is *his* handwriting. If so, it may not be allowed into evidence. I'll have to take this to the county district attorney to get his legal opinion on this. I'm not a lawyer, but I'm thinking there could be potential legal ramifications with something like this," he said.

"Well, you'd know about that more'n me. But I can swear on a stack of bibles that he wrote that and I saw him do it with my own eyes," she said.

"Mrs. Johnson, you may well end up being a witness in this. You keep the letter quiet and the fact that you and I have talked to yourself. Keep a tight lip on this because I don't want Groat or any of his men finding out you've talked to me or that this letter exists. I don't want to tip them off or let them get wind of this. It could possibly be dangerous for you."

"Well, I don't never go anywhere, much. The grocery store once a week or to get my hair done when I can afford it. I stay close by. But I hear ya."

"Good. Now here's my card. You call me on that number right there. That's dispatch. There's somebody there twenty-four hours a day."

"Okay," she said sheepishly.

"I need you to stay safe, now. You hear?"

"I do," she said.

The Lieutenant started to leave, but he turned back to her, extracting the yellow paper from his shirt pocket. Holding it up to her he said, "And he, your husband, he *did* write this? Correct? You'll swear to it?"

She looked up at the Lieutenant, a sad look on her face. She shook her head yes.

———•———

"THE DISTRICT ATTORNEY WILL see you now Lieutenant," the receptionist said.

"Thank you, Ma'am," Lieutenant Berger said, tipping the front of his hat. He removed it as he entered.

"Have a seat Lieutenant," the Brunswick County District Attorney said.

Berger took a seat in one of the two leather chairs that fronted the D.A.'s desk.

"You have a hand-written confession in your possession, you say?

"I do," Lieutenant Berger said, pulling the yellow paper from his shirt pocket, sliding the paper across the desk to the D.A.

"What's been the chain of custody?" he asked, looking at the trooper.

"Just the author, the wife, and me," Berger said. "And of course, now you."

The room fell silent as the D.A. read Easley Johnson's written statement. In the end, he laid the paper on his desk and remained in thought before saying, "There may be a problem with hearsay. The defense attorney will probably claim that since the original author is not present to verify the authenticity of it. The defense may be able to prevent it from being entered into evidence. And without this piece of evidence, you don't have much of a case. This is a highly unusual case—a statement from the grave. But in any event, I like it. Let me do some legal research on this. I know time is of the essence here. I'll get back to you as soon as I've made a decision on this."

CHAPTER 48

"YES SIR, LIEUTENANT. HE'S STANDING RIGHT here in my living room," Richardson Pierce said. "Yes. He says he's willing to talk with you. Okay, we'll wait right here." Pierce hung up the phone and looked at Jack. "He says he's not far away. He'll be here in ten minutes. Sit down and relax, Jack," Pierce said.

"I'd rather stand. I'm kinda nervous," Jack said.

"I don't think the fingerprints are the issue, at this point. I get the feeling that what you heard Groat say about him making people disappear is more what he's focusing on. And you are being completely honest in that, Jack. Right?"

"I am. I feel he was directing it at me, but he threw Rich's name in there as well."

"Then let's nail this son of a bitch, then," Pierce said, just as the knock at the door alerted them to Berger's arrival. "Yes. Come in Lieutenant," Pierce said, opening the glass door for the officer.

"Thank you, Mr. Pierce," the trooper said as he removed his Smokey the Bear hat and tucked it under his arm. "Jack," he said, nodding his head in acknowledgment.

"Lieutenant," Jack returned.

"Jack, I hear you have some information regarding

something you heard Horace Groat say to you, while in your presence?"

"I do."

"You wanna tell me about it?"

"He and I were having a disagreement. Actually, I had just told him that I didn't . . . I *couldn't* work for him anymore. And he said to me, 'You better know I can make people disappear from here. Kinda like Rich Jr did.' Then he added, 'Not that I know anything about that. But you catch my drift?'" Jack said.

"You're absolutely sure about this? He said this directly to you?" Berger asked.

"I'm certain. You don't forget a direct threat like that," Jack said.

"When was this?" Berger asked.

"A week or so ago, I guess. I'm not so good with dates," Jack said.

"Okay. Here's where we are here. I have a handwritten note from an Easley Johnson saying that should something happen to him, should he *disappear*, to look at Horace Groat and a fellow named Jimmy Greer as possible suspects. As it turns out, after an interview with his wife, Mr. Johnson *has* suddenly disappeared. You know of a fellow named Jimmy Greer?"

"I do," Jack said. "He works for Groat. Same as Johnson, I think. That's the guy who owns that red truck I told you about—the truck I saw at the site of the accident."

"Again, here's where I am with this. I need evidence to establish probable cause to be able to obtain a warrant for arrest. That handwritten note is valuable, but it could be a problem in that Mr. Johnson wrote the note, as per Mrs. Johnson, but it could be disputed or thrown out due to the chain of command. That is, the writer of that note, Mr. Easley Johnson, is not available to offer it as evidence, that *he* was the author of that note. Now I'm going to ask you two things, Jack. First, are you willing to sign a statement as to what Groat told you directly about being able to make people disappear, specifically Rich Pierce? If so, along with Ms. Johnson's handwritten note, I feel good, optimistic that we can obtain a warrant for his and Jimmy Greer's arrest. After that, it's in the DA's hands to prosecute the case. But, those two pieces of evidence, as good as they are, could be refuted and defended by the defense at trial. I want to hand the DA a solid case," Berger said.

"I am. No question about it. Prepare the statement, and I'll sign it. So, I'm no longer a suspect? What about my fingerprints on the shell?" Jack asked.

"I already spoke with Ms. Cavanaugh and her version of how those prints got on that shell back up what you told me. No, you are no longer a suspect in this."

"And the other thing? What's the other thing you mentioned?" Jack said.

"Now, you don't have to do this, Jack. You're under no obligation to do this. It *could* be risky, but we need to set Greer and Groat up together, in one place to serve the arrest warrant. But more than that, it would seal the murder charge if we could get Groat to admit to having Rich Jr. murdered," Berger said.

"How would I fit into that?" Jack said.

"We'd need you to record him admitting it," Berger said.

"How would I go about doing that?"

"By wearing a wire. Since you know them and they know you, could you set up a meeting with them," Berger said.

"How am I gonna do that? Groat, as it stands, he wants to do me in. How's he gonna agree to meet with me?"

"A guise. Tell him you want to meet with him under the guise of you wanting to go back to work for him. Tell him you and Pierce had a falling out and that Pierce fired you over Rich's death—that Pierce said you, Groat, and Greer conspired to have his son killed and he wanted you to sign a statement, but you refused. You could say that you now see which side the bread is buttered on—that Pierce was not who you thought he was. Just somewhere in the conversation, you lead him up to the line and make him cross it. I don't care if it's just a step across the line. I want to nail him with his own words. I want him to choke on his own damn words."

"A wire? Damn! This is getting real serious," Jack said.

"It is, Jack. I wanna take this man down. Me—and Richardson Pierce. But this decision to do this has to be yours. Think about it. But the sooner you decide, the sooner we act," Berger said, walking toward the door.

"Lieutenant Berger, you can have my decision right now," Jack said, causing Berger to stop and turn back to Jack. "I'll do it. This man has hurt a lot of people due to his greed and self-centeredness. He's a bully and is willing to take anybody down who stands in his way. And it has to stop! Let's do this!" Jack said.

CHAPTER 49

WITH TWO MURDER WARRANTS RESTING ON HIS LAP, Lieutenant Berger accompanied three officers from the State Bureau of Investigation office who had driven down from Raleigh in their unmarked car.

Berger, in the front passenger's seat, said to the driver, "Just follow 904 on into Sunset Beach. There, it turns into Sunset Boulevard. Once we get into position, you'll have the radio and headset. If you hear Jack say the words, 'Bury the hatchet,' you nod your head, vigorously. I'll have my eyes on you the whole time. If that happens, it means Jack's in trouble, and we'll go in with our guns drawn."

"Gotcha," the driver said.

"Now, on up here a ways, the road will curve to the left. Stay on Sunset Boulevard towards the pontoon bridge. Just before the bridge, the convenience store will be on the right. We'll wanna go behind the store. Groat's office is in the rear, but don't pull in. We'll remain in the car until we see Jack go in. Then you'll come with me, each of us on either side of the door," he said to the man in the back seat. "You other two pull your pieces and stay out here by the car and cover us. When we hear Jack say the code words or if there's trouble, you and I'll rush the door just like we talked about," Berger said to the three

SBI officers. "Okay. There's the store. Ease on around back but park the car out on the road beside the parking lot," Berger said.

The vehicle turned as instructed, its deep-throated engine powering down to a purr.

"Stop right here. We don't want them to see our car. Whose got the warrants? Oh hell! They're sitting right here on my lap." Berger said, laughing, nervously.

At that moment, Jack's Jeep entered the sand parking lot behind the store and stopped at the back door. Jack sat for a moment, composing himself before thumping his cigarette out the open Jeep window. He exited and walked around the back of his Jeep, looking sheepishly around for his backup. He spotted the cruiser, took a deep breath, and knocked on the door.

"Who's there?" came the reply from inside.

"Jack Tagger."

Seconds later, the door opened, and Jimmy Greer looked over and around Jack's shoulder. Then, he grabbed Jack by the arm and said, "Get in here!"

The door slammed, shut and the officers took up their positions.

Horace Groat sat at the Formica table facing Jack. "Boy, you got some balls! Either that or you're pretty damn stupid, you come'n in here like this after what you've done," Groat said.

"I know it. And you're right," Jack said. "But like I told you on the phone, I've had second thoughts about what I did, and I wanna come back to work. Pierce and me had a falling out. He wanted me to admit that I knew you had Rich Junior killed. I lied and told him you didn't. I . . ."

"You *lied* and told him I didn't? You don't know shit boy! What'n the hell you up to? Is this some kinda setup?" Groat growled.

"No. It's no setup. I regret what I did. I'm sorry I quit you," Jack said.

"What damn good are you to me now, Tagger? You've blown it with Pierce. You can't supply me with any information now. *And* you quit me! You know me, Tagger. I don't put up with that shit! And now, here you are, trying to get back in with me! This *is* some kinda set up, ain't it?"

"No, I just lied to Pierce and told him you had nothing to do with Rich's death and . . ."

"Jimmy, rip that damn shirt off and see if he's wired up!"

Backing up, Jack yelled, "Mr. Groat. I just want to bury the hatchet!"

"He's wired," Greer said ripping the taped microphone off Jack's chest.

"I fucking thought so!" Groat said.

The agent in the car nodded his head up and down vigorously. Berger saw the agent's frantic response and immediately opened the rusty screen door and banged on the solid wooden door.

"Who the hell is that? Who'd you bring with you Tagger?" Groat shouted.

"SBI and State Highway Patrol. Open up!" Berger shouted.

"What tha fuck you want," came the reply.

Berger heard what sounded like chairs and tables scraping on a cement floor.

"Open the damned door! Now! Or we're gonna bust it down," Lieutenant Berger yelled at the person on the other side.

"You gotta fuckin warrant?" came the reply from inside.

"I do! Open this door, or we'll break it down and shove the warrant up your ass!"

"Jimmy, put that damn gun on Tagger's head. If he moves or tries to run, shoot him!" Groat hollered.

Greer pressed the barrel of his gun against Jack's temple. "Don't you move, Tagger! Don't even sneeze, or your brains will be all over that table there!"

Seconds later, the door handle turned from the inside. A scruffy-looking man with a day-old beard filled the crack of the door but remained inside. "Let me see the damned warrant," he said.

Trooper Berger said, "You Horace Groat?"

"What if I am?"

"I gotta warrant for your arrest."

"What for?"

"For murder," Berger said, stuffing the yellow warrant into the man's hand.

"Murder? Who'd I murder?"

"For the murder of Easley Johnson and Richardson Pierce Junior."

"Got one for Jimmy Greer too. He in there with you?"

The scruffy man in the door turned his head back into the room. "You hear that? They got one for you too! Don't take that gun off him," he said to the other man in the darkened room.

Trooper Berger silently signaled the SBI agent on the other side of the door with a nod of his head. Both men had their weapons at the ready.

"This is my last warning," Berger said. "Open that door, and come out with your hands up over your heads, or we're coming in. And there's more of us than there are of you."

As Lieutenant Berger finished the sentence, the officers heard a window being pried open on the side of the building. Seconds later, a gunshot rang out. Berger yelled at the two reserve SBI officers to stand their ground and watch the door. Berger and his counterpart rounded the side of the office as a body came slithering horizontally through the opened window.

"Hold it right there!" Berger yelled.

Both officers trained their weapons on the figure now flat on the ground.

"Stay right there! Put your hands out in front of you on the ground, and don't move a damned muscle! That man inside better damn well be alive, or that's another murder charge you'll face. Either that or I'll kill you myself!" Berger said.

Crouched, both arms extended in front of him, holding his weapon, Trooper Berger advanced on the prone man.

"What's your name? Are you Groat? Are you Horace Groat?" Berger asked.

"No. Don't shoot! I ain't him. I'm Jimmy Greer. Horace is still in there," Greer said moving his head up and backward, indicating the office.

Just then shots were fired in front of the office.

"Watch him!" Don't let him move!" Berger shouted over his shoulder to the SBI Agent.

Berger rounded the corner of the building as gun report exploded in the yard. One of the SBI officers was writhing on the ground, shouting incoherently. "Oh, God! Goddam! I'm gutshot! Call momma! Momma! I'm shot!" he screamed as his blood spread out into the sand.

The scruffy man was out in the yard, crouched and firing at the other SBI agent who had taken cover and was returning fire from behind the cruiser. A bloody, mangled left arm dangled uselessly at the scruffy man's side. The SBI agent's left shoulder bore a crimson stain spreading across his white shirt.

The surreal carnage and permeating odor of gun powder brought up sour bile from Berger's stomach, settling in his throat. The scruffy man turned and looked toward Berger and swung his pistol around with his right arm. Instinctually Berger responded, bringing both arms up and taking aim at the perpetrator.

"DROP IT!" Berger yelled "NOW!"

The scruffy man rotated his head from Berger to the agent behind the car then back to Berger. The look on this face said he knew it was over.

Time went into slow motion.

"DROP IT!" both law officers yelled at the same time.

Berger became aware of a fourth entity that had suddenly appeared in the smoky mélange. He saw, standing in the middle of the impromptu circle, a faceless man, looking and walking straight toward the perpetrator whose look of bewilderment abruptly transformed into recognition and horror. Both the perp and the faceless figure stared at one another for what seemed like an eternity in the absurd, slow-motion time warp before the perp's grip suddenly re-tightened on the gun. In a slow ark, he brought the gun up and put the barrel to the side of his head. Staring intently into the soul of the disfigured man, he smiled a grin of acceptance and pulled the trigger.

A drawn-out explosion accompanied the boney crimson and gray expulsion as the man's brains discharged from his skull. Then, the faceless apparition vanished into particles.

Silence followed. Time seemed to stop, until Berger softly said, "That pile of a man laying there'd better be Horace Groat. If not, I'm fucked."

At that moment, the other SBI came around the corner with the detained man in handcuffs.

"Bring him over," Berger said.

The SBI agent grabbed the cuffed man by the scruff of his collar and ushered him over.

Berger stepped up to the man and in his face shouted, "What the hell is your name? It'd better either be Horace Groat or Jimmy Greer. Which is it? I ain't playing!" Berger demanded.

"I'm . . . I'm . . . I'm Greer. Jimmy Greer," he said.

"Good. Now tell me, who the hell that is right there," Berger said pointing to the man on the ground.

"I can't . . . I can't see his face. All I see is a bloody side of somebody's head," he said.

"Okay, smart ass," Berger said. He grabbed Greer by the back of his neck, shoving him over to where the front of the dead man's face lay in the sand. He kicked the back of Greer's legs, bringing him down to his knees. Berger pushed Greer down so that his face was inches away from the front of the dead man's. "How's that? Is the view better now?" Berger asked, pushing Greer's face flat on the ground.

"That's him!" came a voice standing in the doorway.

"Who? *Who's* him?" Berger asked, looking down at the back of the head he was pressing on the ground.

"It's him! Horace. It's Horace Groat," the voice responded.

Berger turned his head and saw Jack standing in the doorway, blood streaming from his head. Berger pulled Greer up by the elbows, handed him over to the SBI agent, and walked to the doorway where Jack was standing.

"Jack. You okay? Let me see that," he said moving Jack's hand away from the wound.

"I'm okay. I was lucky. I turned my head at the last second, just as I heard him pull back the hammer. Then he fired. I think it just grazed me. I'm a little dizzy, though," Jack said.

"Let me see that, Berger said as he parted Jack's hair. I think it's more than a graze. It put a nice part in your scalp. I think you need to go to the hospital. The bullet may have given you have a concussion or cracked your skull." Berger turned to the agent. "Better call an ambulance. Tell 'em we got three to transport. *And* the coroner. But make sure Jack gets transported first," Berger said to the agent. "I believe we're bout done here." Turning back to Jack, he said, "Thank you. This all couldn't have happened without you. We took a bad man down with your help today," Berger said.

"Thank you, Lieutenant. There *is* justice in the world. I feel a sense of redemption now for Mr. Pierce—and Rich!"

CHAPTER 50

"CRICKET HAVE YOU SEEN JACK?" Cassie asked as she entered the restaurant in Ocean Isle.

The ocean breeze followed her, blowing her hair forward over her forehead and into her eyes as she entered from the outside deck. Cricket had just finished with the lunch crowd and was wiping her hands on a dishcloth.

"No, I haven't. I heard he was in the hospital . . . something about a minor head wound, thank God," Cricket said.

"He's not at the hospital, anymore. Mr. Pierce called the hospital, and they told him they had kept him for a twenty-four-hour observation but released him the next day. That was like four, five days ago," Cassie said. You have a minute?" she asked, motioning with her head that they should take the conversation outside.

"Sure. Let me grab my cigarettes. You want one?" Cricket asked.

"No . . . oh hell! Okay," Cassie said.

"Skip, I'm gonna step outside to have a smoke. Be back in to finish up in a few minutes," Cricket hollered to her boss.

"All right. But drag your butt back in her as soon as you finish so we can shut her down and get ready for the dinner shift," he said.

The two women exited the dining room through the screen door and stepped out onto the deck. Cricket flipped open the top of the Marlboro box and extracted two cigarettes. She put both in her mouth, lit them, and passed one to Cassie. Both took draws at the same time and exhaled.

Cassie shook her head and tossed back her hair in the breeze. "I'm really worried about him. His Jeep is in the driveway, but he doesn't answer the door. Jack and I . . . we went away a few weeks ago, spent the weekend at Ocean Drive. We had a great time and got really close that night. But when we got back, I was scared and asked that we cool it for a while . . . told him it was too soon for me. I mean, he was just coming off a broken relationship, so he needed time as well, but that was the last time I saw him. Maybe I hurt him, and that's why I . . . *we* haven't seen him or . . ."

"Or what?" Cricket asked.

"What if Horace Groat has done something to him? Do you know what Jack was going through—with Horace Groat, I mean?" Cassie asked.

"He told me about working for Groat. But nothing surprises me when it comes to him. He's well known around here. From Sunset Beach to Ocean Isle, to Shallotte. My daddy knows him . . . and not in a good way," Cricket said. "What's going on?"

"I guess Jack didn't tell you the whole story. Groat had approached him early on after he moved down here and offered to pay Jack double if he'd get on with Pierce's crew and keep an eye on what he's doing over on Bird. Jack got to a point he couldn't do it anymore, in good conscience. So, he quit Groat. And Groat was really pissed at him. Jack was frightened of him and what he might do in retaliation."

315

"Wait a minute. Go back. You and Jack had a romantic weekend together? And now he's . . ."

"Cricket! I'm sorry. You knew Jack before I did. You guys were hanging out, surfing and all. Did y'all . . . did I step in on you . . . with Jack?"

"Oh no, Cassie. We were . . . *are* . . . just good friends. See, I'm not sure . . . about guys, that is—I mean, whether it's a *guy* I want in my life or not. I'm just confused. That's one reason I'm down here—to try and figure some things out."

"Wait. I don't understand," Cassie said.

"Do I need to spell it out, Cassie? I was in a relationship before I moved down here, but not with a *guy*," Cricket said.

"Oh?" Cassie replied. "I . . . I didn't know you were . . ."

"Gay? I'm not sure I am either. I still consider the possibility that I may be bi. But I tend more toward gay. I like women. Like I said, I'm confused, and so I'm down here to figure out some things about myself. Just like Jack. Like you and like Mr. Pierce. Aren't we all down here trying to work out something in our lives? We came for the salt and sea . . . to soothe our pain?"

"I suppose you're right," Cassie said. "We're all licking our wounds and trying to start over, I guess."

"No better place," Cricket said.

"But Jack, I don't understand his disappearance. I hope it's not because of me. *Or* Groat. Plus, he was avoiding the draft," Cassie said.

"Yeah. I knew that," Cricket said.

"When Jack quit with Groat, he threatened to turn him into the selective Service. That would've been serious—a Federal offense," Cassie said.

"Oh shit!" Cricket said.

Just then, Skip yelled, "Cricket! Get your tail back in here."

"Coming! Now, I'm worried," Cricket said.

"Let me know if you hear from him. Or have him call me, okay?" Cassie asked as she walked down the steps from the restaurant deck.

"Will do. You do the same," Cricket said.

CHAPTER 51

THE SUN WAS LOW ACROSS THE MARSH, Richardson Pierce's favorite time of day—the in-between, soft time. Closing the door behind him, he turned and walked back into the living room, pushing his hands back through his white hair. He was worried. He fixed himself another gin and tonic and walked back out onto the deck overlooking the marsh, Bird Island, and Little River beyond it.

He knew his consumption was more than he'd ever let it be before, but right now, in this time in his life, it didn't matter. The clear liquid in the glass in his hand soothed him as he gazed across the expanse. His thoughts settled on Jack.

Something's not right, he thought. *Did Jack leave and go back to Greensboro after he got out of the hospital? But he would have come by and told me. He would've said his goodbyes. But why's his Jeep still here? Did the draft board find him and spirit him away to some Federal prison?*

Standing on the deck, Pierce looked out and saw a young deer leave the berm they had built for the bridge out over the marsh over Madd Inlet. Grabbing his binoculars from inside the door, he trained them on the deer. He observed a young buck bound and splash across the marsh grass before entering an open pool of brackish water. There, he appeared to sink in the muck up to his underbelly. The buck's frantic struggle to free himself turned Pierce's thoughts again to Jack.

He didn't like the analogy, to think of a free-spirited Jack in that way—mired up, frantically trying to free himself from a sucking, imprisonment. With each twist and lurch, the deer sank deeper until he was up to his neck in water and muck. Through his binoculars, Pierce could see the animal's mouth opening and closing, apparently braying, pleading for release.

The lowering afternoon sun made the image shimmer in the heat. Pierce's hands started to shake. "I've gotta put some brakes on my drinking," he said as he put the binoculars on the railing.

He rubbed the sweat off his forehead with the back of his hand and then retrained the field glasses back out on the struggle in the marsh.

Pierce could take no more. He put his glass of gin on the banister and hurried down the front steps. At the dock, he untied the cleated line and pushed the skiff away from the landing. Two tugs of the rope brought the motor to life as blue smoke exited the motor's exhaust. Pierce turned the steering arm and headed the skiff up the open slew in the entrapped deer's direction. The deer and its location were hidden from the boat and its captain as both sat low in the water, below the taller marsh grass.

"Where the hell is he?" Pierce asked as the boat approached a section of the slew that opened into an intersection of canals. He stood up in the boat and peered over the tall grass. "Over there. Up this slew," he said to himself.

He turned the motor's arm and moved up into a narrow channel close to where he thought the deer might be. *Close, anyway*, he figured.

About halfway up the slew, he cut the engine and let the boat drift. The current was running, so he had no need to pole the boat, but he did use an oar to keep it straight and out of the marsh grass.

As the boat continued drifting towards the anticipated location, Pierce stood. He kept both feet planted against the outer walls to steady himself. Standing, he looked straight ahead and up over the top of the marsh grass for the trapped deer, but he only saw the swaying grass in the cooling breeze. Pierce assisted the current with his paddle.

Soon, the canal widened and then stopped at a wall of marsh grass that prevented him from going any further. The slew ended, but over the top of the grass barricade, he was able to see an open pond that looked like the one where he had observed the deer. His eyes scanned the water, but he only saw the breeze-rippled top of the open pool. The sun was now low in the sky, directly in front of him and blurring his vision, but to his right, over on the berm, inside the tree line, he thought he saw movement.

He watched as the movement continued, coming forward, closer, until the shape evolved into that of a man. As it drew near, the manner and gate of the figure became familiar.

"Jack," he called out. "Is that you?"

At that moment, the figure left the tree line and came down the earthen embankment into the marsh grass. It reached the open pond and entered, wading in up to its knees. Something was strange about its walk, though. The figure was leaving no wake or disturbance in the water as it moved across.

"Jack! Where've you been," he yelled, somewhat deliriously. "We've wondered where you've . . . ."

The sun was just above the horizon now, behind the figure, leaving only a hazy outline.

"Jack! Is that you! Come on now! Quit playing. Come over here. Get in my boat, and I'll take you back! It's gonna start getting dark," Pierce said, waving his arm at the apparition-like figure standing out in the water.

The silent figure turned toward Pierce, facing him. The sun was a sinking blaze behind it, surrounding it in a halo of light.

"Jack?" Pierce said hesitantly. "You . . . you're not Jack, are you?"

At that moment, the sun went below the horizon, and the figure of a faceless man emerged out on the pond.

A message emanated across the water. *I'm not Jack.*

"Who are you? And what happened to your face?" Pierce asked, hesitantly.

The sun sent up its last rays, bouncing off the clouds and scattering its ethereal light across the sky in majestic reds, purples, and pinks. The colors bounced back to Earth, creating an otherworldly effect. At that moment, the figure's face evolved, and a handsome, blond-headed young man appeared.

"Rich!" Pierce gasped.

Yes.

Richardson Pierce's legs faltered, and he almost fell to the bottom of the boat. He caught himself on the gunwales, looked up at the apparition, and said, "Our words. If you're Rich, then you know our words," Pierce said.

I know, Father.

His mouth didn't move when he spoke. Instead, Rich's words entered his father as if a tuning fork was vibrating in his chest.

"You know?"

Yes.

"Tell me! Tell me our words, our message to each other," Pierce said.

Je suis la,' Papa. I am here, Father.

Richardson Pierce reached out for his son, now on all fours in the bottom of the boat. Tears clouded his vision. "Rich! It *is* you! You *are* here! Come. Get in the boat, and let's go home!"

Yes. Home. Finish our home. You will feel my presence there. It will be where our souls meet. You must finish it.

"But with you gone, Rich, it no longer means what it did to me," Pierce said. "I just don't see how I can . . ."

Rich's energy started to drain. His image started to change back to the distorted face.

The Evil One has been dealt with. But to you . . . be in the present. The past is the past. It is not your concern. YOU are your concern. Now, I must leave you. Continue building our dream, and I will be with you there . . . always.

CHAPTER 52

Two years later

THE POLYNESIAN GUEST HOUSE STOOD EMPTY. Cassie Cavanaugh pushed the skiff from the sandy little beach where the dock once stood. The tide was coming in, and the current immediately lifted the boat and pushed it in a wayward direction. Cassie yanked on the cord twice before the motor came to life. This part always scared her. What if . . . the motor didn't start? She and the boat would be at the mercy of the current, and if the tide was going out, they would drift out into the ocean.

Cassie put the engine in neutral and secured the groceries she had purchased from the deli at The Island Mart—a loaf of French Bread, cheese, a bottle of Cabernet Sauvignon, and a quarter-pound of fresh shrimp from Sam Bee's Seafood would be her dinner. Alone.

Cassie crossed the open body of water that ran alongside the pilings of what remained of the bridge. Arriving at the backside of the island, she pulled the boat up to the dock and tied it off on the cleat. She held the bag of groceries in the crook of her right arm and grabbed the rungs of the ladder with her left hand as she climbed to the deck. Putting the bag on the bench, she turned and tended to the boat, giving the rope ample slack it would need once the tide went out. She gathered the groceries and walked the shady sand path to the house.

Putting the bag on the kitchen counter, she pulled out the bottle of red. Opening it, she poured herself a glass and walked out to the gazebo at the front of the house. She pulled her hair out of the tie and shook her head, letting it fall to her shoulders. A breeze from the ocean crested the sand dunes that fronted and protected the house, blowing her hair back onto her shoulders.

Savoring the moment, she closed her eyes slightly in contemplation when a sense of movement atop the dune alerted her attention. Opening her eyes and letting them adjust to the late afternoon sun, she gasped when she focused on a figure standing at the top of the sand dune, its hair blowing in the breeze pushing it forward, covering the face. Startled, Cassie turned and started back toward the house.

A voice called out, "Cassie?"

She stopped. She turned, slowly.

"Cassie?"

The breeze changed directions offshore, and the figure's hair blew back, seaward.

"Oh my God! Is that *you*?" she cried out.

"Yes! It's me."

"Oh, God! Jack! It *is* you!"

"Yeah, Cassie! It's me. I'm back," he said as he walked down the dune towards her. At the bottom of the dune, they embraced.

"Where have you been? Where'd you go? Nobody knew what happened to you," she said pulling back from his embrace to get a better look at him.

"I'm sorry, Cassie. When I was released from the hospital, they were waiting for me. There was nothing I could do. They wouldn't let me contact anyone."

"Who?"

"The prison guards. They had strict rules on who we could contact on the outside. It was basically family, and since I really didn't have any family . . ."

"Prison? You were in prison?"

"Yeah, for resisting the war. They found me, and the penalty for refusing to kill for them was five years in federal prison. I got out in two and a half on good behavior," Jack said.

"So, how'd they find you?" Cassie asked.

"They had some help."

"How? Who?"

"Groat. That son of a bitch turned me in before the gunfight at his office. When I went to the hospital, I had to give them my name and social security number. That sent up a red flag to Selective Service, and they sent the FBI to arrest me."

"We thought that may have been what happened. Mr. Pierce tried to find out for sure, but we never got a confirmation," Cassie said.

"So what happened? I know Groat killed himself, but I didn't get to talk to Mr. Pierce. Does he know that Groat was responsible for Rich's death?"

"Yeah. Lieutenant Berger filled him in on everything," Cassie said.

"Speaking of Mr. Pierce, where is he? Is he here?" Jack asked, heading for the house. "Look at this place! He did it! He finished it!"

Cassie grabbed Jack's arm as he started to pass her. He stopped, looked into her face, and noticed the seriousness in it.

"What's wrong, Cassie?"

"He's not here."

"When will he be back? I told him I'd come to see him if I decided to leave here, but I never got the chance to tell him goodbye—or you and Cricket, for that matter. It all happened so fast . . ."

"Jack! He won't be back. He's gone," Cassie said, tears welling in her eyes.

"Gone?" Jack asked quietly.

"Yes. He passed away about six months ago, but not before finishing it," she said motioning to the house. He left us in his sleep. They said it was a heart attack, but when he learned the truth about Groat ordering Rich's execution, I believe his heart just broke," she said.

"Oh, God," Jack said softly. "That's hard to believe. Mr. Pierce was always so in control," Jack said.

"Let's go sit in the gazebo. I need to tell you some things."

Cassie put her arm around Jack's waist, and they seated themselves on a bench on the circular porch. Cassie took a deep breath and then began.

"Where do I begin? Pour yourself a glass of wine. Better make it a big one."

Cassie told Jack of what had transpired while he was gone and how the truth finally came out—that after Groat was killed in the gunfight with Berger and the SBI, Jimmy Greer was sentenced to life for the murder of Rich Jr. and Easley Johnson. At the end of the telling, she said, "Jack, there *is* a good ending to all this."

"How could there be? This is all so . . ."

"Jack, that day, after Lieutenant Berger visited Mr. Pierce, he went out on the deck and spotted a deer out on the berm trying to cross over a shallow pond in the sound. It looked like the deer got stuck in that pond. Mr. Pierce was drinking pretty heavily during that time, and that deer, in his mind, became you. He really liked you, Jack, and we couldn't find you—didn't know if you fled to Canada or were in prison. Anyway, he got in his boat and headed over. By the time he got close to the spot, the deer evolved again—this time into Rich Junior."

"Jesus! Was he having a breakdown?" Jack asked.

"I don't know. I really don't think it matters. He was certain it happened. *And*, he described Rich just as we saw him. Most importantly, Rich told Mr. Pierce to finish the house and that he would always be here with him in this place, and as you see, he did."

"So, he finally believed what we told him about Bonaparte Landing? That Rich lived on . . . on the other side?"

"He did. He apologized over and over to me. He felt so bad about that. But Jack, it really hurt him that he didn't have a chance to tell you that he believed you," Cassie said.

"I guess I missed a lot. I would've really liked to have heard that," Jack said.

"They're together now, though. Mr. Pierce and his son," Cassie said with a sad smile.

"Yeah. I suppose they are. I sure would've liked to tell him goodbye, though."

"I know, Jack."

"Been some strange times down here the last few years. I never expected all this at Sunset Beach. It's always been such a peaceful vibe down here. It worries me," Jack said.

"I know. It *has* been an eventful time. But why does it worry you? Why now?"

"I don't know. Just a feeling."

"But why? What are you afraid of? Groat's gone. And two of his henchmen, with him. The beachfront between Sunset and Bird Island is not gonna be developed now," Cassie said. "All is well."

"All is well, for now. But there's more coming behind Groat. This beach is bound to change. It's too pristine. And its closeness to the seductive mistress, Miss Myrtle Beach, is bound to bring men and money," Jack said.

"You worry too much about things that haven't happened—things that may *never* happen," Cassie said.

"But things *have* happened, Cassie. When I got out of prison, I had serious thoughts about not coming back here," he said.

"Why?" Cassie said.

"All this death, and hell, a ghost roams the island because of me."

"Jack! Come on now," Cassie said

He looked gently at Cassie and said, "I'm just worried about Sunset. Kinda like the way a daddy might worry about his daughter, pure and untouched. I want to save and protect her. But ugly, greedy men are coming, and I know there's nothing I can do. I can't stop them. Sunset is in their crosshairs. This unspoiled beach has been tainted, soiled by death and greed. And it'll happen again, Cassie. Mark my word! I think I'd rather leave here. Turn my back, walk away, and not see the rape and destruction that's to come."

"Damn, Jack! Now *I'm* depressed," Cassie said.

"I'm sorry. I didn't mean to sound so gloomy, but all this darkness came down after I left Greensboro to move here. It all started with Rich Junior's death, just as I was on my way down. In fact, he was probably killed seconds before we met him on 904. Maybe I brought that darkness with me."

"Oh, don't be ridiculous, Jack! These things happen. You didn't bring or cause it. It was a feud between Mr. Pierce and Groat. Everybody else just got caught up in it. It wasn't *your* karma. It was theirs. Actually, it was Groat's. His poison spread to others. Everyone was a victim of his viciousness. That's the way I see it," Cassie said.

"Thanks, Cassie. You're trying to alleviate my guilt in all this. I know that. But still, I just don't know if I should stay," Jack said. "Deep down inside, I feel like I may be the cause of all this."

Frustrated, Cassie said, "Well why the hell did you come back, then? What was the point in that if that's the way you feel?"

"To see you. To explain why I left so suddenly without saying goodbye to you."

"You didn't owe me that."

"I guess you're right," Jack said turning.

"Dammit, Jack! Wait! Where are you gonna go? I assume, just getting out of the penitentiary, you don't have a job. And I hear making license plates in prison doesn't pay all that well," Cassie said.

Jack turned back around, smiling. "It doesn't. I spent bout all that I made on my bus fare down here."

"So, what are you going to go?"

"Not sure, yet. Wherever my wandering takes me, I guess."

"You can stay here until you begin your next wandering!"

"I don't think that would be right, Cassie. This was Mr. Pierce and Rich Junior's place—their dream. I'd be intruding on them, even though they're gone."

"Mr. Pierce thought of you like a son. No one could replace Rich, but you, he really liked you. I'm gonna tell you something. I'm gonna expose myself here, Jack. I don't know *what* we have or *if* we have anything, but that weekend at Ocean Drive during Beach Weekend meant something. To *me*, anyway. The hurt and loneliness I felt after Rich's death subsided some that weekend. I felt alive. I felt as if I could care again. I told you I wanted to cool it when we got back, but I was just putting off the inevitable. I was having feelings for you, and I was confused. If I hurt you, I'm sorry. But know this. I always wondered what would have happened with *us* if you hadn't gone away," Cassie said.

"I didn't know you felt that way. But I thought about you while I was gone, Cassie. A lot. But . . . ."

"Then, don't go. Stay here. For a while. This place is *you*, Jack! You love it so! Mr. Pierce would've liked that, given the way things turned out. He left this place to me. Rich was his only supporter in this, and since he was gone, Mr. Pierce wrote me in his will. The rest of the family may contest it, but it's a valid will, and when he signed it, he was in full control of his faculties. Always was, up to the end. Maybe we could pick up where we left off after our night on the rooftop and see where it goes."

"Cassie, that's a big decision. Do you think you are . . ."?

"A big decision? Not really. And yes. I *am* ready. Who do we have left, but each other? Our families are all but non-existent. We've both been through a lot. We both need and deserve some peace. Some salvation. What do we have to lose?"

Jack studied her face for a moment and then said, "I think I could take refuge in you, Cassie Cavanaugh. My salvation, as you put it. My *balm*."

Cassie smiled, and in her best George Burns imitation, flicking an imaginary cigar between her thumb and forefinger, she said, "Looks like it's you and me kid."

"Come here," Jack said pulling her into his arms. "Seen any ghosts lately?"

"Only Kindred Spirits." She smiled up at him.

AUTHOR'S NOTE

For decades, thousands of visitors have made the pilgrimage to the Kindred Spirit mailbox on uninhabited Bird Island. People, young and old, joyous and in pain, have written their innermost thoughts and feelings in the mailbox's journals, which have been kept and are archived at the University of North Carolina Wilmington library.

ABOUT THE AUTHOR

The author at Sunset Beach in the mid-90s

After working in the legal profession as an Attorney's Investigator for over twenty years, Tim returned to his first love, writing. Prior to his legal career, he was the Managing Editor at a small newspaper near Pinehurst, North Carolina. He has worked for *USA Today,* the *Greensboro News and Record, Tarheel Magazine* and is a contributing writer for *O. Henry Magazine.* Tim was voted "Best Local Author" in the *Greensboro News and Record's* 2014 Readers Choice Award, runner-up in 2015, and "Best Local Author" again in 2016. The second, revised edition of Tim's first novel, *Curing Time,* is coming Fall 2022 (TouchPoint Press).

Acknowledgements

Sometimes it takes a village . . . or sometimes a family to "raise" a novel. Such is the case with my book, *Madd Inlet*. The "family" at Touchpoint Press *is* a family. From the interaction and comradery among its authors and the guidance of Publisher Sheri Williams, the writers in this "family" are supported and connected in this, sometimes, brutal publishing world. Thank you to, Sheri; Deputy Publisher Ashley Carlson; *my* excellent editor, Senior Editor Kimberly Coghlan; Jennifer Bond, Publicity Manager and Media Liaison; and *all* the TPP staff for making me a part of this family.

Continuing the family tree, I would be remiss if I did not thank the Myrick family of Greensboro, NC for including and sharing their family cottage at Sunset Beach for many a summer beach trips over the years. The memories began there and remain.

Thanks, long-time friend Colleen Keeney, for sharing the surfing picture used at the end of the novel, taken on one of our combined family beach trips. Again . . . the memories! And thanks to Bill Heroy, owner of Old Photo Specialist for bringing the photo back to life.

To my dear friend, Ernie Viers, for his masterful computer intellect in creating and maintaining my website, *timswink.com*. Thank you, Ernie! Your "smarts" amaze me!

And finally, to *my* family for your love and support. To Darin, Andi, Mary Lacy and Evan, Jane and Jack, I love you and am so grateful you all are in my life.

And lastly, to my best friend, my talented and creative wife, Renee, who painted the cover of this novel. I asked her, on a whim, if she would paint me a cover of an angry inlet, but she never heard the word "whim," and the result of her talent graces the front of my novel. Thank you, my love!

Thank you so much for reading MADD INLET. If you've enjoyed the book, we would be grateful if you would post a review on the bookseller's website. Just a few words is all it takes!

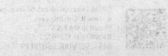

9 781956 851380